THE PLACE WHERE
WORDS COME OUT

B. J. THORSON

The Place Where Words Come Out

Copyright © 2021 by B.J. Thorson

Cover design: Vila Design
Cover art: *Le Paysage* by Emily Carr, 1911, Audain Art Museum

The Place Where Words Come Out is a work of fiction. Any resemblance to actual events, places, incidents, or persons, living or dead (aside from the two Emilys), is entirely coincidental.

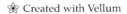 Created with Vellum

For my daughters
Rosie and Eloise

THE PLACE WHERE WORDS COME OUT

By B.J. Thorson

1

I SIT IN MY TENT ON A HOT SEPTEMBER DAY, PENCIL NOT QUITE IN hand but close, and wait. Waiting is a discipline unto itself, and I'd wager I'm one of the best at it of anyone I've met. I'm waiting for a customer to arrive, or at least a curious fair-goer who can be transformed into a customer four times out of five. The fifth ones are too much like hard work, and not worth the wait.

I'm at the Calgary Fair, which they call a Stampede, despite the absence of charging animals, trying to earn enough money to get to Vancouver.

I sketch two little girls – twins – their faces red and luminescent with sugary stickiness from a candy apple gorge. The mother spends the entire session justifying the expense to the father, who never once uncrosses his arms and only exhales with audible judgment at my work as he stands directly behind me. This is something I don't normally allow, but it's already half past noon and I haven't had so much as a visitor in the tent, so I keep my mouth shut and sketch.

Justify the expense. Hardly. My drawings are four bits each and I find myself negotiating with the silent husband by way of the vociferous wife to arrive at a total of 75¢ for this one. I would normally charge per subject, but she argues that I'm only out one sheet of heavy card stock paper rather than two, so that ought to count for something.

I ease my rage at this nitpickiness by imagining the two of them embraced in the heat of their Friday night agreement, her white string-bean body submitting to his meat and potato thrusts with the same rationale: *if I can produce two in your image for the discomfort of one night of violation, then that ought to count for something.*

Despite my vindictive intentions, these daydreams bring about a sense of compassion for her, and I relent on the price.

After the twins, a spinster comes with her dog and makes my day, getting three sketches done at once: herself, her dog, and the two of them together. She says she has a collection of sketches from elsewhere, but these, she confesses, are her first hometown offerings. I ask if she is interested in a proper portrait, with oils and canvas, but she cannot afford it. She says 'cannot', but I only hear 'will not'. I imagine the cost to be a fraction of what she likely spends on her pet, but there's no accounting for taste and priorities in this world.

I eat my lunch, a hard-boiled egg, half a carrot, and a stale corn biscuit without butter, and turn my face towards the East with thoughts of home. My heartbeat quickens, and the sudden rush of blood causes me to catch my breath. It's the thought of being so far from home with nothing tying me back there aside from memories and a continued desire for things to be different.

"You know if you go far enough and take long enough to do it, you'll only end up right next door to where you left."

"O come, Dad," I say, "that's just wordplay."

He laughs when I say this, then wraps me up in a hug as if my hair is on fire.

"My little girl. Have I been so terrible a father that you feel the need to be away from me so much? First Ireland, now this?"

"I'll be twenty in a couple of months, and Vancouver isn't that far away. It's still Canada, just like Halifax."

"Tara," he reasons, "a person can so adjust her thinking that she can be in the same room, within arm's reach, and still be on an entirely different planet. Distance is only what we make it, and space is something we can kill just as easily as we kill time. Don't believe everything you hear. Vancouver is right next-door for some. For others, it's an impossible destination."

"You like to hear yourself say these things, don't you? Like you're Mark Twain or something."

Again he laughs. I am the only one who can ever successfully call him on his linguistic indulgences. A student of his tried once and was immediately and systematically dragged over the coals in the lecture hall. I felt sorry for him, but my father is good with language. The way I want to be with colours.

It is only when I tell him this, and explain my aesthetic reasons for wanting to go, that he finally understands. His protests became warm smiles, and he quickly silences his tongue on the matter. Before I leave him, he hands me a thin volume of Emily Dickinson poetry and a bottle of French wine.

"You'll finish one long before the other", he says, "but they're both for the long journey ahead."

I haven't heard from him since, never staying in one place long enough to justify a return address. I send letters home frequently, though they invariably take the form of a sketch with an accompanying quote from the Dickinson volume that comes closest to expressing my mood. Thank God she was such a melancholic.

"DID YOU DRAW ALL THESE?"

I am shaken out of my nostalgia by a young man standing in the tent looking at the small display of pictures I have hanging on the canvas walls.

"Every last one of them."

"Hmm," he replies. His hands are pushed so deeply in his

trouser pockets that I fear the force will pull his pants right down. Then I notice the leather suspenders. All is safe.

"This one too?" he asks, lifting his chin to a sketch I drew in early June.

"That one too."

"Who is she?"

"The maid of Mr. and Mrs. Allison. She died on the Titanic."

"You knew her?"

"No," I say. "Hers was the first anonymous name published in the paper after the sinking. I felt she deserved a bit more than the dismissive 'maid' she was immortalised as."

He takes in the drawing for some time, masking the clear fact that he knows nothing about the name 'Titanic' or the catastrophe that occurred four months ago off the coast of my home province.

"What's the matter with her eyes?"

"How do you mean?"

"Well, look at them. They're about twice the size of her entire face and bigger than her legs. Was she some kind of freak or something?"

"If anyone is to be called a freak," I say, "I claim the title as my own. I have no idea what she looked like, but I imagine her countenance was as normal as anyone's I draw. I'm a caricaturist."

"A what?"

"Caricatures. Don't look so amazed. It's a popular form of sketch art at fairs like this. Well…not like this one specifically. Others. It's how they sketch in Paris."

"You've been to Paris?" he asks, rubbing his chin with the back of his hand.

"Just last year."

"Well I'll be. Never met someone who's been to Paris before. Guess that explains why you don't sound like you're from around here. Using words like that. What's it mean, you figure?"

I move the stool out into the open, hoping he'll take a seat. If you can get them sitting, then the deal is as good as done.

"Well," I say, setting a crisp white card on the easel, "*caricature* comes from the French – like all great art – meaning to 'overdo'. I imagine it's originally from Latin."

"You imagine?" He says this as he sits down, the smile indicating that he has caught me out in a feign of ignorance, a ploy I'm often guilty of to make people feel at ease.

"You're right, I don't imagine. I know it comes from Latin. It's from the root word for carriage. To load up too much. To overload. Hence the big eyes on the freak."

"My father's a churchman," he tells me. "He knows enough of Latin to 'untangle the mess that was made of our Lord's message' quote unquote, and thought it necessary to teach me what he knows, but he could never make it stick with me."

"Well," I say, "now you know something."

"Your father a churchman too?"

The idea of my father being a churchman sends me into near hysterics. My laughter feels over the top, too much, so I try and calm myself down before my laughter turns to tears. I don't typically talk about my father with complete strangers, but there's something undeniably innocent about this one; the innocence gives me a sense of safety.

"Hardly. Professor of English at a university on the East Coast. American poets, authors, men of letters. Melville, Hawthorne, Whitman. You know."

"So he taught you Latin?"

"He got me started, I suppose, but I learn most of what I know through reading."

"My father claims that to give a woman a book is to give a fox the keys to the henhouse," he says. An image of his father comes immediately to mind: small, bony elbows, one eye forever shut in a myopic squint on the ways of the world.

"You ever consider the fact that your father's an idiot and an ass?"

This comes out before my little sensor can block it. Shit. I could lose this one and I can't afford to lose anything right now. Just keep your mouth shut, Tara, and your hands open, if you want to get to where you're going.

Now it's his turn to laugh, and he does so until tears come to his eyes, which he wipes with a handkerchief from his pocket. He throws it down on the ground like a flag, as if to signal the beginning of a race.

"Considered it a thousand times," he says, "but never had the nerve to dress such thoughts up in words before. This way I get to hear them said without suffering the guilt of saying them myself."

I decide to dive in and start sketching before he can stop me. He suddenly blushes and turns his head away.

"Keep still, please."

"I've never had a picture drawn of me before," he confesses. "How much does it cost?"

"Fifty cents."

He moves his lower jaw out in a frozen moment of consideration.

"Will it take long?"

"If you quit asking questions and keep your mouth closed," I tell him, "I'll have you out of here in fifteen minutes or less."

He stands up as if I'd just shot at him with an aim to blow his balls clear off.

"Four bits for just fifteen minutes work? That makes... what... two dollars an hour! What I wouldn't give to be earning them kind of wages."

The word 'wages' strikes me as odd somehow. I don't consider myself a 'wage earner'. Maybe it was because my father earns a salary, or at worst a stipend, that the word 'wages' connotes for me the sense of someone doing a deed which they take no love or interest in. A passionless exercise, like Sisyphus rolling that boulder up the hill in perpetuity. Wages were something the 'haves' paid out to the 'have-nots' for services rendered, not something you were compensated for in your calling.

"What would you do with a two-dollar-an-hour wage, mister…"

"Snow."

"Mr. Snow."

"Oh please, don't call me Mr. Snow," he pleads. "That's my father and believe me, you wouldn't mistake me for my father once you met him anymore than you'd mistake a ground squirrel for a grizzly bear."

The afternoon sun is coming down hard, and the sharp-edged shadows are unflattering. It's very hot, the dry prairie air sucking the moisture from every saliva gland in my mouth.

I walk over and reach for his hat.

"May I?" I ask.

He turns around, looks over his shoulder, turns back, shrugs, then sits down on the stool. His blond hair falls down like straw and covers the tops of his eyes when I remove his hat. I brush it away, and can feel his entire body tense up with the touch of my hand on his forehead. I come back to the easel and take my first long look at my subject.

It's then that I notice how beautiful he is. His body is that of a child - all limbs, muscles, and joints in harmonic proportion - as though age has not interfered with the perfection of youth in this man. His face… I have never before seen a face like it, and I've stared at many. If I call it an animal face you might misunderstand me, but that is what it is. A thoroughbred animal face, like a fine horse or dog: a blend of man and beast, more beautiful than either.

I don't believe in love at first sight. I don't. I like to think that something as mighty as love takes a little more time to gestate. It's not about that, not at all, it was just… he's like the sky in these parts; something inside of you can't help but stop and look and be in awe.

"You were saying about the wages," I remind him.

"Hmm?"

"What you'd do with a two-dollar-an-hour wage?" I repeat, trying to get him talking some more. The longer he talks, the longer he stays, and the better my chances of selling a sketch. Besides, there's something interesting about this one. Something that goes beyond his beauty. I can't say what, but I'm curious to find out.

"Sugar beet molasses," he answers.

"Never heard of it."

He slaps his hands together, the noise of which could have been herald to a thunderstorm, and rubs his palms as though trying to start a fire.

"If you were a man, would you enjoy a glass of rum now and then?" His voice takes on the tone of a small time hustler, only fun and playful. I can tell he's practiced this pitch a thousand times in his head, but rarely gets a chance to try it out on a potential sucker. I'm happy to oblige as I sketch.

"Sure," I say, "even if I weren't a man. Which I'm not, by the way."

"Right," he says, his eyes flickering to my bosom and then back to my face without the hint of a blush. "Sorry. You indulge then?"

"It's been known to happen."

"Normally I'm just talking to men about this. Other than my father. Never said it to a lady before."

"Rest easy, then. I'm no lady, just a growed-up girl. But for the record, I'm more of a wine drinker. Rum's too sweet."

"That's the molasses talking."

His eyes dart off to double check some imaginary scroll of his rum pitch, then come back to me.

"Rum makes the world a better place for some, " he says, continuing his barker routine, "but it's got to come from some-where. Ask me 'why not here'?"

"Okay, I'll bite. Why not here?"

He's twisting on the stool like a bar room piano player working the crowd.

"Christian temperance," he declares with another clap of his hands. Then he adds, "despite the dancing girls and brothels in towns like this. Whoring and rum consumption are viewed with at least one blind eye, but rum *production* would never escape the full-on glare of powerful churchmen like my father. A fella' would be a fool to dare open a distillery 'round here."

"Something tells me that you're no fool."

"No ma'am," he laughs. His laughter is free of knives, a child's laugh, the sort that's as infectious as a yawn and just as involuntary. I find myself genuinely caught by it and sharing in it; something I don't normally indulge in except with my father.

"So where's your rum empire going to be?"

"About 150 miles south of here. Next door to the sugar beet factory."

That's when it flashes in his eyes, like lightning, and I feel the electrical charge shoot through me.

"Hold it right there," I order him. "Don't move."

As an artist, I've only two things to work with in order to bring off the desired illusion: light and colour. Outside of the illusion of art, light comes from the sun. Or fire. Or kerosene lamps. Or electricity, in places as advanced as here. But a source of light must be imagined to exist in the illusion. Light hits the subject from somewhere, otherwise how could it be seen?

And with light comes the problem of shadow. When light hits the subject a shadow is created; very tricky to show in the illusion. The hallmark of the amateur is to leave shadow out completely. But then the illusion is only half real, and therefore not real at all.

As for colours, I'm only using one: black. A single pencil made of charcoal... the remains of something that once had colour and ever too much light. Charcoal is the colour of shadow, but still I make it reflect the light. It's how I justify the expense.

"Are you finished yet?" he asks.

"Almost. Keep still now."

When a light shines on the outside of someone, that's what you sketch. When it shines on the inside, you can only portray. The light was shining on the inside of this preacher's son and I was caught in the fire that burned from his eyes. I may not believe in love at first sight, but I believe steadfastly that inspiration happens this way. I knew then that I had to paint his portrait.

"Done," I announce as I step back from the easel and he relaxes his pose.

"Well, let's have a look," he says as he puts his hat back on and stands up from the stool.

"Could you come by tomorrow?" I ask. "And the next few days after that? I want to paint you."

"Paint me?"

"Your portrait. With oils, on a real canvas."

"Takes more than fifteen minutes for that, huh?"

"Considerably."

He stands staring at the sketch, hopefully mulling over my offer.

"I wouldn't charge you anything for the painting, of course," I add, trying not to sound desperate. "It would be *on the house,* as they say in the tavern."

"Wouldn't know. Never been inside a tavern before." He laughs again. "Naw, I gotta get home."

"Where's that?"

"Little village south of here. Emmett."

He searches my face to see if I have heard of it, then says something to the effect that no one ever has. Too small and insignificant to register with anyone not from there, and even the residents forget about it when away.

"Not much of an exaggerated carriage here," he says, lazily pointing a finger at the finished image on the easel.

"It's only a sketch," I explain, "a study for a larger work, I hope. I didn't want to caricature you."

"Why not?"

I am as surprised as he is at the drawing. It's my first non-caricatured, freak-less sketch since leaving home. Sketching takes me away from what I've left behind, and I don't think about it while I'm doing it. Since Halifax, they've all come out with overloaded carts. Now, suddenly, this one's different.

It's a worthy effort, capturing a bit of the light inside him. I feel a bit naked all of a sudden standing next to him. Vulnerable. I detect a small measure of defence in his voice, as if he feels inadequate somehow.

"I don't know," I try to explain. "Maybe you're too beautiful for that. There was just no way to ridicule your face, kindly or otherwise."

His reaction – a mixture of laughing pleasure and blushing awkwardness – tells me that no one has ever said these words to him before. Personal beauty must not be a consideration for a man in his family. I understand now that his easy laughter is a way of lubricating himself into a calloused, male world of hard work, hard prayer, and simplicity. Otherwise he wouldn't fit, and when you don't fit into those tight little worlds, the results are often unspeakable.

"Thanks for the picture," he says, "but I really should get going."

"I'm Tara," I blurt out, thrusting out my hand like it's spring-loaded in an attempt to keep him here a little longer. "Tara Hale."

"William!"

The voice comes from behind, at the entrance to my tent. A deep, resonant boom that hits the ground and shakes the earth. Here is the thunder that follows the lightning in my subject's eyes.

"Hey Pop."

The young man named William turns back and winks at me,

as if to say 'watch how I handle this' or 'keep on your toes' or some such silent instruction.

"William," his father says, "where have you been? I've been up and down the grounds looking for you since breakfast."

His father's not a tall man, but I feel in the company of a giant by his mere presence. His beard comes down to his breast, wiry and curled like a mess of inappropriately positioned genital hair, and does its best to conceal a formal dress code of shirt, tie, vest, and jacket. His collar is white and starched and tightly wrapped around his sunburned neck.

"Just enjoying my day at the fair," William says with jovial indifference. "And look here. A genuine original sketch of yours truly."

"So I see," his father says. The disapproval in his voice is evident, though he tries to hide it. I've heard the tone so many times that it's impossible to hide from me. Still, he removes his hat and steps forward with impeccable decorum.

"I'm Charles Snow. William's father."

"That's Miss Hale, Pop. She's been to Paris, and learned how to draw these… what do you call them again?"

"Caricatures," I repeat.

"You know, Pop. From the Latin. Here's one she drew of a maid who drowned when the Titanic hit that iceberg." William turns to me with another wink. "We prayed for three days straight when we heard about the wreck, didn't we Pop?"

So he *had* heard about it. I offer silent pardon to myself for doubting.

"William," he says, as he half turns to his son, "I would appreciate it if you addressed me as your father and not by that odious three-letter diminutive you're so stubbornly fond of." His son mumbles a sorry then winks a third time at me behind his father's back. "Yes, a terrible tragedy, the Titanic. So many souls gone to their Father in Heaven all at once."

He offers his hand and smiles kindly while fixing me with his scrutinizing eyes. I feel like he's looking right inside me, shining a light on every secret and shadow I have locked up and hidden. It's terrifying and fascinating all at once. I can't look away.

"A pleasure to meet you," I finally say, and then add, "I see where William gets his features from, Mr. Snow."

He doesn't respond to this, but turns to his son and says something about hurrying down to the hotel or mother will have the law enlisted. William takes his leave, thanks me again for the 'masterful study' as he calls it, and tells his father that I am owed two dollars.

"Honest wages," he adds, winking one last time. Then he runs off towards the town centre. I take my eyes off him sooner than I would like for fear his father will misread my longing gaze.

"A lucrative enterprise, Miss Hale," he says, "charging two full dollars for a charcoal sketch."

"Your son seeks to take advantage of your kindness and my circumstances," I tell him. "The cost for the sketch is fifty cents."

He hands me a dollar and I turn to my cash purse to make the change.

"Honesty is a priceless virtue, Miss Hale," he smiles. "Worth far more to me than four bits. Please keep it."

He holds up the sketch at arm's length and studies it in silence. I find myself suddenly apprehensive about what he will say, as if he's judging me far more than my drawing.

"Not that I'm an expert in these matters, or even experienced with the art form, but I must say, Miss Hale, that you have a fine hand for drawing."

The compliment comes free of flattery. I attempt some eloquence in my reply.

"Thank-you Mr. Snow, but my hand is only servant to my soul, so in praising my work, you praise not my hand but my very mind and soul."

"And what is your mind and soul, my dear young lady, but an extension of the Lord God your Father? In praising your hand, I praise your soul and by praising that I ultimately praise He who furnished you with mind, soul, and hand."

His voice modulates like an orator's, and such crafted delivery is designed not to elicit a response but to render the audience speechless and awestruck. It works like a charm. It's not that I don't know *what* to say, it's that I simply can't say anything. I feel shaken by him – perhaps the word I want is stricken – and stand like a dumb animal awaiting punishment or instruction from its owner. He waits a moment, expecting some kind of nod or sign of agreement or – who knows? – a jubilant 'amen' or 'hallelujah'! Knowing my voice is going to be dry and cracked and – worst of all – weak, I manage to press some words out of my mouth and salvage some much needed shades of dignity.

"Thank-you for the gift."

I STAY LATE on the grounds that day, spending my gratuity on a shot of rum. I make a silent toast to the portrait that would never be, and sip my drink slowly, wincing at the sugar beet sweetness on my tongue.

As I watch the late day sun loitering in the sky, I cannot get the image of William Snow out of my head, his lightness, his joy. Nor can I rub clear the shadow cast by his father.

To kill time – and space – I sketch a letter home to my mine. A simple profile of the young man who dreams of sugar-beet rum, with a silhouette of his father in the background. I add the following inscription, taken from my book of Emily's poetry:

Had I not seen the Sun
I could have borne the shade
But Light a newer Wilderness
My Wilderness has made –

2

I RETURN TO MY HOTEL AFTER DINNER ON THIS HOT STAMPEDE DAY, only to find my trunk and suitcase hastily packed, awaiting me in the lobby.

"What is the meaning of this?" I demand of the manager.

"You have violated hotel policy, Mrs. Hale. Or shall I say Ms. Hale, if that's even your real name. We have no tolerance for imposters."

"Imposter? How dare — "

"*The Alberta* does not host unmarried women. We booked you a room two days ago under the assurance your husband would be joining you imminently. I see no husband here, nor was there any sign of a man's presence in your room."

I hold up my left hand, with my palm facing me.

"He's been delayed," I say, flashing my ring as proof.

"That's not my concern, ma'am," he replies. "As manager, I have no choice but to suspend the *Alberta*'s hostelry, effective immediately."

A crowd of hats and suits, all men, begin to snort and laugh.

"Where am I to stay?" I ask.

"Try tent city down by the river. Sleep with the Indians," the managing clerk answers with derision.

A young porter takes pity, scribbles a name and address on a piece of hotel stationery, and slips it secretly it into my hand as he moves my trunk outside.

"Don't tell anyone where you got this, hear? It's not the most…" he pauses a moment. "Never mind. It's a bed and a roof. And a meal if you're lucky."

THE MANAGER IS CORRECT. I've fabricated that handy little lie many times as I travel across the vast expanse of Canada. My ring, a modest band of white gold, was given to me in Winnipeg by a distraught mother of four. She had come into my tent with children in tow, and asked for all four to be sketched. She confessed to being low on money, and was up front and honest about her circumstances. Her husband, after years of philandering and drink, had finally been given the freedom he so desperately wanted when she successfully divorced him.

"I got no further use of this," she said, handing me her wedding band. "Don't know if it's worth anything or not, but I sure would love to have remembrances of my children before they grow up and leave. Can't afford no photographs, and can't bring myself to toss this thing in the river. I was raised to never waste anything, you see." I accepted her payment and produced four superb sketches of her children. She was so grateful, she cried.

Most often, I check out of each hotel before my fictional husband arrives. Occasionally, I have to upgrade my lie, stating his train was delayed or work was keeping him a day longer, but I've never been caught outright in my dishonesty and tossed out onto the street.

I realise soon enough that the manager's moral imperative was preceded by a financial one: there are close to forty five thousand people in town this week for the Stampede, so room prices are doubled or tripled and still booked out with ease.

I make arrangements for my trunk to be delivered to the train station in case this lead comes to nothing, then go outside and try to decipher his appalling handwriting. I make out a name with the address: Jennifer Ness. Asking for directions in the street, I go through a dozen apologies from folks who don't live here before someone points me the way. The house is a good ten blocks away from downtown, but closer to the fair grounds.

I manage the walk as best I can, stopping frequently to rest, arms elongated by the weight of my suitcase and bag. I am tired to a degree I've not felt for a long, long time.

NIGHT LAYS DOWN SLOWLY in this part of the country on a late summer night, but my wanderings have left me in the dark. Literally.

"Let me carry them bags for you, ma'am".

I turn and see a moustache, thicker than sagebrush, winking at me. All of a sudden it seems darker than it was moments before.

"Thank you, but I can manage on my own."

"I'm afraid I must insist," he slurs, "being a gentleman an' all." I smell whiskey on his breath as he thrusts his hand quickly forward. I swing my art supply case around my back, out of reach, while he succeeds in clutching the other bag.

"Righty-O. We'll share then. I believe in equal opportunity."

He tosses the bag up and watches it spin one full revolution before deftly snatching it out of the air by its handle.

"Awfully light," he comments as he repeats his spinning trick.

"My husband is right behind me with the rest of our bags, so you best set that down and quietly continue on your way."

He looks behind me, squints his eyes to slits of glassy mischief, and puckers his lips in feigned contemplation.

"I spend many a night seeing in the dark, watching for coyotes and snakes and all, so I reckon I'm pretty good at seeing further than most. Now, unless your husband is the size of a grasshopper, he's either a ghost, a fabrication, or he's found someone better 'tween here and the fair grounds."

He's holding my bag up above his head now, with one hand, pointing it towards the grounds. He then spins it once more.

"Like I say, awfully light. Never known a lady to pack so light before, which means…"

"Put it down."

"You ain't no lady. Figured as much when I saw you doing your doodles this afternoon."

I look towards the saloon from which he emerged. Its light spills out the front door, offering some minimal safety, so long as we stay here.

"Seeing you in them britches earlier, I took you for a fella. But now we're up close and friendly, I can smell you properly."

"Smell me? You're part dog, then?" Just keep him talking, Tara, and someone will walk out eventually.

He laughs, and then howls like a wolf. "I'm pretty loyal and trustworthy. Don't like cats. Can be overprotective of what's mine, so yeah, I may have some canine in me after all." He steps closer. "Come to think of it, there are some things I prefer doing the dog way."

"Licking your own private parts?"

Come on, door, swing open.

He smiles like a demented hyena now, baring his rotting teeth in a hideous grin. "Hell, if I could do that, I wouldn't leave the house. Guess that's where the fairer sex comes in. Now let's get a move on to wherever you're lugging these bags and quit wasting time."

He tosses the bag once more into the air just as the saloon door bursts open with a rowdy cry of patrons. The moustache turns to see who's come out, and I swing my hard case across like a broad sword. The corner of the case makes contact with his jaw. I hear a crack as he crumbles to the ground, and not knowing whether it's my case or his bone that fractured, I quickly grab my other bag and run into the darkness beyond the street.

I can hear him cursing while the others laugh, but don't look back to see which is the more prominent sound.

FINALLY, hours after leaving the hotel, I find the destination I've been seeking. The house boasts no sign of offering lodging, and I momentarily consider the possibility that I'm the butt of a prank by a cruel hotel staff.

It is a large home with a clean veranda and, as far as I can tell in the moonlit night, an array of flowers neatly arranged in boxes beneath the window. I knock, and soon a woman opens the inside wooden door, leaving the screen door closed between the two of us like an upturned drawbridge.

"Yes?"

"Miss Ness?" I ask.

"*Mrs.* Ness," she corrects me. "Can I help you?"

"My name is Tara Hale," I say, "and I'm in need of lodging for the week."

"Where you are from, Miss Hale?"

"Halifax, Nova Scotia, ma'am."

"Are you traveling alone?"

I'm about to answer with a prepared fiction, but find I am too exhausted, too desperate to fabricate a lie.

"Yes ma'am," I nod. "I'm working at the Stampede."

"What do you mean? Working *how*?" She narrows her eyes as she asks, an entire world of preloaded judgment packed into those three letters.

"Please," I say, "I'm offering sketches at the fair, which is what I've been doing all summer right across the country. I'm traveling alone and I miss my father and I'm afraid and…"

Mrs. Ness opens the door.

"You're an artist, then? Why didn't you say so? You're welcome in my home." She puts her arm around me and leads me inside. "Sit yourself down here and I'll be right back with a cup of tea."

Once inside, I can see her a bit more properly. She is about forty, in beautiful figure, wearing a long dress, dark forest green with black trim.

I sink into a red velvet chez lounge with ornate wooden legs on each corner and try to keep myself together until I'm in the privacy of my bed. Only there, alone and unwatched, will I allow myself to cry. It is a cry that's been building since the twin girls this afternoon, brought to a crescendo with the moustache encounter. A large part of me wants nothing more than to go home. Another part of me just wants my dad.

Mrs. Ness returns with a tray bearing a teapot, two cups, sugar, milk, and lemon wedges. I manage a smile.

"Thank-you," I say.

"I know a thing or two about being a woman alone in this dusty, tobacco-spit world. It's anything but easy," she tells me. "Drink your tea and excuse me a moment while I fix you something for dinner."

I start to protest but she raises her hand, her nails beautifully manicured and painted a deep red.

"The fee includes room and board, and you look hungry, so no silliness about not going to the trouble. Please, make yourself at home."

3

It is bright and blue and warm today, the fourth day of Mr. Weadick's Wild West Stampede. Yesterday was soaked by rain, but the arrival of the Duke of Connaught and his royal wife ensured that the crowds would be out in full force. And they are. Today promises to be not only drier, but considerably more lucrative.

Money changes hands faster than I've ever seen: rodeo cowboys compete for large purses, restaurant and hotel enterprises struggle to meet the intense demand, and the spirits of virtually everyone I meet are high and carefree. The *Moustache* passed by the other day, both his eyes blackened and his nose taped down with white gauze. Our eyes met briefly, and the timidity with which he averted his told me I had nothing more to fear from him.

My arm is sore from sketching, and Mrs. Ness has me packing it in ice upon coming home every night, then soaking it in hot Epsom-salt baths for an hour before bed. I somehow managed to overlook the fact that art is a physical activity, and that the muscles involved can be overworked and strained. I don't give in to sickness easily, and feel the same about injury. This is fool-hardy, I know, as I can damage myself beyond repair, but somehow I trust that the body knows when to stop – more so than any doctor – and I'm not there yet.

Mrs. Ness has come by already to deliver a little lunch. This is something she's done for three days now, and though I protest that it's not necessary, she ignores me and keeps me fed. I close up shop with a sign that reads 'back in 30 minutes' and walk with her to a set of benches erected by the river for the Stampede festivities.

She is tremendously hospitable and appears thrilled when I come home every night, fussing around with dinner and ice-packs and questions about the day. I like having someone parent me, so I don't bother to dissuade her attention. Our conversations rarely scratch below the surface of who I've sketched on that particular day, my style as an artist, and the one attribute we seem to have in common: our independence.

"My husband worked for the Eau Claire lumber company here in town," she tells me. "He was manager of operations when he was killed in a lumber accident six years ago."

I nod in sympathy.

"He knew how to take care of me, before and after his death, and for that I'm grateful." She leans in and clutches my hand in a sisterly show of confidence. "But I never loved him."

"How long were you married?" I ask.

"Twelve years. I was twenty-three, the daughter of a Wisconsin shop owner, humble yet self-sufficient. Peter was ten years my elder, pushed into marriage by his father. When the opportunity arose to travel north to Canada and manage the lumber company, he jumped at it. I always longed for adventure, you see, and back then a woman couldn't set out to find it on her own as easily as you can today."

"Trust me," I tell her, "it's not that easy."

"But it's possible."

"Barely," I say.

"I didn't even have that," she succinctly concludes, and I stop arguing.

"Little did I know," she continues, "that a move to Canada was merely a change of scenery, an exchange of wet winters for dry ones, and a considerable drop in the social accoutrements so vital to a woman. Not that there was much to choose from where I came from. In short, I was bored stiff. Peter worked, I puttered, and baked, and made curtains, and resisted the daily temptation to wrap my fingers around his hunting pistol and blow my head off."

Her words shock me. I wince, and ask what stopped her.

"He would have been completely inept at cleaning the mess," she playfully replies, "so I would have had to do it myself."

It feels good to laugh like this, and she is very adept at making me do it.

"Why didn't you go back home after your husband's death?" I ask.

"I thought about it," she confides, "but what was there for me? Besides, I felt it was important to stick out the six months of mourning as he had so many friends and colleagues here. Thankfully, I look stunning in black."

The heat is becoming unbearable, so I make my way back to the tent where a small crowd has gathered, seeking shelter from the sun. One by one they are charmed by my sketches, my personality, my sales pitch, and I happily spend the remainder of the afternoon churning out black and whites in exchange for greens and silvers.

I marvel at how polite and restrained they all seem. Hardly a *stampede* of anything. They should be wilder than they are, almost Bacchanalian, but instead they only pretend to let loose and give over to abandon, which isn't true wildness at all. Another newer wilderness I am forced to adjust to.

This was turning out to be the most lucrative four days I've ever known. My father would be relieved to know of this wind-fall for his daughter. How I wish he was here to bear witness to it.

I'm in the middle of sketching a five-year-old boy — James —

when out of nowhere, another memory comes bubbling up from the underworld of my past. I laugh out loud and entirely out of the blue as far as young James is concerned.

"Why are you laughing?" he asks. His mother is thankfully in and out of my stall, trying to keep an eye on three other children as her son sits still on my stool. She's oblivious to the maniacal sketch artist.

"I was thinking about my father," I explain. "I miss him."

"Where did he go?"

James tilts his little head as he asks this, looking for all the world like a wise and caring father himself.

"He didn't. I did."

He opens his mouth to respond, but his little brain must be forestalling the words as it tries to decipher what I said.

"My father is far away," I try to explain.

"Where?"

"A world or two away. I haven't seen him for months."

"My dad is in a building over there," he replies, pointing towards downtown. "He's been gone all day. He's *working*." I can tell by the way he speaks the word that he's heard it for the first time this morning by way of explanation for an absentee father.

"Is he coming to join you later today?" I ask.

"He said he was but he hasn't yet. Now Mommy's mad at him."

"She told you that?" I lean in as I whisper the question.

"No," he whispers back, "but I can tell."

"When your father is finished with his work," I ask, "what's the first thing you're going to do with him?"

James smiles broadly and squirms in his seat. I capture the happy face of a five-year-old with my black pencil.

"I want to ride the streetcars! But mommy keeps saying no. I think she's afraid to ride it. But I'm not. My dad won't be either."

My hand freezes as a memory pulls up in full-steam colour.

. . .

I AM SEVEN YEARS OLD, sitting next to my father on a train bound for Montreal. I am smartly dressed in what my aunt calls 'traveling clothes', meaning everything is wool and hot and heavy and brown, including the hat that my dad lets me remove as soon as we're seated. My father is handsome with his moustache and hair, curly and dark and without the grey he has in both now. His eyes are blue and his brows above are thick and dark and at once intimidating or comforting, depending on what angle they're set at. He is reading. He's always reading, and this time it's a periodical of some kind, not a book. He's chuckling as he reads, his eyes glassy with chuckle tears, and I ask what he's laughing at.

"A man in Germany has written a book," he tells me, folding the magazine and giving his undivided attention to my question, "in which he says that God is dead. "

God is dead? My eyes go big. This strikes me as the biggest possible news ever. My father looks at me for a long time after he tells me that. He always does this because he's waiting for me to say something back. It's how he teaches.

There was a funeral for a family friend the week before but I wasn't allowed to go. My friend went. He's older than me by three years. I asked him about it afterwards and he said everyone was dressed in black suits and dresses and it rained all day and people were crying. And there was a large box with the dead person inside and then it was buried in the ground and they all had egg-salad sandwiches afterwards with a plate of sweets.

I look up at my father and he's still looking at me with the chuckle tears in his eyes and I draw a picture of a large box with people standing around eating sweets. In the box I imagine the face of the oldest man I can think of, with a white beard, whose name is God and he's dead. I always draw pictures because my dad always gives me paper and pencils to draw, especially on train trips.

"Well, Tara?" he says, still looking at me.

"Well what?"

"What do you think of that?"

"Of what?"

"Of someone saying that God is dead?"
I think for a long time.
"We should tell auntie Helen."

I FINISH my sketch of James. I show it to him and he beams with five-year old pride. His mother quickly pays for it, then grabs his hand and pulls him away in pursuit of the other children. He walks backwards and waves to me with his free hand. I wave back.

Mrs. Ness returns. She's been making the rounds all afternoon with a parasol and wide-brimmed hat. I study how she deports herself, a woman venturing out solo in the world. Her years and defiant beauty work in her favour, and the bodies seem to part for her as if they were water nymphs in the wake of a figurehead sea goddess, bare-breasted and bold on the prow of a ship. She waits patiently as I pack away my pencils.

"We haven't even discussed the lodging fee," I say to her.

"No," she says, smiling as she twirls her parasol on her shoulder, "we haven't."

"I'll be off tomorrow, so I owe you for five nights plus meals."

"Yes you do," she replies, continuing to smile as she pulls her parasol into itself and hooks the frilly ends closed. "As you've no doubt seen in my home, Miss Hale, I am a lover of art."

"Yes," I say, "I've noticed."

"And I've noticed how you have sold yourself short in your claim to be only a sketch artist at a summer fair. You are, Tara Hale, an artist who dabbles in sketches, not the other way around."

I understand the difference in what she says, but refrain from either agreement or denial.

"My fee, if you're agreeable to it, is a sketch of myself by you. If you're not too tired of creating art, that is. And if your hand is up for it."

I feel the sharp prick of pain in the back of my hand, and rub it as I weigh the benefits of her offer.

"That's very generous of you," I say, "but my art, such as it is, goes for four bits a sketch. The deal is weighed heavily in my favour."

"Then you shall be sure to sign it upon completion," Mrs. Ness returns, "and I'll watch it go up in value as your reputation starts to flourish."

"I have no more card stock," I start to explain, but she waves my words away.

"I have. Larger than what you use here, so already the offer is balancing out. I entertained the idea of enrolling in an art class once upon a time, to chip away at the boredom of widowhood, but it never materialised. The supplies I ordered are still untouched. I would be honoured if you would agree."

"Very well," I say, "it's a deal."

"Good," she says with a light clap of her hands. "Now that we have that settled, I am off home to prepare a supper. What would you prefer tonight: Brunswick stew or roasted chicken?"

"How about I treat us to a meal out tonight," I suggest. "It's the end of my Stampede, I have fared well at the fair, and I'm sure we could both welcome the indulgence."

Mrs. Ness raises herself up to full height and gracefully curtsies in a show of acceptance and thanks.

"I will stop by and reserve us a table at the Grill in the King George Hotel," she offers. "I've wanted to dine there since it opened at Christmas, but have not found a suitable dining partner. Until tonight. It's an easy walk from the house."

BACK IN MY ROOM, I climb out of my work clothes and let them fester in a pile on the chair, then wipe myself down using the soap and water basin readily supplied by Mrs. Ness.

A full length oval mirror stands in the corner of the room, and I pivot it to an angle that allows me to view myself in my entirety, from head to toe. The first thing I notice is how thin I am beginning to look. My dark brown hair is pinned back, the natural curls stubbornly escaping - as they always do - the restraints of pin or braid or bonnet. I let my hair down and work it free of itself with my fingers. It rests in bulky weight atop my face, which is not so round as it once was but still more a circle than any other geometric offering. I hold my hands up and frame only my eyes. They are blue and deep, smiling in mischievous knowledge of things secret and devilish. I know these eyes well, having seen them on my father's face every day of my life. On an otherwise featureless countenance, they are my most redeeming feature, and I am grateful for the loan of them.

I pull my one and only dress from the trunk and lay it on the bed. Father bought it for me in Paris as part of his mission to scrub the Maritimes off of me. I've been told it brings out the brilliance in my eyes.

"Ah sweet Jesus..." he sighed as he handed me the dress. "It took years of books and music and opinions to put the brilliance in your eyes, Tara, and only a few simple francs to bring it out."

I step into the simple black elegance of my shoes, and look longingly over at the boots which are far more comfortable. I pull the dress over my broad shoulders, covering the round breasts behind another veil of white. I squeeze them with my hands, the large, charcoal-smudged fingers easily wrapping themselves around the sacks of flesh.

One last look and I conclude that, despite its imperfections, I have a figure that men find alluring. If nothing else, it is a benefit to business. Tonight I shall enjoy showing myself off in the company of my temporary benefactor, and hopefully round out some of the edges in my face with the fat of a fine feast.

4

THE GRILL ROOM IS BUSY TONIGHT, BUT MRS. NESS MANAGES TO secure a small table for us towards the back. I'm more tired than I think, as walking down the stairs from the lobby takes a toll on my legs. The clientele is almost entirely composed of men, and we easily arrest the small pockets of conversation upon our entrance. The room is regal in its design, with a polished marble floor and dark oak arches along the walls. Being in the cellar essentially, below grade, it is wonderfully cool and a great relief from the heat of the day.

There is a set menu available in honour of the Stampede, with only a slightly inflated price of one dollar and twenty-five cents per person. We both agree to order it on the insistence of our waiter. He is about to leave the table when I ask to see a wine menu.

"Miss?"

"What my niece is trying to say," Mrs. Ness intervenes, "is that she would like to order some wine with dinner. Unless you have some unpublicized ruling on lovely women with their old maid aunts ordering a drink in your establishment?"

"Of course not, ma'am," he graciously replies. "And may I say that you are hardly an old maid, aunt or otherwise."

Mrs. Ness bows her head in acknowledgment as the waiter clicks his heels together.

"Gregory!" he calls with practiced delivery. "A wine list, please, for the ladies." He turns back to Mrs. Ness. "My apologies, madame. We are obviously unaccustomed to having such lovely clientele here at the King George Grill."

"I won't tell his majesty if you won't," she offers with a wink.

"Of course." He turns to me with equal civility, only a little more forced. "Miss."

I smile snidely, safe in the protective company of dear auntie Ness.

We decide on a bottle of Bordeaux. She decides, that is, but allows me to place the order. Our first round of Celery en Brancey, Queen olives, and a fresh crabmeat cocktail arrives with the wine. Our waiter pulls the cork at the table.

"How I love that sound," Mrs. Ness says. I smile at her words, as our glasses are coloured a deep burgundy.

"Thank-you for opening your home to me," I announce, raising my glass by way of a toast. "If not for you, I would have been roughing it out in the tent city down by the small river all week."

"The Elbow," she replies as we lift our glasses to each other. "The larger river is the Bow."

She lifts her glass to me and we drink. The wine is warm and delicious. I hold my first mouthful for a long time, bathing my tongue in the tannins and tastes that it hasn't enjoyed for weeks. I have enjoyed red wine since long before I was of an appropriate age to drink it, thanks to my father sharing small sips, and later, glasses with me. I know little about it compared to him, other than I like how it makes my mouth feel. Wet and dry all at once.

"So," she says, "you've never told me what it is you're running away from, Miss Tara Hale from Halifax."

Fear grips me suddenly, and I feel my heart pounding. I smile and cock my head. "What makes you think I'm running away?"

"Oh come now," she says, "I know a fellow escape artist when I see one. At first I assumed it was over a man, a love affair gone wrong, but you've proven yourself far too advanced to be bothered by such a footling matter."

I swirl my wine in the glass, watching the burgundy liquid coat the insides with a faint copy of itself, and can feel the sting of tears hit behind my eyes. "I'm searching, I think, for something that's gone missing in my life. That's part of it."

"And the other part?" she probes, a model of exceptional grace and etiquette as she delicately slices her celery stalks into edible sizes. "What else sent you away from home?"

I stare down into my plate, slowly recalling the images from that night at the end of April.

HUNDREDS OF VICTIMS are being carried into the curling rink. The "death ship" has arrived and is being unloaded. Most of the victims are from Ireland. Some are in boxes, others are bound in canvas. Some merely wrapped in bed sheets.

I CLOSE my eyes as tight as I can to banish them from my thoughts. I want to be free of them tonight, all of them, and enjoy my meal.

"Very well," Mrs. Ness announces, after indulging my silence long enough, "keep your secrets."

"I just needed to get away," I quietly reply. "That's all."

"And so," she says, deftly changing the subject to one more comfortable, "where to from here?"

"Westward," I replied. "Banff, to see what all the fuss is about there. And then my final destination, Vancouver. There's a train departing at 10:15 tomorrow morning."

"So early?"

"It could be worse. I've made arrangements for my trunk to

be delivered to the station tonight, so as not to have to fuss about it in the morning, in case I sleep in."

I unfold the train schedule obtained from the station to double check the time, and stop suddenly as my eyes descry a name I had all but forgotten.

"What is it?" she asks.

"Nothing," I say. "Just a town I've heard of but never been to."

"Which?"

"Emmett."

"Emmett Alberta?" she says with surprise in her voice. "How on earth could you have heard of such a place as that?"

"Do you know it?"

"My husband had some clients from down that way. Emmett is a tiny religious settlement near the border. A strange bunch, to say the least."

"Strange how?" I ask.

"Religious renegades from the USA who branched out to escape persecution in their own country."

"Persecution?" I ask, amused at the scandalous nature of our exchange. "For what?"

"Polygamy," Mrs. Ness confides in dramatic, hushed tones. "Or at least that's the going rumour. They seem hell bent on putting that past behind them, and starting out anew here in the promised land. They're hard working folks for the most part, who abstain from spirits and beer. No tobacco, tea, coffee. No wine with dinner."

"Shame," I say.

"I don't know what the *church de jour* is in Halifax, but out here, the faithful of Emmet stand out like a crucified thumb. How were you raised?" she enquires.

"Roman Catholic, but I'm not a believer," I say, huddled in close as though disclosing a national secret. "When my father told me Nietzsche's pronouncement that *God is Dead*, I took it to heart. I've come to accept art as my religion, and I would sacrifice most things upon its altar."

I take a sip of my wine.

"Except wine and tea," I add with a smile. "Those I could never give up."

"Well then, you best steer clear of Emmett," Mrs. Ness concludes, "as you will be the misfit amongst misfits. They were up here a few years back for some sizeable lumber orders. Difficult to entertain with all those restrictions. Mind you, they were big on desserts. Three of them ate an entire pie in one sitting. Peter found them peculiar as well, but was impressed with their business dealings. 'Good customers' he called them. 'Good as anyone else'."

A small orchestra begins to play their first musical selection of the evening. I flip over the menu card which has the program listed on the other side. It's a sextet from Donizetti's *Lucia di Lammermoor*. Our next course arrives. Cream of celery aux croutons, with some steamed halibut in egg sauce. The food is filling, if a little bland. The halibut triggers a brief longing for home, and I wonder at the quality of fish this far from the ocean. The fried lake trout that also arrives is a bit more palatable, so I leave the halibut behind for the trout and pick at the Parisian potatoes (so called, but I never encountered a single potato prepared this way when in Paris last year).

"So what's in Vancouver for you?" she finally asks. "Or shall I say *who's* in Vancouver?"

"A what by way of a who," I reply, causing her to tilt her head in curiosity. "A chance to be a real artist, I think, and the opportunity to meet one there."

"Perhaps you've fallen in love?" she suggests, baiting me with her tone.

I laugh, and say that one can hardly fall in love with someone they have yet to meet.

"Are you quite certain?" She asks.

"Quite."

"Your conviction intrigues me, Miss Hale. Have you fallen in love before?"

"Of course," I tell her, "I fell in love with music and art and poetry. I fell in love with adventure, with Paris, with travel. All my lovers have taken time and have allowed me to be as patient with them as they have been with me. I have wept for weeks over boys who came to Halifax to study with my father. I have even been proposed to." Why I feel the need to brag about such an event I cannot say, but I colour my words with the bold purple of bravado nevertheless.

"Engaged but never married?" Mrs. Ness is intrigued now, and pushes aside her plate to lean into the table and await my answer.

"Not even engaged," I explain.

"You refuted his proposal?"

"Of course," I laugh. "I was fifteen."

Mrs. Ness winks in response, the shutter opening and closing over that wise, alluring dark eye speaking far more than words. We sip our wine as the next course arrives: breaded veal cutlets and fried oysters. She confesses to having an aversion to oysters, and I gladly pass on the baby cow. Eating the flesh of an infant – regardless of the species – would wrangle with my conscience far too long to justify any culinary satisfaction or curiosity.

"Was your mother disappointed with your refusal of marriage?"

"My mother died when I was born," I reply. "I was raised by my father and, at times, by my spinster aunt Helen."

"But mostly your father," she correctly assumes. "And let me guess. You never told him?"

"I tell my father everything," I answer a bit more defensively than I mean to. "To this day. Given that the young man who proposed was a student of his, he was remarkably restrained in his response. The student, however, was saddled with a reading list that would keep him locked in his dormitory room for the remainder of the term and likely render him blind."

The Grill Room is filling up more and more. Tables of men, dressed in beige linen suits with summer felt hats hanging on every hook and hat rack around the room, talk and cut their meat and smoke cigars. Most have their jackets off and their sleeves rolled up at the table. I can tell just by looking that for many of them this is their first time in a restaurant such as this, likely coming straight off the farms and ranches for a turn in the city. Many dart glances to our table, taken, I'm sure, with my companion's imposing beauty. Because I am sitting with her, I am included in the path of so many wandering eyes.

"He tells me I must yield to nature more," I say, continuing the conversation about my father, "and fight the world less. I'm never sure what he means."

"He worries about you," Mrs. Ness explains, "as he should."

"I can take care of myself."

"I'm sure he knows that, which no doubt adds to the worry."

She senses the line about to crossed, wherein a lodging matron and temporary dining partner becomes too motherly, so she pulls back. I am grateful for her awareness, as I know myself well enough that indignation would soon surface should she nose herself too much into affairs that don't concern her. Especially when it is the affair of me and my father.

"At least you're not falling in love with a religious renegade," she offers with a sly wink. "To Vancouver."

She raises her glass as another course is brought to the table. Roasted chicken, prime rib, Yorkshire puddings and mashed turnips. I am getting full, understanding that such a menu is designed with the appetite of a hungry male in mind. Our glasses are filled once again, and I enjoy the lightheaded cloudiness brought on by the drink, sitting back in my chair to relish it while I take a break from chewing and swallowing.

"To Vancouver," I sigh.

"And your rendezvous with this mysterious artist," Mrs. Ness probes. "What's his name?"

"Emily."

Her mouth is a nest of smiles, and another in a series of grins plays upon her lips.

Dessert consists of a cheese plate, some crispy biscuits, and a humble selection of fruit, including some rare pieces of the tropical variety.

Mrs. Ness rips open a pomegranate and stains the pads of her fingers as she splays the insides out, plucking the kernels.

"Mmmm," she hums as she sucks and bites, "so utterly decadent. I can't remember the last time I've tasted a pomegranate. Certainly never here before."

She reaches her spoon across to me, filled with a half dozen seeds bathing in their bloody juices. I feel a bit self-conscious, and dart glances to my left and right before opening my mouth in the most graceless, halting way.

"Thank you," I say as I bite into them, feeling like a drunken Persephone succumbing to my underworld goddess. "Now I've eaten the food of this place," I say, "I'm trapped here forever."

Mrs. Ness cocks her head to one side, baffled by my reference. I offer a quick and dirty telling of the Greek legend. She listens captively as the efficient Gregory empties the wine bottle into our glasses.

5

THE SUN IS STILL BRIGHT AND HOT AS WE MAKE OUR WAY BACK TO
the house after dinner. The walk is good after so much food, and
I continually belch up the aromatic reminder of each course. We
stroll in silence by the tent city, the smells of open fires and
roasting meats are not so appealing on a full stomach.

A stray dog runs toward us at full speed, and circles in
playful barks. Close behind is a portly woman brandishing a cast
iron fry pan, her reddened cheeks puffing in the sudden
onslaught of physical exertion.

"That your mutt?" she bellows. I am crouched down,
scratching the dog behind the ears. "Best keep her tied up or else
I'll crown the bitch with this frying pan."

"You'd have to catch her first," I reply, unable to resist
pointing out the obvious. I relax knowing that a cunning, four-
legged canine is in no danger from the two-legged bovine.

"Had I caught her," the woman huffs and puffs, "she'd be
stiff as a post and covered in flies by now. Stole a whole ring of
sausages off the fire grate back yonder."

"Maybe she was hungry," I calmly say.

"So are my kids. Keep her on a rope. If my frying pan don't
catch up to her, rest assured the sights on my husband's rifle will

find her easy enough." She turns to my companion and nods a greeting. "Evening ma'am."

She gives one final scowl to the black and tan mutt, turns, and waddles away. Mrs. Ness watches her go then speaks quietly to me as she strokes the dog's head.

"Let's see if she follows us. I have rope at home and we'll get out a bucket of water for her and keep her contained. She found food there once, and she'll go back to find it again."

The dog follows as we walk back to the house. I half hope that Mrs. Ness has forgotten about the sketch promised tonight as I sway with exhaustion. I would happily pay her fee, despite having bereft myself of nearly five dollars for the dinner and wine. A luxurious indulgence, but well deserved. We turn a corner after crossing the low level bridge, and the dog waits on the other side, reluctant – or afraid – to follow.

"Come on, girl!" I slap my thighs as I call. She starts, then stops, circles around as she wrestles with the decision.

"She needs a name, that one," Mrs. Ness says, sucking in her bottom lip as she contemplates.

"George," I suggest. "After the hotel."

"Funny name for a lady," she says back.

I consider George Sand, whose books I am familiar with through my father, but opt out of explaining my suggestion. I've never read anything of hers; she simply made a strong impression upon me by wearing men's clothing seventy-five years ago and smoking tobacco in public. A role model for sure.

"How about Millie? After the artist awaiting you in Vancouver."

"Agreed," I say, and then call her. "Millie! Come on girl!"

Mrs. Ness lifts her fingers to her mouth and lets fly a whistle that would stop a train. Millie tucks her large ears down and sprints effortlessly across the bridge to us.

· · ·

I WALK to the window a dozen times in ten minutes to check on Millie, half expecting a lynch mob to be approaching the house seeking sausage-theft retribution. She's fine, tied to the veranda post, drifting in and out of sleep, interrupting herself to snap her jaws at flies. No sign of a hunting party as the late summer sun sinks into the deep red bed of the western sky.

"Will this suffice?" Mrs. Ness emerges from the kitchen with an oversized sheet of heavy card stock, about two and half feet by thirteen inches in size. "I was thinking of a reclining pose. That is, if you're not opposed to suggestions."

"Fine," I say, smiling as I answer to mask my complete lack of interest in the activity looming now in the air.

"The light will be more favourable upstairs," she suggests, "and I've arranged an easel and chair for you there, as well as an oil lamp for later."

I tell her that I'll change into my work clothes and meet her up there shortly.

When I open the door to my room, I am immediately assaulted by the lingering smell of sweat and sun and Stampede emanating from the pile of clothes on the chair. Having had no intention of donning them again in the morning, I took no pains to ready them for wear. I cannot stomach the thought of climbing into them again tonight so I slip a light cotton dressing gown over my shoulders.

The last thing I want to do is work, but shall do my best to translate this woman into art. This is what she wants, after all, and I am not above bartering whatever talents I may possess in exchange for board and room. Only this once, of course. Were I to pay my way with charcoal and parchment all the time, the currency would soon lose its value and I would bankrupt my soul.

"Sweet Jesus on the cross," I can hear my father say, "it's just a sketch, Tara. Just clean your teeth and draw the damn picture so you can get to bed. *Your soul.*"

I listen to his voice in my head as I pull my stockings off. I like feeling him close in these moments. I shake my head and laugh at myself as I brush my teeth. This is what happens when I stop and think too much. The one sure way I know to silence the thoughts is by working. I will lose myself in the lines and shadows and forms and light.

6

"COME IN."

The knock on her heavy oak door hangs like an echo in the air of the silent house as she responds. I open it and feel the refreshment of a slight breeze from the open window. The floor-boards are distinctly cooler in here, and my bare feet eagerly embrace the drop in temperature. My eyes catch glimpses of the view from the second floor bedroom, and I'm amazed that I can see the campfires and canvas structures from the tent city, as well as dwindling activity on the fairgrounds this Friday night.

"I've poured a cup of tea for you, and I took the liberty of opening this," Mrs. Ness says, revealing a bottle of port wine. She is wearing a full length silk dressing gown, heavy and ornate, its dark forest green so much richer looking than the humble cream colours of my own. The sleeves on her gown are enormous; for all I know, she could have pulled the bottle out from there like some sideshow magician.

"It's only a ten-year-old port, but still a good vintage," she informs me, and without asking if I want a glass or not, pours out two. The thick, red nectar bloodies a small crystal goblet, which she hands to me. "To the creative act, and other marvellous mysteries."

She raises her glass to touch with mine. My eyes quickly widen at the pretentious and ominous toast, and she winks at me when she sees this. I'm uncertain if the wink is an acknowledgment of the inflated address or in reference to something else.

"Mmm. So sweet. Thank-you," I quietly say after taking a sip.

"Thank *you*," she responds and takes a large pull of her drink. The glass is empty after two full drafts. "It's from my late husband's reserve in the basement. I seldom have anyone here worth sharing it with, and I don't dare open a bottle alone. It is a pleasure to have you here, Miss Tara Hale of Halifax."

I take another sip and she promptly fills my glass and her own, the bottle still in her hand. She is gazing intently at me now.

"I have money, as I'm sure you've no doubt surmised. I want to be up front about my motives here. If all goes well tonight with the sketch, a full portrait in oils would not be out of the question. At a generous rate of commission, of course."

She continues to wrap her eyes around mine, like two large black stars seeking out a child to wish upon them. How can such light pour forth from such deep, bottomless black? The paradox – along with the hint of my first full commission – couples with the sticky sugar of the port, all of it mixing in my head to bring on a sweet state of dizziness. I break eye contact and search out the room for something else to look at.

"Everything is here for you," she says. "Easel, sketch pad, card stock, pencils. Is there anything else you need?"

"No, no," I answer, "this is more than fine."

"Interesting work clothes," she comments.

"Yes," I say, crossing my arms and curling my bare toes in a sudden wave of self-consciousness. "I chose not to wear my working clothes after all. They stunk."

"I'm sure they were fine," she says, "but so long as you're comfortable, then that's all that matters. Don't you agree?"

"Absolutely," I say, and after we drink one more time, she fills the glasses one more time. "Shall we get started?"

The pencils are new and a good quality, far nicer than what I can afford. I move the easel aside and pull the chair forward towards the bed. I sit, consider the light, then move the chair again, this time to the opposite side of the bed. It is now beneath the open window, and I can take full advantage of what remains of the day's light and the cool breeze on my back from the west-facing opening. When I finally settle, sit, and look up, I see that Mrs. Ness has removed her long robe and is reclining nude upon the bed.

"I hope this is not presumptuous of me," she says, reading the shock in my expression. "You've done nude studies before, I assume. In art class at the very least."

"Dozens," I say, with as much nonchalance as I can summon, using the lie to hide my reaction. The sheer perfection of her naked body married to the unexpected shock of seeing it on full display mere inches away from me has me at once bounding forward and held back, like a balloon cornered by the wind. "Hundreds." I laugh, with the expanded second tier of my fib, and my subject stretches out, cat-like, in confidence and comfort.

"Thank god you're not uncomfortable with it," she purrs.

"Not in the least."

"To be sketched while dressed would be wrong somehow," she says. "I'd feel like I was modelling the latest fashions for an Eaton's catalogue."

Part of my job as an artist, I try to convince myself, is to mask my inexperience. Artists are worldly, sophisticated. We are meant to shock, not be shocked. I tell myself this as I look at the beautiful woman on the bed. Her skin is naturally of a dark tint, almost brown, and free of blemishes. Every curve and lift on her breasts and hips are proportionately perfect, and her long auburn hair flows like ribbons of silk. Her legs are crossed as she reclines on her hip, modestly hiding the triangular tuft of hair in her middle. I somehow feel less of a woman in the presence of so much of one. Both of us female, but as if we are of a different species altogether. What should feel natural and easy is rife with constricted breath and a nervous shake in my hand. I down my drink.

For the past three months, my subjects have been clothed and sketched from the neck up. And exaggerated in the most freakish ways. What I lack in education, I compensate with imagination. Creativity is a far more reliable informant than experience.

Her beauty, the possibility of a commission, the port, the breeze, it all converges together in me as I hold my pencil in a state of recalcitrant stupor. But there is something else, a tiny mole of an intruder, tugging at my sleeve for attention, or at the very least recognition of its presence. I quickly lay the sketch pad on my lap and instruct my subject.

"I'm going to do a few trials in my sketch pad first," I say, "and then move on to your piece of card stock. Lay very still. Don't move."

She holds her pose by holding her breath. She hasn't posed before.

"But you can breathe," I tell her.

I get to work, connecting my hand directly to my eye, moving one across the white of the page as the other crosses the browned white of her skin. I silently pray to a dead god that my sketch does not come out as caricature.

She is easy to draw, true beauty being so readily captured. Like that preacher's son at the fair. What was his name? His face flashes in my mind like lightning; gone before it fully arrives, bumping into itself on the way out, and I focus in again on Mrs. Ness.

"Tilt a little towards the light, please. Too far. Yes. Hold there, please. And breathe."

And breathe. I should listen to my own instruction as I find I am holding my breath as I work, as if sketching under water for seconds at a time. I come up for air in the form of a drink. First of port, then of tea. I flip the pages of the sketch book quickly, as if I am the page turner to a pianist during a performance of a Rachmaninoff piano concerto. Fast, passionate, grueling. No time to breathe.

"Can I stretch out my –"

"No," I almost shout, "stay still. A few more minutes, then you can stretch." I say the words as I smudge a line of her lower thigh into a shadow.

I turn my head over my shoulder to check the light. There's not much time left. Thank god for these long summer nights on the prairies. An oil lamp will cast all the wrong shadows. I must finish the basic form with natural light.

"Take a moment to stretch now, if you like. I will start on the large card stock when we resume. We haven't much time left with the daylight."

"Of course," she says with excitement. "A quick stretch, a drink. Hand me your glass."

I do so out of reflex, then stand with my newly filled glass at the window. I look out at the setting sun as I sip, trying to decide if port is sweeter than rum. My eyes are growing heavy, and a bit cloudy from the excess of this night.

"How do you want me?" she asks when we get back to work.

"Just as before," I say, "with your leg up and slightly bent."

"Like this?"

"No. More this way. Not so much. Now bend it. Like before. No."

"Sorry, I..."

Without asking or thinking, I stand and lift her leg into place. The skin of her thigh is unimaginably soft and smooth, and her leg muscles relax into my hand like an enormous snake. She gasps as I touch her.

"There," I say, "don't move." I curl her hair behind her ear before returning to my seat. This is unnecessary, I realize, as I won't sketch any details of her face until later. The oil lamp is sufficient for that. I perform the gesture anyway, sit back down, and lay the card stock on my lap.

As I sketch, the urgency relaxes. I could close my eyes and

draw now from memory, still ripe and fresh as a newly peeled orange. The light is soft and warm and perfectly suited to its subject. The two of them, Mrs. Ness and her light, are one and the same for a brief moment. Both aging, but showing no signs of weakness, offering the best of who they are to one another. And I am the lucky witness to this most sublime and ephemeral of marriages. I am spectator and secretary, both seeing and recording the meeting.

"Mrs. Ness," I whisper, not so much a summons as an expression.

"Please," she says, "call me Jennie."

"Yes, Jennie. You're very easy to sketch, I have to say." *Because you are beautiful.* "Like you were already here, on the page, before I ever came along."

"How lovely," she says in between breaths. She's breathing heavily now, as if taking my reminders too much to heart. Her sighing shifts the position of her arm.

"Your arm, please."

"Yes?"

"Can you return it to where it was?"

"I'm sorry," she says. "I didn't realize it had moved. Where?"

I stand and replace it for her. It's only a matter of an inch, but such is all that's required to move from soft light to unforgiving shadow. The back of my hand accidentally brushes her breast in the process.

"I beg your pardon," I whisper. She says nothing in response, but only sighs. I notice her nipple sit up straight, as if a slouching student was suddenly tapped on the shoulder by her schoolmarm.

The light is barely hanging on, but I continue with the sketch. The intensity of creating something beautiful tricks me into feeling completely sober all of the sudden, and thirsty. I reach for my glass of port and drink it down in one mouthful, its syrupy texture coating my mouth and tongue like sweet paint. My head spins as my hand steadies, and I feel as if I am entering some kind of trance.

This is it, I tell myself, *this is what all great artists must feel all the time.* I feel as if I've graduated into some mysterious, secret society of privilege and knowledge. I sketch her breasts. Breast, really. Only one is exposed, its sister buried behind a silk sheet and silkier arm. I feel as if I am still touching it, brushing it with the back of my hand over and over.

The intruder is back, demanding now to be noticed.

Arousal. I am aroused by her.

No. Am I? How could I be? Why shouldn't I be?

I try to shake the intruder from my thoughts, but the tiny mole has moved in and will not be so easily dismissed. I set down the pencil, and lay the card stock aside.

"Are you finished?" Jennifer asks, confused.

"For a moment. Please, relax, stretch, do what you need to do."

And she does.

Jennifer stands and lowers herself down to me in one swift movement. I feel her lips press against mine, and the wet, sticky taste of port on her tongue meets the same on my own. I snap my head back as if my lips have just brushed against the hot belly of a stove. My body is way ahead of my mind, and I react before fully understanding what I'm reacting to. I instinctively pull back, rejecting her and her kiss. My heart rate seems to double, and the innocuous intruder of arousal from seconds before turns to fear.

"Don't be afraid," she whispers as she pulls me closer to her, and I realize just how strong she is.

I place my hands on the upper position of her chest, above her breasts, and push with all my strength. She lets go of my back and I spring to my feet instantly, trying to step away as I do so. The sudden rush of blood disorients me, and I knock over the crystal glass of port as I step out of the invaded space.

"I'm sorry," I say. "You misunderstand... I'm not..." The

words are incomplete, insufficient to diffuse a situation such as this.

Why am I apologising? I ask myself the question the same time I notice the sharp pain on the bottom of my foot. I lift it sideways, on an angle. Blood. I've stepped on the port glass, crushing it with my bare foot. Shards of glass have embedded themselves there.

"I'm sorry if I led you to believe…" I say, apologising again. Have I brought this attack on? Yes, attack. I am being attacked and wounded in the process.

"Stop being silly," she says, "and come sit down."

She's right; I am being silly. *Aren't I?*

Though I've never been the object of a woman's affections before, I've seen homosexual women together in Paris, and never considered the coupling to be wrong or threatening in any way. Why am I reacting so strangely now? I should relax. I should be flattered. I should breathe.

"My foot," I say, "it's cut."

"I'm sure it's fine," Jennifer calmly responds. "What you need is a drink. Let me fetch you another glass." She starts to search for her robe, her exposed flesh entirely void now of allure and beauty. The mere mention of another drink triggers a reflex in my stomach and I taste the acidic bile of vomit in my throat.

"No," I quickly say, "I must go. Now."

"Go? Go where? It's the middle of the night. Now stop this silliness and sit down. Please."

I sit on the edge of the bed; not so much due to her invitation but because my head is reeling and I think 'better to sit than fall'. I recline back and see the ceiling of the room spinning before I pass out.

7

I FEEL MY LEG RISE INTO THE AIR AND OPEN MY EYES TO FIND JENNIE kneeling before me, holding my calf, wiping away at the base of my foot. I pull back but she holds it firm.

"Hold still, my little bambino," she admonishes. "You have a nasty little cut here."

A bowl of water sits on the floor, along with some white gauze bandages. How long have I been out? Jennie holds a pair of tweezers, which cast large, long shadows across the room from the oil lamp's light. The tenderness of her touch and ministrations draws my attention away from nausea and I settle down to being nursed. Her robe is over her shoulders but still open, so I keep my eyes averted.

"There, that's all the glass," Jennie says as she reaches around and pours some whiskey into another white bowl. "Do you want a shot of this before I disinfect your sweet little footsie? It will hurt like the devil."

I shake my head, feeling my teeth starting to chatter.

"Suit yourself," she says, taking a long pull on the bottle herself. "On three."

I feel her hands firmly on my leg, just above the ankle, the bowl of whiskey directly below it.

"One. Two. Three."

My foot is forcefully plunged into the little pool of alcohol, and I let fly a scream as I try to jerk it out. Jennie holds it firm. Tears come to my eyes from the unbearable stinging at the other end of me. I lean back on my elbows and grit my teeth.

"That should do it. Well done, my brave little lady."

I feel her wipe my throbbing foot with the softest towel in the world, then wrap it in clouds of gauze. She pulls my sketching stool over and folds the towel on top of it, then loads it up with two pillows from the bed.

"You need to keep it elevated," she tells me.

My nightdress falls open slightly as she lifts my foot up, sinking down towards my hips exposing more and more leg in the process.

"Lay back some so your foot rests higher than your heart. That's a good girl. Now try to relax."

I close my eyes tightly, hoping to shut off the throbbing pain of my foot, which has now joined with the nausea in my stomach and the ache in my temples. I am a wreck, and I concentrate on the past to pull me through the unpleasantness of the present.

I'M FIVE YEARS OLD, and suffering from one of the dozens of mild flu viruses that gather and spread in universities. It is the middle of the morning, on a Sunday, and I am sitting on my father's lap in a rocking chair. I know it is a Sunday because my father is home and my nanny is away at church. My father gently rocks in the chair, humming as he holds me close to him. Upon my lap is an empty chamber pot for when I am sick. I feel safe and comfortable and momentarily rescued from the loneliness of quarantine my nanny always insists upon in bouts of illness.

"Feeling better?" my father asks and I nod. Just as I'm beginning to believe that I am feeling better, a wave of sickness rises with tremendous efficiency, and I aim my mouth at the chamber pot's opening. My father is not alarmed, knowing all along it would happen. As I am

finishing the expulsion from my guts, my bladder decides to join in the fun, and I wet myself and – by extension – my father. I start to giggle uncontrollably.

"Well, well, well," he says, laughing with me, "I've heard of muling and puking in the nurse's arms, but even Shakespeare never conceived an event such as this. How infinite the love a father feels for his daughter, as he holds her pissing and puking upon his very lap." He lightly runs his finger up and down my arm, making no great effort to get up and change himself. Or me.

I FEEL the same light touch of fingers up and down my arm and open my eyes. I was dreaming the memory, more vivid than a simple recall. Jennie now lay beside me, her breasts exposed, as she runs her fingers up and down my arm.

"You drifted off there for a while," she says. "Feeling better?"

I am afraid to move my arm. Afraid there will be another incident. My foot is numb. I am half asleep and less than half awake. My eyes burn when open, so I keep closing them, struggling to stay alert.

"Shhh," Jennie whispers as she presses a cloth to my forehead. "Go back to sleep my little doe, back to sleep."

I open my eyes in intervals, each time her face is closer to mine. I can smell her breath now as she continues to whisper, as if I am a tiny little candle she is trying to blow out. I am sinking deeper into the bed, giving over to it, and giving over to Jennie's advances. I have no fight left in me, my entire battalion of energy gone to my foot, my head, and my stomach.

"Shhh… there, there… just relax."

I feel her lips just above mine, and think I should not be afraid, not be averse to this. I am an artist, I am on an adventure. I should try this. I tell myself that this is just the sort of experience I have been looking for without knowing it. I part my lips and close my eyes. She kisses me, and I don't pull away. I don't breathe either, and lay perfectly still, frozen, offering her a corpse but nothing more. She presses harder, searching for something beyond compliance, some evidence of active participation. Her hand begins to stroke my breast.

I turn my head to the side, sharply.

"Stop." I say the word like I'm slapping her face.

Jennie freezes for a second, and then abruptly pulls herself off of me.

"Go," she grumbles, "get to bed."

I roll over and start the difficult job of sitting up, lowering the pins and needles in my leg to the floor.

"Quickly, please." She is angry. I would be too, I suppose, if I was her. How could I ever be her?

"How dare you invite my love and then so childishly refuse it," she snaps at me.

"Invite?" I have to stop moving in order to ask the question.

"Yes, invite. You travel alone, exuding a confidence and experience well beyond your years. A young woman, unwed, wearing men's trousers. What would you have me think? Seducing me with your invitation to dinner, inviting yourself to my room, allowing me to strip and pose before you."

"I..."

"And speaking so freely of love and art. Love and art are one and the same thing, young lady. Both are infernos reserved only for the most capable of hands. You are a petty amateur, no better than a teasing dilettante. Lucky for you I am not a man, seeking vengeance upon you for leading me on and then refusing to perform. Rest assured, child, that a man would speak less with his voice and more with his hands, turning words to fists."

I limp towards the door, the soft warm glow of the oil lamp dancing on the glass knob.

"A word of advice," she says, in no way kindly, "behave like a whore and you'll be treated like one. You and your infantile sketches, your fond memories of 'dear daddy'. I mistook you for a woman, a human being, a person of passion and intelligence and warmth. How foolish of me, to let my blood be heated by the flame of your lies. Away with you. Child."

I limp in the blackness of the upstairs landing, feeling my way for the stairs. The darkness is swimming in my tears as I grope like a blind soldier, wounded from a battle she was suddenly thrust into. I hear the door slam behind me as my hand finds the staircase railing.

Downstairs I quickly dress into my traveling clothes, squeeze my throbbing foot into my boot, lace it up tight, and hastily throw as much as I can find into my bag.

OUTSIDE THE SKY is dark with a thin scar of pink in the East. My heart stops when I feel a pressure against my legs. It's the dog, the stray we rescued a few hours earlier. Is that all? A few hours? The joy and innocence of the evening before seem to belong to a different era. A different Tara.

"Millie. Come girl." I untie her from the veranda post, and she licks the salty stains from my cheeks. I hang on to the rope as I try to get my bearings.

"Which direction is the train station?" I ask out loud. West of here, towards the downtown buildings. I can see their shadowy tops in the near distance. I start to walk, limping more than walking, telling myself that I will board the first train that comes and let it take me wherever it chooses. A momentary lapse of panic floods through me as I feel through the contents of my bag for my money pouch. I find it, feel the bulk of it, and assure myself that it is all there.

We make our way to Ninth Avenue and limp slowly towards the station. Some all-night fires are burning in the tent city, but both Millie and I keep focused on the road ahead. Thankfully the early morning air is only slightly cool, and it's no hardship to wait outside for the sunrise.

My trunk arrived safe and sound last night, and I shudder to think that I may have forgotten entirely about it if not for that foresight. Millie stays close and well behaved as I limp along the platform.

The ticket officer is in his wicket, but the window is closed. He must have only arrived a few moments before me. I tap on the glass.

"Good morning," he says without looking at me. "I'm not quite open yet. If you could come back—"

"I need a ticket now, please. Westward. Vancouver, Banff, whichever train is leaving next."

"Like I was saying, ticket sales will be open fifteen minutes before the first train departure, but I'm afraid it's not going west. That train doesn't leave for another five or six hours."

Too long. I'm convinced that either Jennifer will come looking for me, or I will bleed to death sitting on the platform. I can't bear the thought of walking to find a doctor, or spending another minute in this town.

"When is the first train out of here?" I ask.

"Miss, if you can give me a few minutes to sit down and take my coat off, I'll be happy to —"

"Please," I beg. "It's an emergency."

He tilts his head down and looks at me over the lenses of his spectacles, which are pinched down low on his nose. Assured he isn't aiding a fugitive, he consults a schedule pinned to the wall beside the service window.

"The CPR line, southbound, leaves in thirty minutes, and the C&E line, northbound for Edmonton, leaves in just over an hour."

North or South? Which to take? Both seem equally arbitrary and innocent, neither getting me any closer to Vancouver. There will be a cost involved with either choice, unnecessary costs of lodging and food and return to Calgary to board the proper train westbound. Not to mention the throbbing danger of my injury.

North or South? Up or down? We have no idea what unintended consequences will result from the simplest of choices. What adventure awaits in this direction? Which in that?

Up until this moment, I have carefully planned out every aspect of my itinerary, always aware of what I was heading towards. As much as I could, at least. It was always another fair, another chance to sketch and earn money.

Another few miles away from father and the curling rink morgue that home had become.

The summer is nearly over, and the fairs are pretty much finished. I know nothing about the towns and offerings in either direction. As far as I'm concerned, each route will drop me into a wasteland, and all I will have is time.

I know I said at the beginning that I'm good at waiting. Better than most. I could wait it out up north or down south, what difference could it possibly make?

So I choose. It's hasty, reactive decision making, and may come at a price. But a choice needs to be made, so I make it.

All to save thirty minutes of waiting on the platform.

8

"WHAT'S YOUR DOG'S NAME?"

I am dreaming of sand and ocean when I feel a tug on my skirts.

"Miss? Missus?"

I open my eyes to find two adorably dressed children, a boy and girl, about five and seven-years-old respectively, sitting across from me. They feed small chunks of dark bread to Millie, whose tail is polishing a spot on the rail car floor in gratitude.

"Millie," I say after clearing my throat. They look at each other and smile broadly, sucking in air as if I had just revealed a long held secret.

"We have a danty named Millie," says the girl.

"Danty Millie," the boy nods.

"We're going to her house."

My dog. I hadn't thought about possession in any sense until the children ask about her. I guess she's mine now. Or I'm hers.

"She doesn't bite," the girl tells me with all the conviction of a supreme court judge.

"Who?" I ask.

"Millie."

"Your auntie? Heavens I hope not." Their laughter summons

Mother, who is sitting down towards the end of the car. I see the plump woman squeezing down the aisle to my seat.

"Hush now, children," she says, "don't bother the gentleman. I'm sorry if they're disturbing you."

"Not at all," I say. "I love the company of children."

Realizing that I'm not a gentleman at all, her doughy face puckers and reddens, and she drags her children away by their wrists. The boy looks back and I give him a wave. A yank on his ear snaps his head forward before he can return the gesture.

I ensure my ringed finger is in full view, but the over-protective matron is not seeing it.

My foot feels on fire, and I attempt to walk off the pain by going up and down the aisle of the train car. It only makes things worse. I settle into my seat and give in to sleep, the beginning of a fever starting to pinch my temples.

Sometime later, I'm awoken by the train pulling into a station. With no idea where I am, or when, I gather my bag and limp woefully onto the platform. I can no longer put any weight on my foot, aware of it only by its numbing absence of feeling. A porter is kind enough to go back for my trunk, and as I search for a coin, I ask him where we are.

"End of the line, ma'am", he says officially, with the slightest of nods.

I've never taken a train to the end of the line before. So final.

"And the name?" I ask. "This town. What's the name?"

"Emmett, ma'am," he says as he sets my trunk down on the platform. "Emmett Alberta."

THE LATE DAY sun is somehow nearer to the globe in Emmett, and I have never felt closer to burning or melting - depending on what I'm truly made of - as I do right now. I hobble towards the edge of the platform and pull a yellowed kerchief from the front pocket of my trousers to wipe my sweaty brow.

Standing upright, watching the porter unload my trunk,

shoots fire from my foot and up my leg. I reach out to lean on something but there's nothing there. I nearly tumble over on the platform, the heat and my hunger not helping at all to maintain some sense of equilibrium. I am forced to quickly put my bad foot down with considerable weight, and another sharp bolt of pain lightnings up my leg. In a flash, I relive every smell from last night: tent city fires, oil from the lamp, perfumed skin, port-drenched breath, the funky smell of desire, dog hair, blood from the cut.

The cut. The cut. The cut.

The memory of my injury skips like a phonograph record, and the image of glass needling into my foot waves over me again and again. I need to sit down. I make my way to the trunk - all but dragging my foot now - and flop down on top of it.

I realize all of a sudden that I have no idea how to get from the platform to a hotel, or if there is even a hotel at all. How will I move my trunk?

I try to unlace the bindings of my boot to rescue my aching foot from its cage, but even the slightest touch near the foot is excruciating. I've really done it now. I must get this looked at, and soon...

Blinking my eyes brings me back to alertness. I blacked out for a moment. I look about me, hyper-conscious all of a sudden, and take stock of my bag, my trunk, my dog.

Oh sweet Jesus!

"Millie!" I call, and then try to whistle, but my mouth is dry. Damn it, I'm thirsty. "Millie! Come here, girl!" My voice cracks shamelessly. If I was listening to me (and seeing me in the state I am in), I would conclude that here is a woman about to fall apart. I am, because I've lost the only friend I have in the world. My dog is nowhere to be seen. I limp my way back to the railway car and call around, but no luck. Besides, the station master is clearing the platform borders to allow the train to pull out.

"My dog," I whimper, "I think my dog is on the train."

"No dogs allowed in the passenger car, ma'am," he says without looking at me.

"No," I mumble, "you don't understand. My dog..."

"Please step back, miss, the train's moving out."

"Millie!" I call again, suddenly understanding how easily the mind can break, how fast the slip from concern to panic to hysterics. Had I the energy, I would have used it to scream and hit the station master with my fists.

The train slowly pulls itself away like an old man getting out of bed, puffing itself into locomotion. My eyes flit back and forth on every window, waiting to see Millie's face and paws pressed up against the glass. Guilt swells in my chest and chokes me into breathlessness. How could I have forgotten her so soon? As the repercussions of my selfishness resonate, I turn and scan the platform and beyond for someone to assist me.

That's when I see him, the young man standing in the shade of the station house, his hands pushed deep into his trouser pockets. I recognise the pose at once.

Of course. Emmett.

What was his name again?

I slip my faux ring off, hiding it in my pockets. My eyes moisten and a smile cracks the dry skin of my face. Like he's a brother home from battle. Like he's the messiah in the wilderness. Like he even knows who I am.

"Fancy meeting you here," I say as I limp towards him, wishing for all the world he would see me as some kind of goddess approaching.

He looks up and squints at me as he tries to place my voice and face in his mind.

"Tara Hale. I sketched you the other day. At the Calgary fair."

"Well I'll be," he says as he pulls off his cap, letting fall that crop of straw atop his head. "Never would have recognised you in a thousand years in those breeches. You look like any number of ditch-digging boys showing up in town looking for work, only a bit prettier."

The heat - both from the air and my foot, which is quickly climbing up my leg - causes me to falter.

"Careful now," he says, reaching out to steady me.

"Thank you," I say, and then want to add an explanation of some kind, but don't.

"You look hungry," he says, as he carves a wad off a chunk of reddened jerky with his pocketknife.

I eagerly chew on the offering. It's salty and good but hard as leather and my jaw begins to ache.

"Did you forget to hop the train somewhere important or did you lose a bet or have you just plain hit rock bottom or what?"

"Pardon?" I grunt, struck dumb with the salty salvation of the meat.

"What are you doing in Emmett?" he asks. "I'm afraid there's no fair here."

I look out across the wide stretch of brown grass and dirt that goes on indefinitely, newly exposed by the departed train. There, far in the distance, like a black fly stuck against some endless windowpane, is Millie, hard at work chasing a ground squirrel. The shade and mini-snack restores my wits somewhat, and I smile back at him.

"I'll tell you if you answer me this. Do you typically spend your afternoons hanging out at the train platforms?"

"Have been for the past three days," he explains, "and you're the first person of any interest to arrive. We're waiting for a cheese-maker to come from Ontario, and pop's been on eggshells since Thursday when he was first expected. Therefore, every day at this time, I'm sent with a horse and buggy to fetch someone who never arrives."

I hear the squeal of a kill, and watch Millie stand over her prey, holding the fresh corpse in place with her front paw as she digs in for her meal while I continue to struggle with mine.

"I've got a buggy ready and willing to drop someone some-place. Sure would be a waste to head back to town empty handed. Can I offer you a ride somewhere?"

"The hotel," I say, "assuming there's one here."

"Hotel!" he laughs. "Not quite. You're not in Paris anymore, Ms. Hale. Sister Talbot lets out rooms upstairs in her house. She's sour as a lemon and twice as yellow. But the place is nice enough by Emmett standards, which means you're assured a roof, bedding, and plenty of suspicious eyes if you're checking in as a single woman. What more could you ask for?"

He gestures for me to walk towards the buggy, and I wince when I step on my sore foot.

"You all right?"

"Fine, I think. Just a cut on my foot the other night. I'm sure it's nothing. I hope it's nothing."

"Not the way you're limping it, it isn't," he says. "Best have Mother take a look at it before anything else. Last thing you want is an infection. How'd you hurt it?"

"Long story," I say. "Is your mother a nurse?"

"Nurse, cook, bottle washer, and drill sergeant all rolled into one. She'll fix you up, and likely feed you in the bargain. Unless, that is, you've got something against a home-cooked meal."

He helps me to the buggy, and as I watch him load my trunk and bag, I whistle for Millie to come around. For all I know she might have been using me to get a free ride south and upon arrival will easily leave me cold. I call her a second time. Her oversized ears point up, she comes running and leaps up into the cracked leather seat of the buggy.

"Millie," I say, "this is…" but for the life of me I can't recall his name.

"William," he smiles. "I didn't know you were traveling with a companion."

"Nor did I 'till last night. Get in the back, girl. Go on. Git!" Millie's ears go down as she hops over to where I point and snap my fingers.

"My father has little love for animals of any kind," William explains, "so we haven't got any at the place. Mother, however, grew up with as many pets as siblings so she'll be happy to see this mongrel. Where did you find such a fleabag?"

"Calgary," I say, "and she's no fleabag. Looks as bad as you or I would without a proper bath in weeks or months. She's a fine dog and I love her to no end. Isn't that right, Millie?"

"Be sure to keep her tied up at night," William tells me, "or the coyotes will make a meal of her the way she just did of that poor gopher out there."

THE RIDE into town is slow and easy, but I suffer from a pounding headache for the duration of it. William talks continually about the history of Emmett, and the surrounding area.

"Yes, it's true," William says, answering a question that I have not asked. "Everyone asks eventually, so I'm skipping to the chase, as it were. Yes, the area was founded by polygamist outlaws, men of faith on the run from men of the law."

I look to him, no doubt with a vacant stare due to my discomfort. "I only have one mother, if that's what your look is asking. And no wife - or wives - of my own." He points across to his left and resumes the tour guide persona. "That there is Lee's Creek, a tributary of St. Mary's River. The fishing's not bad, so long as you..."

The sound of his words trail off as I close my eyes, the bright sun no friend to the thundering behind my temples. All my faculties are engaged in keeping myself from vomiting, as my body begins to pulse with nausea and fever.

9

WILLIAM'S VOICE DRIFTS IN AND OUT, AS WAVES OF FEVER AND nausea rise and fall. The trail from the station is rough going, and each bump of the buggy wheels echoes with shoots of pain up my leg.

He's explaining something about the arrival of the cheese manufacturer, how it's of immense importance, growing region, healthy survival. I have an image of this place as a small child needing its bottle of milk in order to grow. Except the child's head is the size of a hot air balloon, and the bottle the size of a sewing thimble. I'm fading quickly.

"Miss Tara Hale," William announces, "you remember my father, Charles Emmett Snow."

I try to sit up to attention, and find myself mumbling a repetition of his middle name. "Emmett?"

"Founder of the town that bears his name," William confirms. "The idea of a town named Charleston sounded far too American for the new world's taste, and the very idea of naming a place after 'Snow' immediately spelt doom. That's how Emmett came to be chosen, first settlement of the blessed brethren outside of the United States. Population – to date – four hundred and ninety five." He leans over and asks with a hush, "How long are you staying?"

Before I can answer, he changes the number in a loud proclamation.

"Four hundred and ninety six. Ninety-seven if you include the mutt."

"A pleasure to see you again, Miss Hale." Mr. Snow extends his hand as he speaks.

I squint and offer my hand.

"I must say, you don't look well at all. Is everything all right?"

"She sliced her foot open," William offers on my behalf. "We're on our way to Sister Talbot's now, but suggested that Mother take a look at her wound right away."

"I see," his father nods, and then turns towards what I assume is the front door of their home and calls. "Sarah, dear. Can you come out please?" He turns back to his son. "Shall I assume, William, that Mr. Ibey was not on the train?"

"You shall. But Miss Hale was, and I figured she was a much prettier arrival than Mr. Ibey."

"Yes, yes of course, of course."

A woman comes out of the house, wearing an apron tied around large floral skirts, wiping her hands on a dish towel. She nods to William and then looks to her husband.

"Ah, my dear," Mr. Snow says, "allow me to introduce Miss Tara Hale. She is the artist responsible for the drawing of William."

"Very pleased to meet you, Miss Hale," she offers, but no hand or warmth is forthcoming.

"Miss Hale," William announces, "this is my mother. Sarah Evangeline Snow."

"A pleasure, Mrs. Snow," I say as I shift my weight in the carriage to extend a hand. In doing so, my foot is pressed against the side and I cry out in pain.

"Mother, I hope you don't mind, but I told Miss Hale that you would take a look at her foot. I think it might be infected."

"It's not as bad as that," I say. "I was careless and stepped on some broken glass with a bare foot."

"Nasty business," Mr. Snow says, "a cut on the foot." He offers sympathy in this way, simply acknowledging the obvious, careful not to judge or coddle too much.

"Father, would it be all right to continue on to Sister Talbot's? I have Miss Hale's belongings already in the buggy."

"Of course. Your mother will go along with you and help our visitor get settled. Sarah?"

"Let me get the medical kit," she says. "I'll only be a moment."

"Really," I protest, "you don't need to fuss so much. I'm sure it's fine."

"No trouble, Miss Hale," Mr. Snow graciously returns.

All at once everyone is moving in all directions on my account. After being self-sufficient for so long, I cannot deny the drunkenness I feel with such a glut of doting. It lowers my defences, and the fever takes hold with a vengeance.

Suddenly I hear Mrs. Snow coo with delight, and the gurgling moans of pleasure I have come to identify with Millie.

"Told you she loves dogs," William whispers, and then assures me that Millie will be fine, promising to put a bucket of water out for her first thing.

"He'll need to be tied up on the north side of the house," Mr. Snow instructs. "He'll have some shade in the evening there."

"He's a she, Pop."

"I'm afraid Sister Talbot, proprietress of the boarding house, is even less charmed with dogs than I," Mr. Snow informs me, "and won't let your companion within 100 yards of her establishment."

"Thank you, Mr. Snow," I say. "You're very kind."

He flicks his head in a quick nod, lifts his hand away, then positions himself aside the horse and checks the harness with a quick tug. He is not a man for small talk, especially with a young woman outside of his home. Thankfully Mrs. Snow is soon out the door and climbing into the buggy. She carries a neat tin box beneath one arm.

"Unload her trunk, Son," his father mandates. "Then straight back home and see to the dog."

"Will do, Pop."

Mr. Snow deftly hands his wife up into the seat of the buggy beside me.

"Supper's on the stove," she tells him. "You and William eat at the usual time, then send him with a plate for Miss Hale after he's done. Be sure to wrap it well so as to keep it hot. Save mine in the warmer until I'm home."

"Very good, Mother. Give my regards to Sister Talbot at the hotel." He points this instruction up, no doubt to assuage any concern over a single woman seeking a room at the village hotel.

"Understood," Mrs. Snow says, as she pats her husband's hand, then turns to William with a nod.

He clicks his tongue and reins the horse into motion. I watch his father lift his hat in farewell as we turn, and hear Millie whimper as she watches me ride away.

"As I said," William announces, "Pop hates animals."

"Your father hates nothing in this world, William. He has love for all God's creatures."

"Dogs are pretty low on the list, Mother. A notch above Catholics."

"Enough now," she says, trying not to laugh. "Concentrate on the reins."

We arrive a few moments later. William lifts me down from the buggy as his mother begins to make the arrangements for my room. Despite my febrile state, this small display of kindness is moving me greatly, and I have to pull my lips into my teeth and inhale deeply through my nose to prevent tears. The sudden intake of breath leaves me dizzy, and I feel my body become overwhelmed with heat, as if a pile of coals lie at the bottom of my boot, stoking me up like a blast furnace. I bend over to catch my breath, leaning on William's arm as waves of heat flush over me.

"Miss Hale?" he asks with alarm in his voice.

"Just a little dizzy all of a sudden, that's all," I try to assure him. "Give me a minute."

Limping through the door of this simple, two-story house, I catch snippets of the conversation between Mrs. Snow and the proprietress. She is trying to explain who I am and what I'm doing here.

"An artist from the fair in Calgary. She sketched William's portrait."

Pursed silence emanates from the woman. I feel myself about to faint, and sit down on the trunk, opening and closing my fingers against the brass edges to busy myself with a conscious activity to forestall passing out.

"Brother Snow is aware of her arrival in town, and sends his regards," Mrs. Snow adds.

The woman lifts a registry up to the table - albeit with reluctance - and fusses around for a pen and ink. William is standing at the back of the lobby, ready to carry my trunk and bags up to my room. If a room is to be granted me.

"On top of this," Mrs. Snow continues, "the lady is injured and I would like to tend to her foot and be home in time for the evening fireside, if it's not too much to ask."

Miss Talbot turns to me with a forced smile, and I force one back. She is in her late-forties, with a face like a well-used pin cushion. Her hair is parted with severity down the centre, and then pulled back in the tightest bun imaginable at the crown of her head. I notice her mouth moving ever so slightly, as if constantly chewing something, as she forces that smile at me.

"If you'll kindly sign our register, Miss..."

"Hale," I say, standing with uncertainty.

"Miss Hale. I'll have young William take your trunk up to room number three." With a nod, William effortlessly lifts my trunk and starts to climb the stairs. "It is a pleasure to welcome one of God's children to Emmett, and we hope your stay is pleasant."

As I'm about to sign my name, the pen slips from my fingers, and I collapse to the floor.

I'M BEING CARRIED UPSTAIRS, but feel like I'm falling. My eyes open and I hear the voices around me, but can't see anything clearly. I'm laid upon the bed, and sink deep into the mattress. I feel wet, hot, and scared. I hear Mrs. Snow take control.

"Set the trunk there, William," she commands, "against the foot of the bed, front side out, and leave it closed. Take this pitcher downstairs and have it filled with hot water, then bring it back up immediately."

The mention of pitcher and water makes me thirsty. I try to ask for water, but find I cannot speak. Mumbles of a plea escape my lips, but no one takes notice.

"Wait a moment, William. Light this oil lamp before you go so I can get a good look at Miss Hale's foot. Quickly now."

I feel her rolling up the leg of my trousers, unlacing the straps on my boot and prying it off with considerable effort. The pain is excruciating, despite how slowly she is removing it, and I scream and writhe, clutching the simple knit bedspread in my fists. I turn my head to the side and open my eyes, trying to pull myself out of the darkness I have slipped into. I see William gazing in a frozen stupor at my leg, the jug still in his hand. Either my foot is a bloody display of grotesque infection, or else he's never seen the bare leg of a woman before. Likely a combination of both.

His mother snakes him out of the room with a fierce hissing, then gently begins to unravel the bandage wrapped around my foot. Mrs. Snow has a touch that is both gentle and purposely efficient, and I shut my eyes once more as the fever heralds me back into darkness.

10

"WATER. WATER."

I move my lips in an effort to say the word, but the sound is dry as dirt. I mouth it in request; my intention is to ask for it, but soon I'm describing it. The heat that originated in my foot and radiated through my entire body is fading. And fast. I'm suddenly cold, freezing, and soaking wet. I try to squirm my way out of this feeling, but my arms and legs don't easily move. I gasp for air, feeling the pressure tighten around my chest brought on by being immersed in cold water. The shock to the respiratory system comes next, followed by a retardation of muscular control, and finally the involuntary shaking.

I open my mouth to scream, but cannot catch my breath. The sky is dark and cloudy, and I hear the slap of water up against my ears.

I am in the ocean, floating, and freezing cold. In the distance, I see a ship engulfed in flames. I start to make my way towards it, hoping the heat from the fire will warm the water and stop my teeth from chattering. I kick my legs with as much energy as I can summon, but it's slow moving. The ocean is littered with debris, obstructing my route to the fire. I check my distance to

the ship and find that it is further away than when I started. The
fire is getting smaller.

The Titanic is burning, sinking, and the water is freezing. I'm
there suddenly, one of the passengers trying to survive in the
unforgiving Atlantic. I have no sense of time. Past and present
are one and the same.

I kick harder, but make no headway. My legs keep hitting
something, making it impossible to propel forward. The water is
still frigid, but I am overheated with the effort. I don't understand how I can feel this in water, but my body is breaking out in
a sweat, so I stop moving.

Suddenly there's a loud explosion behind me, and the sky is
lit up. For a few seconds it is daylight. I see the ocean around
me, filled with hundreds of bodies. My heart stops upon seeing
the open eyes on their faces, carelessly gazing to the heavens
above, as if enjoying a harmless outing on the lake. I try to
scream but can't, my chest squeezed again in the vice grip of
freezing water.

I LIFT MYSELF UP, and feel the pressure of two hands on my shoulders, another pair against my head. I am back in the hotel room
in Emmett. A small glow from the kerosine lamp softly lights the
room, and I see Mrs. Snow at the foot of the bed. She looks
terribly concerned when she catches my eye, then smiles reassur-
ingly at me. I see her mouth form the words 'all right' and
'father', but the sound is muffled.

There are two men standing above me. One is Charles Snow,
but I don't recognize the other. Again, the sound is muffled, as if
I'm under water trying to hear what's being said above the
surface.

I close my eyes and sink back into the soft mattress.

. . .

IT IS day at the hotel. I see the bright summer sun pushing against the drawn curtains, the slivers escaping from either side blinding me instantly.

"Eileen, hold her down while I change the dressing." The voice is Mrs. Snow's.

Another set of hands press into my shoulders, and my exhausted strength is no match for them. I am pinned down into the bed, and blink the perspiration out of my eyes. I try to focus on the person holding me down, but she is in shadow, back-lit by the bright summer window. She smells of barn - a distinct aroma of animal, shit, and hay wafting off her arms, her face - and I find it oddly soothing. She senses my temporary lapse into relax-ation, and leans down to whisper in my ear.

"Forsake this place as soon as you are able. Leave and never come back. Forsake. Forsake. Forsake." Her repeated use of the word echoes in my ears like some unknown music, and I am away once again. Calm, easy darkness swallows me, and I float on the smell of hay and a country girl's warning to 'forsake' this place.

This short-lived bout of tranquility is bitten in half by the teeth of another vision, and my febrile mind sends me reeling into another locale.

I AM HOME IN HALIFAX, in my aunt Helen's kitchen, but I can't smell the sea. I can only smell hay and animal hair and shit. The windows are too high for me to look out of. I try to stand, but each attempt only results in my falling down on the dirty wooden floor.

My aunt calls me over to her, and I try to walk but can't. I look at my feet. They are small, baby feet. Impossibly small, looking more like swollen pink blisters at the ends of my legs.

She calls me again, and I crawl to her. My entire body weight rests on my arms and the floor is hard against my hands. Afraid I will collapse, I stop moving and my aunt laughs as she effortlessly picks me up. I am no bigger than her hands. She fusses with the buttons on her blouse, and a pink breast emerges with a brown, milky nipple standing straight out. She puts it in my mouth, and I begin to suck.

The milk is sweet and soothing at first, but quickly turns hot and sour. I try to pull my head away, but it's being forcibly held there. I hear moaning and look up to see it's not my aunt's breast I'm suckling but that of Jennifer Ness. I bite down hard, and feel a sharp slap against my bottom. I am pulled away and handed to the country girl who smells of barn.

"Forsake or be forsaken." She whispers this in my ear as she rocks me back and forth. Across the room is Mrs. Snow singing a hymn. Her breasts, too, are exposed. They are large and full, and growing larger as I watch her. The weight of them pulls her forward, and she sings louder and louder to keep from falling over altogether. The words to the song gradually become clear, and drown out the barn girl's whispered 'forsakes' with their soothing effect.

I am a child of God,
And he has sent me here,
Has given me an earthly home
With parents kind and dear.
Lead me, guide me, walk beside me,
Help me find the way.
Teach me all that I must do
To live with Him someday.

11

I open my eyes to see Mrs. Snow rocking in a chair at the foot of my bed. A massive, unfinished quilt cascades off of her lap. It is composed of a series of patches, discarded fragments of material gathered over a century it seems, with no two patches alike. She holds a section of the quilt in her hands as she stitches two patches together with bright yellow thread.

She sings the hymn from my dream as she works. I glance around the room, taking stock of its contents: a tray of dirty plates and cups atop the dresser; a large basket filled with yarn and knitting needles beside Mrs. Snow's chair; a small collection of mittens beside the basket, knit, I assume, by the same hands that have been caring for me. On the other side of the bed, towards the dresser, stands a collection of white gauze bandage material, looking pristine next to the bucket of reddened ones at its side.

"Welcome back, Miss Hale," Mrs. Snow says as she approaches the front of the bed and sits down at my side. She lays her open palm on my forehead. "You gave us all quite the scare, young lady."

I lick my lips into life and moisten my mouth to speak, but my words fall like chalk.

"You've been... You've..."

She smiles as she shakes the mercury down in a thermometer.

"Seven minutes, under the tongue. Let's see just where we stand before anything else."

"You've been with me all night?" I ask, managing the question before she inserts the cool glass into my mouth.

"All night?" Mrs. Snow says as she smiles broadly, a slight sting of pain registering in her eyes. She looks tired, the dark shadows below her eyes testament to a lack of sleep. "My dear, you've been out with a deadly fever for three days."

My mouth peels open in shock, but she gently presses upward on my chin to close it down again.

"Lips tight against the thermometer, now. No cheating."

Three days? The news hits me like a slap, and I feel my face contort itself in a mixture of gratitude, humility, and sadness.

"Heavenly Father loves you so very much, my child. He's been watching over you, not calling you to His bosom just yet, giving you more time upon this earth."

A knock at the door is answered by Mrs. Snow's calm voice.

"Come in."

A young woman, about sixteen, steps into the room. Her instant shock is due, it would seem, to my being awake. Mrs. Snow addresses her while continuing to cradle me in her arms.

"Eileen, tell Brother Snow that Miss Hale's fever has broken and that she is awake. And bring some broth and biscuits back to the room if you please." She turns down to me. "I imagine you're hungry."

I nod as I suck the saliva back in that has been escaping between my lips.

"That will be all. Thank you, Eileen." The girl sharply nods, just once, and departs without saying a word.

"Charles has been worried sick about you," Mrs. Snow tells me as she takes the thermometer out of my mouth and holds it up to the light. "Ninety-nine point seven. I would call that a divine improvement, coming down from the 104 you were at this time yesterday. Charles has been trying to find a way to contact your parents, but since we never got a chance to know where you're from, it's been slow going."

The thought of a telegram going home sends a shudder of grief through me, and my eyes moisten once more. I try to think of my father, but his image is mixed up with something to do with the Titanic and fire on the water. A fevered dream, I expect.

"He's been in contact with our local police detachment," Mrs. Snow tells me.

"The police?" The unspoken 'why' in my question causes Mrs. Snow to turn towards me and take my face in her hands. A serious gesture to issue an equally serious declaration.

"Truly," she begins, "we did not know if you would live or die, Miss Hale. We were all a bit scared, I must say. Even Charles, who seems to be afraid of nothing in this world. Thankfully, you are a healthy young woman. Your body was able to fight it off, with the Lord's help of course."

"I don't... I don't understand." My voice is still dry and cracked, and together with the struggle for breath brought on by weeping, words are a great effort.

"What's the last thing you remember?" she asks.

"Riding in the buggy with you and William. I was afraid... I would be sick there..."

She tells me of how I passed out downstairs, was carried upstairs by William, and laid out on the bed.

"I set to work removing your boot," she informs me, "which was finally achieved with a great deal of difficulty. Your foot was severely swollen and every time I touched it, you would scream in agony. William and Sister Talbot had to hold you down as I peeled your boot off and unwrapped the bandages. The dressing was filthy, wet with blood and pus and dirty from your boot. I imagined that was how the cellulitis set in."

"Cellulitis?"

"Your infection. It was wiggling up your leg like a hungry

snake. Your fever was climbing almost as quickly. A cursory inspection of the bottom of your foot revealed that there was still glass fragments lodged inside the wound, which made matters much worse."

I start to feel light-headed at her words, reeling from the account of many hours of cleaning out glass, alternate applications of warm compresses and herb poultices to draw the infection out.

"When I was finished, I was so worried for you. Your fever continued to climb, and I had done all I could. The closest doctor lives in the next township, which would put him at close to six hours away by the time he was fetched and brought. While I sent William off for him, I had Charles and one of the other priesthood holders here administer a blessing to you."

My eyes widen with the trigger of a memory of two men with their hands on me.

"Yes," she explains, "you woke during it, but your wakened state was short-lived. I'm surprised you recall it at all."

"I don't remember," I stammer, "what they said... their words..."

"Thank the Lord," she replies, "for 'twas He that saved you most of all. I was just doing what I was taught. What anyone else would have done."

Another knock at the door, and the young girl enters again followed by William.

"Thank you, Eileen. Bring the tray over to Miss Hale please." The girl hesitates slightly. "Come now, she won't bite you."

Eileen brings the tray to me, and sets it on my lap. I immediately pick up the scent of hay and horsehair, the smell triggering a memory which lights and fades like breath on a coal.

"Thank you," I say.

She nods sharply again, holding her position for a second or two longer than is necessary, as if not sure what to say or whether to step back or forward or move at all.

Mrs. Snow lifts a plate off the bowl, the steam of a simple

broth floating upwards now. Two warm biscuits are on the tray, wrapped in cloth. My nurse sinks a spoon into the earthy, oily liquid and lifts it to my lips. The taste - so exceedingly basic and yet so explosive - fills my entire mouth.

"You've all been so kind," I stammer. "I don't..." Once more, my words are choked away with emotion. I lower my chin upon my chest and try to pull myself together.

"Father's gone off to notify Sergeant Parks that Miss Hale has recovered," William announces, then turns his face to me, removing his hat as he does so, causing that blond hair to fall once again upon his brow. He brushes it aside once, but it returns as soon as his hand has left his head. "Otherwise he'd be here too. He sends his best wishes and hearty congratulations, Miss Hale."

I nod to him as I curl my lips inside in an attempt to close the faucet of my tears.

"Oh. I almost forgot. Your dog is doing fine, too. If her constant tail-wagging and licking of my hand are any reliable form of communication, she sends her best wishes as well."

Millie. I had not thought of her since coming around, forgetting entirely that she was even in my life. The mention of her stirs the pot once again, and new tears flow with ease. Never have I cried so much in so short a time.

"All right, you two," Mrs. Snow says, "let's give Miss Hale a little privacy. She has an exhausting three days behind her, and can look forward to at least a week of recovery ahead. There will be plenty of time to visit soon enough."

William and Eileen take their leave, and I return to my dinner, serving myself spoonful after spoonful of broth and digging into my biscuits. Never has food tasted so grand.

"How does your foot feel now?" she asks.

I stop eating for a moment to search for an answer.

"It feels fine," I say. "In fact, I can't really feel it at all."

"It's probably a bit numb from the elevation," she replies, and then dismantles a tower of cushions from beneath my heel, gently lowering the injured limb down onto the mattress. "Can you feel my hand upon your heel?" I nod with mouth full. "Wiggle your toes a bit."

I do as she asks, and can feel the newly created apertures in the pad of my foot. Strange to feel an opening where there was never meant to be one. The sensation is slight, but there, and I manipulate my foot out of curiosity to feel it stretch to the maximum.

"Ah!" I cry, as pain explodes in response to my curiosity. I suck air through my teeth. The crumbs of biscuit in my mouth hit the back of my throat, and I cough and choke as a result.

"Careful," Mrs. Snow tells me. "It's going to be awfully tender down there for some time. The cuts are not wide enough for stitching, but the glass made its way deep into your foot. May I take a look at your leg?"

She lifts the bedspread over and draws the bottom of my nightgown up, a nightgown I have no recollection of putting on. "Oh yes. Much, much better. The redness is fading into a healthy pink. You're recovering quickly and well, Miss Hale."

She tucks everything away again, under cover, and collects a new batch of white gauze bandage. "I'd like to change your dressing. That is, if you don't mind me doing so while you eat."

I shake my head and try to speak, sighing heavily every three or four words.

"I'm nearly finished. It was the best soup I've ever tasted. The biscuits are delicious."

"That's more the hunger and lapsed fever talking, but thank you all the same." She unwraps the dressing from my foot, the redness growing darker with each round, and deposits it all into the bucket in the corner. She begins to hum a familiar melody as she wraps it anew.

"That song," I say, recognizing it at once, "it's beautiful. What is it?"

"One of the hymns from our church," she answers with a smile, and softly sings the words to the song that I awoke to earlier, the song that led me out of my fever and back into health.

I am a child of God,
And so my needs are great…

She comes to my side when she's done. "Can I have Charles send a telegram to your parents for you?"

"I'll write a letter," I reply, far too quickly as I notice her brow raise, "and post it home this week."

"Are you sure? It would be no trouble and I'm certain they'd love to hear that you're all right. Parents have a way of knowing when their babies are in trouble. I would hate to think they've been suffering without word from you."

"I'll write as soon as I'm able," I tell her. "That's the best way."

"Tell me about your family," Mrs. Snow says, as she sits at the side of the bed.

My heart stops for a moment. What can I possibly say? The truth would be too painful and a lie would be so terribly improper after all she's done for me. "What would you like to know?"

"Well… if you were at home right now, what would your mother have to say about the glass in your foot?" She is smiling when she asks this, and her relaxed state in turn relaxes me.

"If this had happened at home," I explain, "I imagine one of the nurses at the college would be waiting on me."

"The college?"

"King's College, in Windsor. I spend most of my time in my father's apartments near the university."

"And your mother?"

"My mother died when I was born," I explain.

Mrs. Snow nods, without pity or surprise. "I see," is all she says.

"I have an aunt. My mother's sister. She is the closest thing to a mother in my life, but lives in Halifax. We're not terribly close, I'm afraid."

"I'm sorry to hear that."

"Trust me," I say, "we all function much better with distance between us, like the oak trees in Point Pleasant Park. Too close and we'd surely strangle one another."

Mrs. Snow smiles and reflects on what I've said. I fear for a moment she has taken me literally.

"Family is the most important part of God's plan for us," she says. "We are His children, and to have a healthy, loving family is the truest way to worship him."

"I assure you, Mrs. Snow," I tell her, "I'm closer to my father than anything in the world. He is my advisor, my friend, my mentor, my one true love. Without him, I -"

A sharp bolt of pain and I retract my foot.

"It will do that from time to time, Miss Hale," she informs me. "All part of the healing process."

I breathe in and out in a succession of quick breaths, as if trying to blow out an endless array of candles on a cake.

"Tell me more about your father. Best to keep your mind off the pain."

I close my eyes and search for something to say, but all I can see is the image of a fire burning on the water flashing across my mind.

"Another time, perhaps," my caregiver quietly concedes. "Rest now."

12

I AM AWAKE FOR HOURS BY THE TIME THE KNOCK COMES AT THE door. The sun is shining through the window. I know, for I watched it come to me to say good morning. William and his mother enter the room after my 'come in' is called out. I prop myself up and pinch a little red into my cheeks.

"Well, you're looking much better this morning," Mrs. Snow announces as she sets a tray before me consisting of a bowl of porridge, a glass of milk, and some cold chicken. "You'll need to start building your strength back up, my dear. I've taken the liberty of adding some molasses to your porridge. I don't care for it myself, but it's the only way William will eat it. Besides, a little black glue is probably not a bad thing. Let me know how it tastes."

I thank her and begin to devour the offering before me. As I slurp and chew, I notice William is brandishing a book, rather thick and bound in leather. He passes it from hand to hand as if it were too hot to hold.

"Doctor Snow here says you'll be laid up for a couple of weeks," he says, "so I thought you might like some reading material to help pass the time."

"How thoughtful of you," I say, excited at the prospect of

losing myself in something thick and adventurous. "I hope it's filled with intrigue, insight, and an array of characters burning away on the bonfire of plots and subplots."

He hands me the tome as his mother wraps the dressing on my foot. I fan its thin pages, blackened with minuscule type.

"You want intrigue? Plots? Characters? Then that's the one for you," Mrs. Snow tells me. "Our Book has it all with the spirit of the Lord present on every page."

"Forgive me," I say as I flip through it, "but it looks like the Bible, only with chapters I've never heard of before."

"Another testament," William explains, "an addition to the Bible, if you will. In many ways it's the perfect book for reading during convalescence, as some sections are so exciting, they'll keep you awake and engrossed for hours, making time disappear. Other sections will put you to sleep in no time flat."

"Enough now, William," Mrs. Snow says, "show some respect please."

She turns back to me and beams as she speaks. "I still remember the first time I read it. I don't know how many candles I used up reading late into the night, or how many hours I filled with daydreams about the ordeals those people went through. It is indeed the most perfect book ever written, and the reason we are who we are today."

I don't buy her endorsement at all. Firstly, because the most perfect book ever written doesn't exist because it's never been written. And how boring would perfection be in any piece of art? I'm immediately discouraged and try to keep a polite smile on my face. Hopefully there are other books around this peculiar little hamlet.

My foot all bound and set, Mrs. Snow lifts it up onto the stack of pillows and begins to gather the tray of breakfast dishes. William automatically takes over, and his mother thanks him with a soft hand on his back.

"Now, if you'll excuse the two of us, we have a number of chores to tend to. I'll send young Eileen with some lunch later."

"Thank you again," I call out, "both of you. For the food and," holding up my new book, "food for thought."

The two of them utter their goodbyes as they close the door behind them. A brief silence, just enough for me to sigh, and the door flies open with the force of William's enthusiasm. I jump out of my skin with the surprise.

"Let me know if you have any questions about the book," he barks, and then closes the door, leaving his words behind him.

I soon settle back into my skin, and the bed. The door flies open again. I jolt, but don't jump the second time.

"Not *if*. *When*. Because you will. Lots of them." The door closes abruptly once more.

I wrap my fingers around a morsel of biscuit, cock my arm, and take aim at the door. Sure enough, it flies open a third time. I fire a pitch that lands squarely between William's eyes, and the biscuit bursts into a cloud of crumbs. Some land in his mouth, which is open for the purposes of speaking. He claps it shut without breathing a word, smiles with a quick raise of his eyebrows and exits the room, closing the door behind him.

It remains closed for the rest of the morning. I have no idea what he was returning to say the third time.

13

EACH DAY BEGINS AND ENDS LIKE THE ONE BEFORE, AND I SOON LOSE track of the calendar. The boredom that I thought would be my demise has become like any other routine. It's amazing how we grow accustomed to anything that repeats itself over and over, and grow to accept it as 'the way things are'. I fill the hours with some light sketching, visits with my entourage of caregivers and meal providers, and enormous sessions of reading, if I can even call it that.

Their so-called 'holy book' is wholly unreadable. It as if the writer took the shadow from the old testament and light from the new, and mashed them both together in a paste of forgettable grey. Dipping his pen into this bland ink, he then attempted a new portrait of Jesus the Nazarene. I can only assume his intentions were sincere and genuine, but alas, the result is a caricature in words, entirely lacking in irony. Something not quite scripture and so very far from literature. It is laughable while managing to be completely bereft of humour.

A question begins to cook as I burn through the pages: have I been duped by this preacher's son and his mother? Is this mockery of the Bible a private joke they share, springing it upon unsuspecting visitors, all for a laugh? Surely they can't take it as seriously as they professed upon presentation.

The narrative is implausible, but then so are the narratives of a thousand other books, some of which are considered great works of art. Certain passages lend themselves well to quotation and moralizing - what else would one expect from pseudo-scripture? - while other sections lie dead upon the page. I am compelled to finish it out of courtesy to them. They saved my life, and I find myself driven by some primitive rite to do their bidding, whatever it may be. If reading their 'most perfect book' carries me even a fraction closer to paying the highest of debts back, than read it I shall, regardless the toll on my intelligence.

Though it be the equivalent of an emetic in print, I'd memorize it word for word if they asked me to, and sing it out like some medieval troubadour, lute firmly in hand, my voice quavering with every 'And it came to pass' born out of its pages (and there are literally hundreds of them in this literary catastrophe).

YOUNG EILEEN IS my most frequent visitor. This is somewhat unfortunate, as she is also the quietest. My longing for conversation is only enflamed by her reticence for it, so today I am determined to coax her out of her shell.

"Good afternoon, Eileen," I cheerfully say.

"Ma'am."

She curtsies, as she always does, careful to not upset the bowl of soup that is balanced on her tray. She wears a clean, cream-coloured dress today. Every other time I've seen her, she has been cloaked in the same dingy floral print affair. Clouds of yellow permanently stained below the arms, the collar frayed and grimy. But today, she is well turned out, despite the fact that her hair has lost a fight with a brush and is arranged with pins and combs in a pretty fashion.

"You look very pretty today, if I may say so."

"Ma'am."

"Surely you didn't dress up just to bring me lunch."

"No ma'am. Church this morning."

My mind flips back over the days. Is it Sunday already? Have I really been calling this bed, this room, this town home for a full week? I lower my head and rub my eyes, trying to account for the disappearance of seven days. She steps closer, setting the tray on the dresser.

"Do you want me to fetch Sister Snow?" she asks, reading my incredulity as discomfort.

"No, no," I say, "I'm fine. Just surprised to hear that it's Sunday. So soon." I look out the open window, the thin curtains lightly dancing in the breeze. Sun and blue and the smell of warmth. "It looks like a beautiful day."

"It is, I guess." She lifts the tray again, eager to set it before me and be out of here. "You're sure you don't want me to fetch Sister Snow?"

"Yes, I'm really fine. I'd be happy if you just sat for a moment and talked with me."

Eileen's eyes widen all of a sudden, shift around in quick, bird-like darts, and finally end in a curious squint.

"Talk about what?"

"Anything, really. It's so bloody miserable here, made doubly so by how lovely it is outside. I'm stuck here because of these damned bandages."

My little curse ignites a spark behind her eyes. She sets the tray on the table and sits on the edge of the bed. She clears her throat, folds her hands upon her lap, unfolds them just as quickly, and clears her throat once again, all the while keeping her eyes averted from mine.

"How'd you hurt your foot?" she finally asks.

"Cut it," I say, "stupidly, on some broken glass."

"Is it feeling better?"

"Very much, thank you. And thanks again for bringing my lunches all week."

"Sister Snow asked me to," she quickly replies.

"I know. But thanks all the same. It's very kind of you. I'm sure you have better things to do than to bring a meal to a stranger."

I doubt she has anything better to do, knowing that the prime entertainment in towns like this revolves around the mysterious arrival - and extended stay - of a stranger. We sit in silence for a few minutes.

"How was church?" I finally ask.

"Same as ever," she answers, and then waits, and then asks a question back. "Have you been to church before?" She's getting the hang of conversation easily enough.

"Yes," I tell her, "but not for a long time."

"It's kind of boring," she confides, "except for the shopping."

"Shopping?"

"Sacrament meeting," she explains. "It's the best part. You get to see all the boys with their hair combed and fine clothes up front with Brother Snow where they sit as priesthood holders. It's the best shopping day of the week in Emmett."

"It sounds like damn good fun," I say.

She blushes again at my pocket-sized profanity, looks over her shoulder, and when certain the empty room isn't watching, smiles broadly.

"When I was first here, during the fever, you spoke to me, didn't you?" I ask her.

She is silent a moment, the smile running from her face like a child caught with her hand in a candy jar.

"Maybe." She throws the answer like a dart. "I might have said something. Something like 'you'll be all right' or something."

"*Forsake*. You said *forsake*."

The word comes to me without my searching for it, though I had tried to recall it many times before these last few days.

"I remember, because it struck my ears as an odd word, like it was right out of your holy book." I hold the collection of *And it*

Came to Passes up as a reference. "Not a word I'd have thought someone like you to use. *Forsake*."

She shrugs in silence and swallows in nervousness.

"Tell me, Eileen, have you read this?"

"Supposed to," she says, "but I can't concentrate that long. Besides, Brother Snow reads it plenty enough every Sunday, so I figure I'm getting through it that way."

"It's really terrible, isn't it?" I offer. "I mean, it's so horribly written."

My companion's eyes widen in shock, as she pulls her head back. "It's the word of God," she says in a whisper.

"Well then," I offer, "God must have been having an off day when he wrote this, because it's dreadfully unreadable."

She looks at me with that expression of shock for ten or fifteen seconds, and then suddenly opens her mouth into the first laugh I've ever heard from her. Her teeth are as close to perfect as any I've seen. This surprises me, as I was expecting the opposite.

"You're wickedly funny, Miss Hale," she says, still in hushed tones, covering her mouth as she continues to laugh. "Never heard anyone say the sort of things you say before."

"And I've never heard of anyone shopping for a boyfriend in church before," I quickly reply, and she pivots her head side to side quickly, conceding my point.

"It's all just for fun," she confides. "I'm going to marry William, anyway. We've been promised to each other. "

I'm less surprised at the content of this news than I am at how easily she discloses it. I'm tempted to ask how many potential wives William has had promised to him, but refrain.

Arranged marriages, though somewhat outdated elsewhere, make sense here. Tight religious communities such as this prefer to fold into themselves, and I can imagine the Snows arranging things with her parents long ago.

But I can feel the warning in her voice as well. If she perceives me as some sort of competition to William's affections, then it is no wonder I was urged to forsake this place. Her way of saying 'hands off what's mine.'

"How wonderful for you," I say, placing my hand on hers in a gesture of congratulations and, I hope, alliance. "Has a date been set?"

"As soon as he's back from his mission," she confirms.

"Mission?"

"For the church," she blurts out, then adds with a friendly laugh "don't you know nothin, Miss Hale? Every boy goes on his mission as soon as he turns nineteen. Then comes back and gets married. It's always been this way."

"I see," I tell her. "I'm sorry, I'm not familiar with the ways of your church. How long will he be gone for?"

"Two years," Eileen confesses, with a touch of sorrow in her voice.

"Ouch! That's a long time to wait. When does he leave?"

"End of next month."

I nod and pat her hand. I have a momentary vision of William preaching to the natives out of a mud hut, this deplorable book in hand, his hat still upon his head.

"Well then, that explains it. If I only had a few weeks to spend with my husband-to-be, I'd tell a single young woman who suddenly showed up in the middle of my arrangement to forsake this place too."

Eileen swallows and blinks her eyes three or four times as she fusses and fidgets. "I never said anything like that," she lies, terribly I might add, and so painfully obviously it's almost sweet. "I don't think. You sure it was me?"

"No," I say, needing no more confirmation of her warning than I already have. "I'm not even sure if it was anybody. I was in such a state, with the fever and all. A pig could have flown into the room and dropped diamonds out of his ass and I would have thought *how lovely.*"

Eileen laughs once more, louder and longer than before. "You're so funny, Miss Hale."

"Oh come," I say, "aren't we on a first name basis yet? I won't call you 'young Eileen' as Mrs. Snow does, for I think you're much older in so many ways. Nor will I call you 'sister'. I will call you Eileen, and you'll call me Tara. Agreed?"

She's suddenly very pretty as she smiles.

If my fate is to be stuck in Emmett for another week as my foot heals, I vow to kill the boredom of being here before it kills me. Eileen, my new ally and friend, will help me do it. Through her, with her, and in her, I'll set about unraveling whatever mysteries this place has to offer. And if there was more behind her instruction to *forsake* it than a romantic rivalry.

14

THE LAST THREE DAYS HAVE SEEN ME ON MY FEET, TAKING STEPS around the room as I reacquaint myself with my legs and the fine art of walking. Eileen has been appointed as my human crutch, and she handles my body weight with the greatest of ease.

"This is why they call you Eileen, I suppose." My pun thankfully falls flat, as I lean on her broad shoulders. Like most cheap word plays, it sounded clever in my head, but dead upon my tongue.

Mrs. Snow has prescribed sunshine and fresh air, so today we're attempting a walk outside. Eileen successfully aids my descent from the upper floor room, and to our mutual surprise, William is waiting outside with a cane. He is humming a tune as he waves the cane in the air. No, 'humming' is too generous a verb; he pushes sound through sealed lips resembling, somewhat, a tune. Like a body pulled from a fire, it is badly deformed but recognizable.

"Is that Rock of Ages you're attempting to find?"

William uses the cane as a conductor's baton, humming louder and even more off key to his imaginary choir. He's the musical equivalent of a termite, destroying a great work of art even as he burrows into it. I look to Eileen for affirmation, but she is focused on keeping me vertical.

Last night, my temperature was 99.6. I've been a point or two above or below this all week; a fever low enough to trick me into feeling healthy, yet high enough to keep me in bed. My attempts at walking around the room are enough to raise the mercury a notch or two, but I believe my foot is rapidly recovering.

"Miss Hale, forgive my skepticism, but I would not have believed it had I not seen it with my own two eyes," William offers by way of greeting.

I raise my hand in mock imitation of a fiery preacher and intone the following: "Now I ask you: is this faith?"

"I beg your pardon?" he says.

"Let me see if I can remember it by heart. *Yea, there are those who say if thou wilt show us a sign from heaven, then we will know for sure, then we shall believe. Now I ask you: is this faith?*"

"Pretty close", William confirms. "A few words different here and there, but that's it in a nutshell."

He sits down on a tree stump, his hands folded across his lap like some holy pontiff in his chambers.

"You've gotten all the way to Chapter 32 in less than a week?" he asks. "I'm impressed, Miss Hale. It took me months to read that far."

"Au contraire. I've read the book in its entirety once through, and have gone back over several passages many times since."

"You've read the entire Book on your first go?" Eileen asks, her eyes widening as she speaks.

William studies me with those deep blues of his, searching my face for a question or comment that he could not come up with on his own. He sits amazed, quizzical, enflamed… the way I have sat while looking upon certain paintings in the past. The way I want others to look upon mine someday.

"May I ask," he says, "what it was about that verse that caused you to commit it to memory?"

"Aside from sheer boredom and absolutely nothing else to

do?" I quip. Eileen stifles a laugh, but William maintains his focus.

"It didn't affect me much one way or the other when I first read it," I explain. "I liked part a few verses earlier much more, the analogy of faith to a seed that one lets grow within one's bosom. A metaphor simply expressed and easy enough to understand. In fact, I don't think I remembered the quote I just recited at all, at least not in a conscious way, until I read the very end of the book."

"Which?" William asks.

"Something or other about asking God to prove the truth of everything written," I say, trying to recall the exact words. "By the power of the Holy Ghost."

William nods as I speak, correcting me on the final line. "*And by the power of the Holy Ghost, ye may know the truth of all things.* Isn't it wonderful? Pray to the Lord and He will manifest the truth of all you've read."

"And how would he do that, Mr. William Snow?" I ask.

His eyes light up as he searches the sky for the right words.

"He just… does," William says. "And you know it when it happens. A feeling washes over you, like a shower of flames, and you feel it… here." He lays his hand upon his breast. "It's an unmistakable burning sensation. That's the Holy Ghost talking to you, and you understand the truth of all things."

"Like a sign from God?" I ask.

"Yes, that's exactly –" he starts to reply when his shoulders drop abruptly, and the elation whistles out of him via the hole I've just pricked into his effusion. His words fall low, defeated and resigned. "I see what you're doing."

"Mr. Snow," I protest, "I'm not 'doing' anything. There is one prophet in the book telling me *not* to look for a sign and he makes a convincing argument for faith and then another is urging me *to* ask for a sign, so that I'll know for sure that the book is true and *not* have to take it on faith. Don't you find that a heavy contradiction?" I look to Eileen. "Don't you?"

Her eyes flash momentarily in terror, and her cheeks redden as she attempts to form an answer.

"Well…" she begins, but William cuts her off before she can proceed.

"I don't see it that way," he calmly responds.

"Oh? Tell me, how do you see it?"

"Human nature being what it is," he tries to explain, "we are always seeking to know things, to have certainty. The Lord provides it to those who have read the scriptures. All you have to do is ask, and he provides."

"So the whole idea of faith is inconsequential," I counter. "Or at best secondary to knowledge?"

"I never said that."

"But you must admit that the one cancels the other out," I say, "rendering it superfluous."

He is silent for a moment, considering his response, weighing his words, never taking those penetrating eyes off of mine.

This is fun.

"Let me ask you this, Miss Hale. Have you personally accepted the invitation and sought surety from Heavenly Father in prayer?"

"No sir, I have not."

"Don't you have a desire to know?"

"To know what?"

"If what you have read in the Book is true," he says.

"It doesn't matter to me, Mr. Snow, if the Book is true or not. What matters is if there is truth in it. I'm not satisfied that there is any to be found within its pages."

William holds my eyes for a moment longer, and then suddenly claps his hands together, shattering the dome of intensity, and shouts a jubilant 'Amen' at the top of his lungs.

"You really ought to talk to father about these things, Miss Hale," he triumphantly suggests. "I know the Book pretty well, but have little skill in the art of debate. Pop would be impressed, I'm sure. I don't think anyone has looked at those two passages in quite that light before. Yes ma'am, you have an interesting way of piecing different things together."

"It's my job," I say. "It's what I do best."

He begins to pace, running his fingers through his hair, then clapping his hands together twice then thrice, with a mighty force.

"I didn't quite know what to say," he admits. "I was just making it up as I went along. I did all right though, didn't I?"

Before I can determine what he's referring to, let alone give an answer, he is off again.

"Nobody's ever asked me questions like that before. It was exciting being an authority on scripture. Didn't you find it exciting?"

His enthusiasm is contagious, and I nod in agreement with him. I notice that he ignores Eileen almost entirely.

"A good thing for me to practice, seeing as how I'll be doing a great deal more of it soon enough."

"Oh?" I ask. My question yields no further explanation, as he is speaking far more to himself than to me. I doubt he even hears me.

I look to Eileen for an explanation, but she purses her lips in silence. I trust she'll tell me later.

"Here," he says, as he reaches out his hand. "You best get some movement under your feet or Mother will chastise both of us for not doing our job."

I take his hand and pull myself up, as Eileen helps on the other side. William picks up the book and carries it as we amble around the outside of the hotel in short, slow steps.

I feel a sense of pride wash over me as I walk. Contradictions abound in the Bible, and they're no secret to anyone, but something tells me that few have culled this Book of scripture for them. The fact that my question was not answered by William is of little importance. Besides, I much prefer the ocean of a question to the trickle of an answer. You can't swim in an answer. Then again, you can't drown in one either.

"What's your favourite passage, Eileen?" I ask her, in part to remind William that she's here. He seems determined to ignore her entirely and put all his attention on me. But I also am curious to hear if any part of this religious screed has sunk in for her.

"Chapter 26, verse 14," she replies, perhaps a bit too quickly.

"Oh come on, Sister Owens," William moans, like a child who must chase after a ball poorly thrown. "Pick something original at least."

She shoots him a hard look, her face going stone as she rebukes him for his criticism.

"It happens to be my favourite part," she defends herself. "And besides, she wasn't asking you, she was asking me."

William throws his hands up in mild frustration. "Fine."

Already they behave like a married couple.

"I don't know the reference," I say to Eileen. "What's Chapter 26?"

"The children, speaking to our Lord," she explains.

"Wondrous and marvellous things," William jumps in, helping her flesh out the Word made flesh.

I do recall that bit now that she has brought it up. I found it equal parts preposterous and sad. Children, as young as two, opening their mouths to speak, preaching essentially, to the masses.

"Yes, I recall," I tell them. "But could find no record anywhere of what they purportedly said."

"It was all forbidden by our Lord to be written down," William explains.

"But surely you must wonder," I say, then turn to Eileen. "Aren't you curious? What could they possibly have to say?"

Once again, before she can formulate an answer of her own, William cuts her off.

"That, Miss Hale, is between those children and their Father."

Something in the way he says 'Father' sends an icy wind through me.

I am back in Halifax, at the curling rink-come-morgue, the ice cold wind blowing in off the water. It is dark and cold and frighteningly silent. I had no idea it would be like this. I was not prepared to be amongst the living charged with ferrying the dead.

"Miss Hale?" Eileen says, perhaps more than once.

I snap out of my reverie. My heart is pounding and my brow glistens with sweat.

"Are you feeling poorly again?"

I bury my face in her sleeve to stifle a sob, and turn away from William.

"Thank you for helping with our exercises, Brother Snow," I hear her saying to William with protective authority. "She needs her rest now. I'll see her upstairs."

"Of course," William says as she leads me to the door of the house. "I enjoyed our talk very much, Miss Hale. I'm sorry it has disturbed you so."

"Shoo now," Eileen snaps to him, as she closes the door with her foot. I offer nothing by way of a response.

It's only when I am back in my room, and I hear the door latch closed as Eileen takes her leave do I give over to the memory in full. The relentless sobs follow hard on the cold wind of recollection.

THE MACKAY-BENNETT, a rescue ship, had been dispatched to aid in the recovery effort of the tragedy four hundred miles off the coast, and had arrived at the naval port that morning. Horse-drawn hearses had spent the day carrying an endless cargo of bodies up the hill to a curling rink. There were close to fifty undertakers called in to embalm the dead, of which one was a woman. She was charged with the female victims and the children. My aunt Helen, trained as a nurse, was one of her assistants.

It was nighttime, and Helen had been there for the entire day. I wrapped some cold sausages and went to the temporary morgue. The curling rink was heavily guarded, so as to dissuade the reporters and the curious. One of the men minding the door was a student of my *father's, and he let me in. I don't know what I was expecting. I knew there had been casualties, but somehow I had it in my head that there would be at least an equal amount of survivors on board, that the scene would have contained some joy and celebration, that I'd find grateful men and women wrapped in blankets, sipping hot broth, counting their lucky stars that they had been saved. I could not have been more wrong.*

The silence at the rink was deafening. Even the water, out of respect, was calm and quiet. What couldn't be heard was felt a thousand fold: the wind, the sorrow, the immense weight of the catastrophe. I was riveted by what I saw, both horrified and fascinated. Yes, fascinated, I cannot deny it. People were moving all around me, bodies were being received, embalmed, and stacked. Some in caskets, some in canvas bags. Most just wrapped in simple bed sheets. Many of them had been ravaged by birds and hungry sea creatures.

The worst, I was told, the ones beyond recognition, were buried at sea.

Never to be identified, recovered, or returned to their families.

15

THE REST OF THE DAY PASSES SLOWLY, AND I AM RAW WITH SORROW by dinner time. I try to sketch, to take my mind off the haunting memories of that April night, but am only partially successful. I'm grateful for the little scraps of distraction.

I attempt to render the scene that Eileen liked from their holy book: a small group of infants speaking to a sea of adults. When I try to capture the wonder of such an occurrence, however, it comes across like a Victorian Christmas card, a Dickensian illustration of baby carollers singing 'God Rest Ye Merry Gentlemen' to stupefied onlookers. Finally I throw my pencil across the room and drop my sketch pad to the floor in defeat.

I check my temperature: 99.9. Not good. I feel exhausted, both physically and emotionally, and notice that my foot is beginning to burn anew. I have no appetite for supper when it arrives, delivered by Mrs. Snow.

"Please don't feel obliged to eat if you're not hungry, Miss Hale," Mrs. Snow tells me. Her words come across as kind and filled with understanding.

"I'm sorry," I say, and press my hands to my eyes in an effort to push the tears back from whence they are springing.

"It is I who should apologise to you," she says, "for this morning."

I pull my head back and look at her with confusion.

"William acted inappropriately. He should not have disturbed your time with Eileen. This was not as I had arranged."

I sniffle out that I was not bothered by his visit in the slightest. "In fact I rather enjoyed it. The one bright spot of my day."

"Be that as it may, it was outside the boundaries of propriety, and he should have known better," she explains. "William is a responsible young man, and I have every confidence that he can distinguish right from wrong. Still, in the eyes of others - including Sister Talbot below - the visit of a young man to a pair of young women unchaperoned, is a result of poor judgement."

"Your son was every bit the gentleman, Mrs. Snow."

"Of that I have no doubt," she nods in agreement, "but obviously he said something that upset you considerably. He confided in me his concern for you upon leaving your walk this morning."

I sit up quickly and feel a wave of dizziness blacken my vision. I tilt my head back and forth in an attempt to regain some equilibrium.

"Sorry," I say, disoriented. "It's been a difficult day. I've eaten nothing since last night's dinner."

Mrs. Snow glances over at the neglected breakfast tray balanced precariously on the night table beside the bed.

"My fever is up again, my foot is aching, and I just... sorry... I just want to be on my way, and no longer a burden on you and your family."

My voice cracks and crumbles like stale bread, and I 'honk' my words more than speak them. Every three breaths I must try to catch it anew while the veil of fever passes over me.

"But it wasn't William's doing, Mrs. Snow, believe me. I have such terrible pictures in my head and I can't rid myself of them."

She lifts the skirts of her dress and climbs atop the end of the bed, pulling the bedspread out to tuck her crossed legs beneath it. She then takes my hands in hers, and looks deep into my eyes.

"Tell me. Unburden you heart of its sorrow, my dear. Your Father in Heaven loves you so, and has sent me to you so that you may divest yourself of pain. Share your sorrow with me and give yourself some peace."

Her invitation unlocks something inside of me, and I squeeze her hands tighter, hanging on to her as I slip back into the abyss of memory, the edge of which I have been teetering on all day long.

"It was a Tuesday night," I begin, "two weeks after the sinking of the *Titanic*…"

I feel her hands squeezing mine. The warmth from them battles the iciness of my tale, and I am numb as a result. I am at the Halifax rink and in this small Albertan bed simultaneously, my fever pulsating with the clarity of memory. I am everywhere and nowhere, killing time and space, subject to neither.

"Someone must have sat me down on a bench, because I don't remember doing it. My aunt soon found me and took me home. I laid in bed for three days."

Mrs. Snow remained silent.

"I couldn't bear the thought of staying there, the land of the dead, any longer. I boarded a train and headed west."

I hang my head for a number of minutes after speaking, attempting to remove myself from that time and place and restore myself here. My hands are still in the hands of my life-saver, and when I finally lift my head, I find her leaning towards me. My story has made her younger somehow, and her eyes are filled with a mixture of pity and admiration.

"You're very easy to talk to," I say. "Thank you."

"I am a child of God, Miss Hale. My mission in this life is to bring peace wherever I can. All thanks are due to my Father in Heaven, who listens to you through me."

We sit like this, in silence, for some time.

"I know our faith must seem strange to you," she says. "Contradictory at times."

I look to her with a question in my eyes.

"William told me of your questions this morning," she continues, "and I completely understand. Trying to know our ways just by reading a book would be like trying to understand the world of art just by holding a brush."

She stands and crosses to the door.

"You'll be up and on your feet by Sunday, provided nothing further interferes with your convalescence. Be our guest at church then, and meet some of our other members. After that, you're free to be on your way."

I rainbow a 'thank you' through my tears, and nod.

"It would be unfortunate if all you took away from your time with us was a collection of misinterpreted passages from scripture and a belly full of porridge. Come see our faith in action for yourself, give your foot a final test, and then continue on your adventure."

After she leaves, I consider her invitation. No harm in attending church. Besides, the promise of some stained glass and inspired architecture sounds enticing after a fortnight spent in this plain, beige box of a room.

I eat my dinner and then hobble across the room in search of my hastily discarded pencil.

I capture Mrs. Snow in a sketch, her beloved book in one hand and a paint brush in the other. I select a piece of verse from dear Emily D, and inscribe it below the large, matronly bosom caricatured on the paper.

> *How well I knew Her not*
> *Whom not to know has been*
> *A Bounty in prospective, now*
> *Next door to mine the Pain*

I'll ask Eileen to post it home for me tomorrow.

16

I AWAKE SUNDAY MORNING CRAVING COFFEE LIKE NEVER BEFORE. Maybe it's the air in this place, very dry, and the never-ending circle of a horizon that fuels the craving, but there it is. My foot feels considerably better, but I refrain from unraveling what I hope is the final round of dressing set in place last night by Mrs. Snow.

I eagerly bury the bottom of my thermometer under my tongue, but know already that it will read exactly as I want it to. I hobble out of bed and open the curtains on the window, allowing the sun to properly announce itself. These past two weeks notwithstanding, I am typically an early riser, and can see by the position of the sun and the quality of the light that it is not much later than eight. Not much time before my carriage arrives for services.

Soon a wagon approaches, but I don't recognize the occupants. A man behind the reins, pulling on his stiff white collar and hastily tied tie, a portly woman beside him, his wife, I assume, with cheeks as rosy as apples and a large brim hat shading her eyes, and two young girls in the back. They are engaged in a sequence of cat's cradle, their hands adorned with string as they sit facing one another.

"Good morning, Miss Hale," the woman announces from her perch in the front. "Sister Snow asked us to fetch you as she was called away on some last minute something or other. I'm supposed to check your temperature before we go."

"Running late, Mother," the driver reminds his wife, and then tips his hat to me with a reserved 'good morning'.

"I promise you," I say, shielding my eyes from the sun with the back of my hand, "my temperature is normal. I just checked it."

"The Lord hath wrought a miracle indeed!" she exclaims, clapping her hands and raising them to the sky. "Sister Snow near had me convinced that you'd be sent packing back to your room, but I knew in my heart that Heavenly Father would keep His promise and restore you to health. Oh, she'll be so very happy to see you there. I had no doubt, of course."

"Of course," I say.

"Splendid," she claps. "Then let's be on our way then."

She turns her head to the back and issues a stern command. "Eileen, wake up, girl, and help Miss Hale into the carriage. Honestly, child!"

I lean back and descry my friend and ally pop down from the rear of the carriage. She's wearing her Sunday best again, which I now assume to be her Sunday *only*.

"Quickly, child," her mother barks.

Eileen helps me into the backseat of the carriage, and the two of us sit together facing backwards. Mr. Owens clicks his tongue and the horses move us all forward with a slight jolt.

"We brought along a crutch for you," Mrs. Owens calls back, "courtesy of the Snows. You'll want to be using it for the next few days. Mind you, with the power of the Lord working his ways with you, I've no doubt that you'll be running through the coulees in no time at all. Mark my words! No time at all."

I look to Eileen and she rolls her eyes as her mother speaks. Once we are safe in the silence of the ride, she leans in and whispers to me, "I'm glad you're feeling better."

"Me too," I say.

"I'm glad you're coming with us to church, too."

"Best shopping day in Emmett, I hear."

THE SMALL CHAPEL stands beside the creek with a dirt road leading to its door. Some folks travel here as we do, by horse and buggy, some walk, and at least one family arrives on bicycles. The building itself is more of a meeting hall than a church, with nary a religious symbol or reference to be seen. No colours or images stain the glass of the windows, no vestments or costumes adorn the minister, no crucifix hangs around the necks of any of the congregation. My hopes for beholding some grandeur in the architecture are instantly dashed.

I seem to be the object of attention, as I am met by everyone with a handshake and constant assurances of how welcome I am in Emmett, and what a pleasure it is to have me here. I immediately distrust everyone, and detect not the slightest bit of sincerity in a single voice.

Once we are gathered in the hall, Mr. Snow starts off the service with a formal welcome to me before the entire congregation. I feel examined and exposed with so much public attention. I prefer to arrive and visit anonymously, but the town seems to have other plans.

We listen to a pair of brief, emotional speeches from two different members of the church. Eileen provides a play-by-play of sorts, whispering that this is what they call 'bearing one's testimony'. There are many tears shed in these testimonies, by both the speakers and those listening. I listen as free of scepticism as I can manage, but find the vulnerability of both speakers forced and fabricated. I am unmoved by their words.

After the testimonies are shared, there is a prolonged sermon by none other than Charles Emmett Snow. He begins by reading a story from the Bible; one I've heard before. It famously ends with 'Lord, I believe: help thou mine unbelief'.

He pauses for a long time after the reading, with great effect, and then raises his eyes to the group, slowly repeating the words of Christ.

"*If thou canst believe, all things are possible to him that believeth.* Notice, my dear brothers and sisters, the choice of words our Lord employs here: *believe*. He does not say 'if thou canst *accept*, all things are possible to him that *accepteth*'. *Believe*. I tell you today, my brothers and sisters in Christ, that the act of *accepting* and the act of *believing* are two very different things. And I know that there are many of you, sitting here today and listening to the spirit speaking through me, that cannot distinguish between acceptance and belief. Our church, our great way of life, asks us to believe in many principles, many ordinances and directives, but I know many of us merely accept them. Why? Because we cherish the community, because we are reluctant to draw attention to ourselves, because we do not want to make waves. But what of the waves you make in your heart of hearts and soul of souls when you accept without belief? I tell you now, acceptance without belief is an empty compromise, and our Father in heaven deserves better from His children."

He holds the room - myself included - in the net of his voice and not a single pair of lungs draws in breath during his caesura. I have to admit, he is extraordinarily gifted as an orator.

"But we also know of God's children who are *not* here with us," he continues. "Do we believe in them as we do in ourselves? Or do we accept the idea of them only? If we accept the idea of them, then they no longer live and breathe as we do. They are ideas. Concepts. Illusions. A very convenient way for us to separate ourselves from their loneliness, their isolation. Is this how we treat God's children? Would we treat each other so coldly? Shake the hand of the man to your left, embrace the child to your right. Speak to them. Go ahead, make contact with your brothers and sisters in the here and now."

Each of us turns and shakes hands, saying a warm 'hello' and 'good morning' to one another, I being the only one who has to introduce myself repeatedly.

"Very good," Mr. Snow says, "very good. You see them. You hear them, and touch them, and smell the tonic in their hair. You believe that they are here, now. You believe in them. Now close your eyes, all of you, close your eyes."

Again, we all do as requested.

"You can no longer see or feel them, but you believe they are there. Nothing to accept. Only belief. Now close your eyes more, my brothers and sisters. Close them even tighter, and think of those Children of God who are *not* standing beside you. See them. Hear them. For the sake of our Father in Heaven, hear them. 'Lord help thou my unbelief'."

I sneak a peek and look around at this point. Most of the group is concentrating deeply, with heads lowered in a reverence that could pass as grief. Some of the women let tears loose from their tight-shut eyes and dab their cheeks with kerchiefs. The mood quickly shifts from excitement and rapt attention to self-directed reflection and melancholy.

This display of grief, in contrast to the earlier testimonies, is genuine and real. I feel it. It is as though we are suddenly at a funeral, collectively mourning the dead. What is this? Is there some kind of magic at play here? It triggers memories once again of the curling rink, and I am deeply moved along with everyone else.

"To the young men of our faith," Mr. Snow says, turning his attention to the few young men sitting near the front beside William. "I say you are beautiful, each and every one of you."

He goes on about ordinances and principles, and I look around. Aside from William, there were hardly any young men there at all. I count four. Compared to at least eighteen young women.

I crane my neck around to view the congregation behind me. Not another young man to be seen, aside from the five up at the front.

I take in the families with children. Again, plenty of girls, but so few little boys.

This is beyond strange. Why such an imbalance?

This was the shopping day Eileen was so excited about? The shelves are bare. I look to her, hoping she'll see the confusion in my eyes and offer an explanation, but she is silently listening with her eyes closed. Perhaps she has fallen asleep.

"I promise you," Mr. Snow continues, "if you only accept the principles and do not believe, as men you will fail. Just as the father of the child we heard of in the scriptures failed. You will fail in passing these principles on to your wives, who will depend on you to help them carry the weight of such beauty and truth. They cannot do it alone, however strong they appear to be. And no single family can carry it alone. Only with our entire community, all who dwell in Emmett and its surrounds, and by extension our brethren in Cherry Creek, only with all of us believing can God's great work be realized."

After another well placed pause, and I can see the congregation nodding in agreement.

"And it is a great, great work. I know this. I believe this, as I believe in the sky and the earth and breath inside my lungs. It is a heavy, heavy beauty my friends, so much so it still brings tears to my eyes. Excuse me," he says, turning away for a moment, either out of genuine necessity or effect (or, like all great orators, a savvy combination of the two). "Look at me. Fifty-seven years old, a tower of God-given strength, yet I am reduced to tears when I contemplate such beauty and truth."

He composes himself for the final argument of his sermon, and delivers a blast that I cannot help but feel is directed almost exclusively at myself.

"There are those outside the fold who choose neither to believe nor accept the ways of the children of God. They are in the clutches of Satan, living a life of deception and immorality. Alas, this is not news to us. I say to you today, my brothers and sisters, that those of you who choose to accept and not believe are no closer to God then they are."

I half expect applause after the last words are spoken, so well-modulated are they. It's all I can do to stop myself from nodding in agreement like everyone else here.

"I know that the Church is the one true church, and I know that President Leonard C. Wooley is our prophet and revelator. He helps my unbelief. In the name of God the Father and Jesus Christ. Amen."

AFTER CHURCH, I make use of my newly gifted crutch and walk back to the boarding house with Eileen. Her mother and sisters choose to walk as well, along with the Snows, who all lag behind mired in post-church chatter.

"Can I ask you something?" I say to Eileen as we walk. She shrugs a yes. "Mr. Snow mentioned a prophet at the end of his sermon."

"President Wooley, you mean?"

"Yes," I say. "I've never heard of him before, nor do I recall his name coming up in your book of scripture. When did he live?"

"What do you mean? He lives right now. In Cherry Creek."

"A living prophet? And revelator too?" I ask with obvious incredulity in my tone.

"Mm-hmm", Eileen nods, as though we're discussing something as common as a shop keeper. "He's the president of the church."

"God speaks to him?"

"Yes ma'am. Why wouldn't He?"

I am trying not to laugh, and so I take a breath and speak through a smile. "I don't know, it just seems so… incredible. Prophets, for me, are old, wild men who eat honey and locusts, wearing animal hides…"

"President Wooley wears a suit, just like Brother Snow," she says. "At least he did the few times I've seen him."

"Right. I guess that's it. A suit-wearing prophet who speaks with the authority of God. It doesn't seem strange to you?"

"No ma'am," she replies, again with that shrug.

We walk on for a few more moments, and I voice another oddity about the service.

"And another thing. Don't you find it odd that there are so few young men in church, compared to young women?"

"It's awful," Eileen answers with a heavy sighing nod. "I have William, but the rest of my friends will likely have to seek out husbands from Cherry Creek or elsewhere."

"But why?" I ask, unable to shake the strangeness I felt seeing so few of them in attendance. "Why such an imbalance? It doesn't seem natural."

A voice directly behind us suddenly bellows out a piercing cry, sending both Eileen and I screaming with heart-stopping terror. As the high-pitched shrieks subside, the sound of laughter rises to take its place on the air. We turn to find William Snow at our heels, slapping both of his knees in jubilant revelry.

"Gotcha!"

Seeing Eileen stutter and awkwardly respond to the prank - her shock and shyness competing to be the overwhelming emotion - causes me to pull inwards and remain stoically unexpressive. Although my heart is racing, I find I can steady my voice enough to appear unmoved.

"Mr. Snow," I begin to say.

"Heavenly Father forgive me," he says. Despite his words of contrition, he continues to giggle and revel in his accomplishment. "But it sure was funny to see you both jump six inches in the air like that."

"And what if Miss Hale had jumped as high as you say," Eileen scolds, "and landed poorly on her foot. State she's in, you could cripple her for life."

"Relax, Sister Owens," he replies, again with the tone of one who despises a spoil sport. "Her foot's none the worse for wear, though I reckon her heart skipped a beat or two. Am I right, Miss Hale?"

"I'm entirely fine," I say, and then add "your purpose achieved, can we assume you'll allow us to walk home in peace or will there be another display of childish pranks to look forward to?"

"No ma'am, I'm done. I simply came over to walk home with you both if that's all right. Mother and Father are jawing away with your ma, Sister Owens, and going at a snail's pace to boot. You're moving twice as fast, even with your crutch, Miss Hale. Just couldn't stand to listen to them any longer."

I look over to Eileen whose eyes are darting from William to me to the ground in rapid, bird-like tilts of the head. She's holding her breath, evinced by the rising crimson of blood to her face.

"What do you think, Miss Owens?" I ask. "Shall we allow this ruffian the pleasure of our company for a spell?"

Eileen swallows once then twice, her eyes widen and refocus, and she squeaks out:

"If he behaves himself." William watches her with a slight crinkle of disdain in his curiosity.

"You sick or something, Sister Owens?" he inquires.

The blood that so readily pooled in her cheeks and forehead turns tail and retreats with his question, reducing Eileen to a ghostly pallor in a matter of seconds.

"A slight bout of the autumn cold, isn't that so Eileen?" I offer in her defence. She nods. "Nothing to alarm yourself with, Mr. Snow, as I'm sure she's past the phase of contagion. To be safe, however, why don't you walk beside me on my left?"

I position myself between Eileen and William, giving a wink to the former who squeezes my hand in grateful relief.

"We were just discussing an issue which has left me entirely in the dark," I say. "Perhaps you could shed some light on it."

"I'll do my best," he nods. "Shoot."

"Where are all the young men in this town?" I ask.

William stops for a moment, as if I had just spit on his shoes. He holds his gaze downward, and then looks up with his disarming wide smile and holds my eyes for a moment.

"Maybe if you were a bit more specific on the type of young man you're looking for, Miss Hale, I could give you a more specific answer."

"You know full well, Mr. Snow, that there was only you and a couple other boys in church today," I say. "Can you explain that for starters?"

He looks up to the sky and spreads his arms wide as if to point to an answer in the blue and white and the occasional flight of a grasshopper.

"It's coming on harvest season, a beautiful day," he says. "I imagine most are working on their daddy's farms."

"And last week?" I ask. "And the week before that? Eileen tells me it's always like this in church."

"Farming is a busy job, Miss Hale. Especially at this time of year."

"But you're always there, I'd wager."

"My daddy doesn't farm," he answers and pulls a long blade of wild grass from the ground, breaks off the end, and sticks it in his mouth like inserting a feather in his cap.

"Listen, I'd be more than happy to find you a collection of eligible young men if you were fixing to stay on here in Emmett," he offers, "but I understand you're taking the evening train north to Calgary tonight."

Eileen looks to me with a wince in her eyes. "You're leaving? Tonight?"

"I'm sorry, was that not public knowledge?" William offers by way of apology. "I only ask because Mother told me to have the buggy ready for you at Sister Talbot's to take you to the train station."

"Yes, I did discuss that with Mrs. Snow," I say, looking back over my shoulder at her, engrossed in conversation with Eileen's mother. "I was going to tell you back at my room," I say to Eileen. "Maybe enlist your help to pack."

"I'll leave you to it," William says with a mischievous smile. "Oh, and let me know about the type of young man you're looking to find, Miss Hale. Always happy to help."

"I'm not looking to find any, Mr. Snow," I tell him.

"Well," he croons as he nods towards Eileen, "whoever it is that's looking."

We arrive in the centre of town and stop to take our leave of William.

"Thank you both for the walk and the stimulating conversation," he says. "It was certainly much more colourful than anything that my folks would have offered on the way home. Enjoy the rest of your day."

He squeezes the tip of his hat with the thumb and index finger in an exaggerated gesture of civility.

"I'll be by around half past five to fetch you, Miss Hale," he says as he turns towards the path that leads to his house.

17

WHEN WE ARRIVE AT THE LODGING HOUSE, EILEEN ASKS ENDLESS questions all afternoon about where I'm going. I can tell she is one part saddened by the loss of a new friend, and nine parts relieved to see a potential rival depart.

My trunk and bags all packed, I make my way downstairs to settle the bill for the room with Ms. Talbot.

"It's been settled, Miss," she informs me. "Compliments of Brother Snow."

I am surprised and humbled, my money purse in my hand, untouched since I left Calgary two weeks before. I turn to Eileen.

"Will you walk with me to the Snows, so I can offer my thanks before William hauls me to the train station?"

"If you like," she replies.

I turn back to the pin cushion face as she is turning away, and enquire about some food. "A sandwich for the train, perhaps? And do you have any more of that pie from the other day? I'll take whatever's left to the Snows as a thank-you gift. It was quite delicious."

"Fast Sunday, I'm afraid. Nothing until supper time." She consults a grandfather clock ticking in the corner. "Which, as you know, is not for another ninety minutes." She attempts to leave a second time and I stop her again.

"I'm sorry, but there's nothing at all? No left over beef or biscuits? I don't mind fixing it myself if it's a problem."

"Sorry," Sister Talbot unfeelingly responds, "Fast Sunday. We follow the direction of the church and Brother Snow. Not our stomachs. Good day, Miss Hale."

I'm instructed to leave my trunk and bags outside the door for pick up, as Ms. Talbot would prefer not to be disturbed later on.

"It's not fast Sunday," Eileen tells me as I hobble along with her up the road to the Snow house. "Sister Talbot just plain don't like you."

"Yes, she let me know that in more ways than one during my stay."

"She don't like anyone much, but especially outsiders."

"Why in the world would she run a boarding house then?" I ask.

"That's her calling," Eileen explains. "Every adult here has a calling, and that's hers. Emmett needs a place for visitors to stay. She's got a nice house with no one living in it, no family to fuss with."

"So who calls her?" I ask, fascinated by the glimpse into the machinations of how this place runs.

"What do you mean?"

"The callings? Who decides their recipients?"

"Heavenly Father, of course" she answers, appearing genuinely amazed that I'd be so thick as to ask.

"A calling? From God? To run a boarding house when you don't like boarders?"

Eileen laughs less at my logic, it seems, and more at my incredulity.

"Seems so," she says with a shrug.

"And everyone has a vocation here? A calling?"

"Pretty much, yeah. Brother Snow's is to lead us all, and

ensure we follow Heavenly Father's plan. Sister Snow tends to the sick. My ma teaches the young women, pa the young men."

"And you?" I ask. "Do you have a calling? Does William?"

"Not yet," she answers. "But then, we ain't adults. I'm sure we'll get ours after he get gets back from his mission, and we're married and all."

I shake my head at the social order at play, and marvel at how stifling such a life must be. Callings are vocations, in the truest sense of the word, not a job roster that needs filling.

I'm about to bring this up when I hear a call of an entirely different nature.

Millie catches my scent as I approach the house, and begins to howl with excitement. I hand my crutch to Eileen, kneel down in the dirt, soiling the knees of my skirts, and receive my long-lost friend. We enjoy a slobbery reunion, and I let her lick my face and mouth repeatedly as I scratch her belly. A large bucket of water, along with another lined with kitchen scraps is within reach for her, as is a purple blanket matted with dog hair. I'm overjoyed to see her.

William greets us at the front door.

"Looks like she missed you," he says. "I let her off the rope every day for a run, and walked her along the creek for a spell most evenings."

"Did she behave?" I ask, as I run my hand along Millie's back.

"We each make it back in one piece and haven't missed supper," William replies, "so I figure that's pretty much model behaviour for both dog and man."

Mrs. Snow comes to the door, an apron tied around her waist, wiping her hands on a towel. I limp towards her with outstretched arms, and take her hands in mine.

"Thank you for all you've done for me," I tell her. "If not for you, I shudder to think…" She hushes me with a pat of her hands.

"I did what anyone else would have done," she assures me.

T"The Lord saw fit to heal you, so you were healed. Just glad I could help in His work."

She glances down to the dog hair clinging to my skirts. "I see you've said hello to your companion. Such a fine dog, that one. I can tell."

She offers her arm to me, and the two of us walk around to the western side of the house. William and Eileen tag along behind, silent as they follow.

Mrs. Snow regales me with an abbreviated history of the building. "When we arrived here almost twenty years ago, we lived in a tent all that summer while Charles built this house. Can you imagine?"

We turn the corner and find Mr. Snow sitting at a simple wooden table, aglow in the afternoon sun, scratching out a letter with pen and ink.

"Charles, dear, look who dropped by," Mrs. Snow announces.

Her husband takes his time finishing his missive, then sets his pen down and stands up, pulling his suit vest down snugly as he does so. He wears the same suit as he had this morning at church, sans jacket, which hangs on the back of his chair.

"Miss Hale," he begins, "what a pleasant surprise. I see you're back on your feet, and steady as a rock."

William and his mother move to stand beside him, and Eileen hands me my crutch as she crouches down and busies herself with Millie, who gorges on the attention.

"I understand that you settled my room fee with Ms. Talbot," I say with a slight bow of my head. "Very kind and generous of you, but entirely unnecessary. May I reimburse you now?"

"Not at all, Miss Hale, it was entirely my pleasure," Mr. Snow replies. "Though the circumstances that brought you here were unfortunate, your presence these past two weeks was most fortunate indeed, for my wife, my son, and young Eileen here. Some felt blessed to have a pet around the house. Myself not withstanding."

"What Father is trying to say," William speaks up, "is that we

loved having you here. Millie too. In fact, we hate to see you go
so soon."

I look to Eileen, who seems to be listening as she plays with
Millie, but I can't say for sure. I'm certain she's does not hate to
see me go.

"Would you consider extending your stay, Miss Hale?"

Mrs. Snow's question catches me off guard.

"We've discussed it as a family," she continues, "and would
like to offer you a commission of sorts. William mentioned that
you expressed an interest once upon a time to paint his portrait,
and while it's not something we would have considered essential, it is an opportunity we'd like to capitalise on. As I'm sure
you can appreciate, artists of any sort are few and far between
around here, so we'd like to take advantage of your presence
now if we possibly can."

I am rendered speechless by this. I stand in my dumbstruck
silence, staring at the three of them, unable to respond.

"We'd pay you, of course," William adds. "Far less than what
you'd command in Paris or Calgary, but something. Wouldn't
we, Father?"

A breathless silence follows, wherein the sound of Millie
barking for Eileen to throw a stick is seemingly amplified. Up
until now, I was oblivious to any agenda in their generosity with
the boarding fee. The point of it all is now stripped naked and on
display and I find myself excited by the possibility of what
hangs in the air.

"How much would it cost for you to paint -" Mrs. Snow
starts to enquire, but is interrupted.

"I must confess my discomfort at talking business on the
Lord's day," Mr. Snow exclaims, cutting his wife's question off at
the knees, "and shall therefore excuse myself from the rest of the
conversation. Normally I would not allow it at all, but circumstances being what they are, it is unavoidable. My wife will work
out the details of the fee with you, and see to ordering whatever
supplies you need, again at our expense. Now, if you'll excuse

me, I must get back to writing my report to my superiors. If you choose to accept our offer, I will see you again. If not, please go with God's speed and the blessings of the Father upon you."

He nods curtly to his wife and son, gathers his papers and pen, and retreats into the house he built with his own two hands.

"Sorry about Pop," William offers once he's gone, "he takes the rule of no work on the Lord's Day more seriously than most."

"As do we all," his mother admonishes, "but timing is such that we needed to ask now. If you accept, Miss Hale, we can work out the details tomorrow."

I consider the lodgings and Ms. Talbot. The thought of holing up in there for another minute, let alone a few days, repulses me.

"I doubt I'd be welcome back at the guest house," I say, "and I'm sure Ms. Talbot —"

"We have arranged to have you stay with the Owens family," Mrs. Snow quickly replies. "Again, at no cost to you. Eileen and yourself have become close, it seems, so they were happy to have you join them there. In fact, Sister Owens mentioned the possibility of having you offer some instruction to the young women in the art of drawing."

"Father's always going on about how he wishes there were more opportunities for education amongst the youth," William offers.

"True," Mrs. Snow adds. "Your presence here is a divine opportunity for the betterment of our ward. It would be a shame to refuse Heavenly Father's offer."

"Not to mention a sin," William adds, with that charming wink of his.

I consider their offer. Wouldn't it be better to arrive in Vancouver with some portraiture experience to speak of? After all, I do want to make a good impression with the artist there. A handful of caricature sketches from country fairs will mean little to her next to a commissioned portrait.

I look to William, and see the beauty that was so overpowering upon first meeting him in Calgary. He is lit from within now as he was then. I am deeply stirred by this, and my resolve to leave is weakened by his imploring eyes.

"Please say yes," he quietly speaks.

I remind myself that my vocation, my calling, is that of an artist. I set out from the land of the dead to pursue my life in inks and colours, and here is my first bonafide opportunity to prove it. I would be a hypocrite, not to mention a fool, to refuse.

"I accept," I reply, and instantly feel a flood of nervousness and excitement wash over me.

"Wonderful," William claps his hands loudly once again. "Settled!"

And just like that, it is. *Settled.* He sounds authoritarian when he speaks the word. Like his father. Yes, that's it. He sounds exactly like his father.

Charles Emmet Snow would have declared the same after scrambling around this dry, wind-swept corner coming from god knows where, and driving his makeshift stake into the ground. *Settled.* And so it was. The sheep would have flocked to their shepherd, heads lowered, feet shuffling along, seeing only the arse-end of the settler in front.

I'm suddenly aware of a silence behind me, and turn around to see both Eileen and Millie gone from the yard. How long have they been away?

I wonder if Eileen knows of all this. If so, does she welcome it? And why did she not say anything to me earlier?

18

THE COMMISSION GETS OFF TO A SLOW START. WE ARE ABLE TO MEET for an hour on Monday morning, and then for about twenty minutes on Tuesday. Both times are with a chaperone in the person of Mr. or Mrs. Snow. Wednesday morning is cancelled as neither parent is available to attend. Due to the demands of callings and followers and running the mini planet of a religious community, both are swamped with running off here and there.

The long-awaited cheese maker arrives on Wednesday afternoon, and I don't see William or any of the Snows for the next two days.

I share a small room with Eileen's younger sisters at the Owens house. The first three nights were late and scarce of sleep. They lay in bed talking, thrilled to be sharing their space with a grown up, much to the envy of Eileen, which they also relished.

She may not have a calling of her own, but Eileen's parents keep the poor girl occupied around the clock. Between a plethora of chores, errands, and minding her sisters, she barely comes up for air.

Finally on Thursday, after a late lunch, I turn my attention towards Eileen and attempt to steal her away from her chores for a walk.

"It will be a slow one," I add, more to assure her mother than her, "and not very far, but if you can spare a few moments, I'd love to get some air."

Eileen clutches her hands together like a child that has just discovered a litter of kittens in a box, and rises to accept.

"If it's all right with you, Mother?" she asks.

"Yes, yes," Mrs. Owens distractedly replies. "You've worked hard all day. Enjoy your walk."

The two younger girls give quick cries of disappointment at not being able to take a walk with 'Sister Hale' (as they've come to call me). Their complaints are quickly silenced by a single look from their mother.

I whistle for Millie to come along, and watch as she jumps up to the both of us in search of attention. Eileen's eyes, however, do not return Millie's solicitations. They are fixed straight ahead, and I can easily guess what the conversation will be about.

"What do you want to paint William for?" she asks, implying, perhaps, I have ulterior motives with the portrait.

"Many reasons," I say. "Firstly, I was asked to. Secondly, it's my job *and* my calling."

She looks to me with a tilt of her head.

"I'm an artist, Eileen. It's how I make my living."

"Uh-huh," is all she replies. She's upset with me being here. Threatened, I imagine.

One thing my father taught me about problem solving is to give a little bit of what the other wants, so they can let go of wondering whether they're wrong or right, and work towards a solution. But just a little.

"And thirdly," I venture, trying his theory out, "why wouldn't I want to paint his portrait? William's beautiful. There's no other way to say it. You'd have to be a blind fool not to notice him."

"That's the problem," she cries. "*Every* girl notices him. Even the fools."

She drops her guard long enough to let me back in. Perfect.

We walk along in silence for a while, and she turns her head back three more times before the house is out of view.

"And he never notices anybody," she sighs. "Not even me."

"That's how boys are," I say, with a laugh. "Don't worry. He won't be a boy for much longer. He'll take note of you once he realizes that he's a man, and then he won't stop looking your way."

"He notices you."

"That's only because I'm a stranger to him. I'll admit he may be infatuated with me, Eileen, but he is promised to you. Let me assure you, as your friend, I have no interest in William Snow, other than to paint his portrait. I am staying behind here to do that and that only. Once done, I'll be on the train out of here before the oils dry upon the canvas, and will be forgotten by William and you and everyone within three days."

I stop and take her hands, looking into her eyes. The soft afternoon light is flattering on this young girl, and I notice the firmness of her body. Beneath the awkward, shy, and socially maladjusted child, an alluring woman awaits. Shakespeare's Viola comes to mind, and I peruse the diver's schedule of her beauty: item, two lips, indifferent red; two eyes with lids to them; one neck, one chin, and so forth. Youthful and fresh, yes, but such youthfulness surely drops and fades before too long. No doubt she will leave many a copy of her beauty behind. I suddenly feel a stab of jealousy course through my blood.

"You have nothing to fear with me," I say, resuming my walk. "If you weren't so busy, I'd invite you attend the portrait sessions, just to put your mind at ease."

She exhales a colossal sigh of relief, and smiles once again.

"Tell me more about his mission," I ask, curious to know, but anxious to put her thoughts back on him and away from me. "When does he leave again?"

"Day after his nineteenth birthday," she tells me. "We'll have a traditional Acceptance Dinner with his family on the night he turns nineteen."

"Acceptance Dinner?" I ask.

"Before a young man departs on his mission, he must accept the calling. So the family celebrates with an Acceptance Dinner. Only him, his family, and his promised wife attend."

"Wonderful," I squeeze her hand with my words. "It sounds like a lovely tradition. When does this happen?"

"Acceptance Dinner is on the 31st of October," she explains. "He leaves on November 1st."

I stop walking again. Much more abruptly this time, as if a snake had just slithered across my feet. My skin is instantly covered with a clammy film, and a dizziness blows over me, causing me to temporarily lose my footing. I grab Eileen by the arm.

"Are you all right, Miss Hale?"

"Just my foot," I lie. "Little phantoms of pain come and go still. Nothing to worry about."

The ancient Celts believed all the souls who've departed in the past year will finally be released from their purgatory at this time, and travel to their final resting place. Heaven or hell, depending on their fate.

If I am to have a religious heritage at all, I'll come closest to honouring the tradition into which I was born. I don't believe in such stories, drummed up to frighten children into submission, like every other religious fable, but then I've never seen death up close as I have this year.

My body is two steps ahead of my beliefs, valid or not. I feel my stomach rise on warm air, as if I have crested a tremendous wave in a tiny skiff. The reaction comes as such a shock, I have no idea if it is based in fear or truth.

"Where does he go?" I ask this - hopefully - without betraying a hint of the tempest that is raging inside of me. "On his mission?"

"Don't know," Eileen tells me. "They don't find out until a few days before they leave. That's when the Holy Ghost lets the church leaders know, and they in turn inform the missionaries. Probably England or some other place a million miles away."

We arrive at Lee's Creek, bested here by Millie who is up to her belly in it, and I turn us to the left, knowing that there's a large rock nearby where we can comfortably sit down. It is I who needs to sit, but so long as I pretend it to be Eileen who is in need of comfort, I will keep my secret hidden.

"Two years is not so long," I begin, desperately trying to distract myself from the familiar sights and scent of death, coming at me now in relentless waves. "Surely he'll be home for holidays and vacations. You'll be able to see him then."

"There are no holidays when you're on a mission," she says, shaking her head. "The church doesn't allow it."

I do my best to stay present for her, while keeping the ocean of sorrow inside of me from spilling over the dykes.

"Well then. You can always write. Love letters are sometimes far more romantic and effective than face-to-face courtship."

"Letters between family members only," she explains. "And he can only write to them. It's as if he disappears for two whole years. Completely gone."

We arrive at Rose Rock (which I named for the wild rose bush that grows beside it), and I sit myself down to catch my breath. I can't remove all those faces from my thoughts, and the two of us sit there, Eileen and I, each imagining a different set of eyes. She sees one set, living, with golden hair falling over his forehead, while I see another set, lifeless and vacant, staring into nothingness.

A heavy grief fills me, moving fast, and I cannot stop my tears.

"He'll not forget you," I cry, then add with forceful conviction: "You must ensure that he'll never forget you."

"How?" Eileen's voice also betrays the crack of weeping. To my great relief, she is interpreting my sorrow as pure empathy for her own. "Tara?"

"Hmm?"

"How do I ensure that he won't forget about me?"

I take her hand in mine, feeling the sweat on my palms moisten the top and bottom of her dry, calloused skin.

"I don't exactly know, my friend," I confess. "But if you don't find a way to tell him now, you'll regret it the rest of your days."

19

Late September stirs feelings of returning to school. A mixture of joy at getting to go back myself, and sadness of having to see my father leave the house in Halifax and return to his apartments at the University. It is always offset by seeing him back for his birthday on the Ides of October, which I have looked forward to every year, almost more than my own. This will be the first year I've not been with him for it.

I sketch two souls - silhouetted against the setting sun - walking hand in hand atop of clouds. It will be his birthday card this year. I find some lines from Ms. Dickinson.

> *Birthday of but a single pang*
> *That there are less to come -*
> *Afflictive is the Adjective*
> *But affluent the doom -*

"Less to come" indeed.

My evening with Emily last night was difficult, contemplating the souls who will migrate on the 31st of October. It is a fiction, I know, but like all good fiction, it can strike deeper than truth. It will prove nothing, however, compared to the separation

I'll feel on the 15th when my father migrates from forty-seven to forty-eight.

AUTUMN IS TRAGICALLY short-lived in southern Alberta. We're barely past the equinox when I wake to find a blanket of snow has been tucked under my chin during the night. The tips of the evergreen branches are dipped in a heavy white, as if someone had started a paint job and was then called away, or became disenchanted with the effort, and left it partially started, partially finished. I had not anticipated being on the prairies come winter, and am therefore at a disadvantage for apparel, not having brought any boots or mittens or mufflers appropriate to the climes.

"The snow won't last," William assures me when we sit for our session after breakfast. "It'll all be gone by mid-afternoon, and then we'll be in for a bit of an Indian summer. Should take us to late October, most likely, perhaps even into November. Then the real winter will commence, putting this childish imitation to shame."

"By then," I tell him, "I'll be settled on the coast, washing away like the rest out there with the rain."

"Why there?" he asks.

He is relaxed today, easy to be with. No humming, no pranking, no swaggering bravado. Perhaps it's not relaxed at all, but more behaved, having his father with him this time.

Mr. Snow sits close by, watching me sketch. He is like a student, studying a master, though I'm hardly qualified to serve as mentor to anyone. Still, he keenly observes every choice, every technique I employ. It may settle William to have him here, but I am knotted with nerves.

"There's an artist there," I explain, "whom I want to meet, and with whom I plan to study."

He raises his eyebrows in search of a name.

"Emily Carr," I tell him.

"Your dog's namesake, perhaps?" Mr. Snow asks.

"Mille is named after her, yes, as well as a different Emily. A poet from America."

"Ms. Dickinson," William says. "Yes, I noticed the book in your bag. One of your favourites, I take it?"

"It was a gift," I explain, with a clearing of my throat. "From my father. A valued possession, and she's gotten me through quite a lot since I left home. I'd be happy to lend you my volume if you're interested."

"Much obliged, Miss Hale," he says. "I'm curious to read her poems."

"She achieved with words what I hope to achieve with oils," I tell him as I sketch. "Not pictures, not just that," I say, searching for the words, "but a guide to some kind of greater image. Something that exists only by way of its lesser messengers."

My words seem to fall off William like droplets of melting ice on glass, but I see that his father is listening, absorbing all I say. He centres his eyes on me - it feels as if for the first time - and a playful smile spreads between his moustache and beard.

"We are much more alike than either of us gives credit for, Miss Hale" he comments.

"How so?" I ask, sketching mindlessly now, more drawn to the electricity that pulses from the father's eyes than the son's.

"We both seek that which can only be found by the indirect path. As if we are always looking into mirrors, seeing reflections, glimpses only. Never directly face to face."

"Face to face with...?" I am curious to hear how he will connect my pursuit of art with his own pursuit of God.

"Face to face with True Beauty," he replies, capitalizing the words with his voice as though they are a title or geographical destination we can somehow travel to. His eyes are glazed now with moisture, and he stares off into that world of which he has just spoken.

Like his son before, Charles Emmett Snow is lit from within. In an instant I understand how so many would have followed him here, pulled up roots and left all that was familiar to travel north, willing to endure hardship, cruelty, illness and possibly death. Here is the soul of greatness. Had he an affinity for music, perhaps another Bach or Beethoven; for literature, another Hawthorne or Whitman; for science, perhaps a Newton. But it was religion to which he has devoted his life. I understand the struggle to make smaller minds comprehend, to bring others to the fire that burns within. The endless parade of failures, the temptation to rule by fear, to exercise the blunt wallop of power verses the pure expression of yearning, of vulnerability. I understand how he is and why he is and how he feels in this instant.

I look to William, and see the father in the child, the child in the father. William will not only succeed him, but will surpass all that his father will have accomplished. He is genius in waiting, while Charles Emmet Snow is brilliance in exodus. My portrait, I can see now, will be a combination of the two of them. Youth and age, innocence and experience, light and shadow, all mixed together and birthed by my hand.

"You're right," I conclude. "We are not that far removed from one another."

20

THE INDIAN SUMMER DAYS ARE DRY AND HOT, BUT GIVE WAY TO cool, refreshing nights and damp, chilly mornings.

I busy myself with the work, tirelessly devoting hours and hours to the portrait. My sessions with William are usually limited, but I manage to capture enough of him to allow for studies and practice. One day it may be his nose (classic Greek style, long and straight, a leader's nose, noble without calling any special attention to itself). Another day it would be his jaw (protruding and square and commanding of attention, despite - or because of - its baby smooth skin). I spend a few days on the eyes, secretly transplanting his father's for his own. I am trying to replicate their deep, cobalt blue, their icy penetration, their ability to express multiple emotions at once. This is a tall order for any artist; herculean for a novice. If the devil is in the details, I sell my soul to him a few hours at a time.

The young women of Emmett, including all three of the Owens girls, gather on Tuesday evening for a lesson in art. I've never taught before and discover as I do it for the first time how little attention I paid to how I was taught. I feel as if I am constantly reinventing the wheel when I teach these sessions.

The girls are eager and polite and playful, but have no reference to art or artists, books or legends, poems or plays.

I discover that it's very difficult to start teaching with a blank slate. Having watched my father and his colleagues for so long, I understand now that what they are really doing is connecting things together for their students, drawing conclusions and filling in the blanks. The students somehow understand this, and each one brings an attic full of disparate parts and pieces that are sewn together into something new.

Through this obsessive indulgence in work, I start to formulate my credo as an artist. Or rather, it forms itself and is slowly revealed to me.

Essentially, everything began connected in some forgotten universe or dream, a secret life we all used to lead, and our job as artists – whatever the discipline – is to reconnect that which has separated. When something works, when a book is read or a symphony heard or a painting viewed, there is a recognition deep, deep down that affirms for us that things have been brought back together again. When something really works - when genius is at play - we see not only the connection of things but feel in our very marrow that *we* are connected to it as well. This is a private and ineffable experience - and deeply personal - but when it happens, the universe feels exactly like it should.

A blank-slated student is conducive only to complete indoctrination of someone else's ideas. Basically what I'm doing is creating little versions of myself: mini Tara Hales, sketch artists for hire. If I ask them to draw a picture of a cathedral, for example, I have to draw one first because no one has ever seen one before. They could draw the meeting house here in Emmett where services are held, but not anything with spires or arches or steeples. Thus whatever I draw, they draw. Some are better copyists than others.

The young men also meet on Tuesday evening, and go off with Mr. Owens for their lessons. Once again, I am flummoxed by the low turnout. Indeed, there are so few of them gathered, the meeting could be held in the outdoor latrine.

This is no longer a curiosity for me, and I find myself bothered by the gender imbalance, and increasingly angered by the complete dismissal of it. I bring it up once again with William at the end of our next session. We're in the chapel this time, where I've not been since church that Sunday two weeks ago. His mother is with us, and I make sure my observation is voiced loudly enough for her to hear.

"I notice the young men's night is as poorly attended as Sunday morning service."

"What about it?" William calmly replies.

"There was only you, Mr. Owens, and a couple more. Were the other boys working on their daddy's farms even then?"

"I don't know," he replies. "You'd have to ask them. I'm afraid I don't keep tabs on the brethren."

He leans forward to steal a look at his mother, who catches his eye and holds her gaze steady. Does she nod an instruction? I can't tell. William shakes his head and shifts a toothpick he's been chewing on from one end of his smile to the other.

"Young men's night is and always has been a boring chore of a meeting. I have to go, you see, because my father's in charge, but most of the other fellows in and around town skip out. They drum up some excuse or other about being needed at home, and then Pop chastises them and their families the following Sunday. The next week is packed, of course, but slowly they drop off, week by week, until the blast from the pulpit again."

"I thought your father controlled this town," I politely say. "If he wanted them there, who would dare refuse?"

William laughs, pulls the toothpick from his mouth, and turns it slowly in between his fingers.

"Don't get the wrong idea about my father, Miss Hale. He's in charge, yes, and charged with the spiritual welfare of the entire region, but he also knows when to give and take. Besides, everyone has a choice to come to the meetings or not. If the other boys don't want to come, nobody's going to force them. Well, their mothers might, maybe their fathers, but certainly not mine."

I steal a look to Mrs. Snow. She is smiling with what I can only identify as pride.

"If Father is content that they're working for the betterment of the community – whether it be digging ditches or peeling spuds – then he's happy to let each family decide for itself."

"What about the girls?" I ask. "Is it the same for them? They came out in droves for young women's night."

"The girls go because they like each other's company and the chance to jaw a bit. They came to your night because they find you fascinating, I guess."

"Fascinating?"

"Most of them, if not all, have never met a non-member before. The fact that you aren't the Devil with horns and a burning fork has them baffled. Not to mention that you're different from most women – church members or otherwise."

"Different how?" I ask, but William only shrugs and pops the toothpick once more into his mouth.

I notice Mrs. Snow has turned her attention away, and is gathering her knitting materials together.

"Mrs. Snow," I ask, a bit persistent and a bit impertinent, "do you have any idea what William is referring to?"

"The difference between you and the other women these girls have been exposed to?" she repeats. "I would think it's obvious, wouldn't you?"

She, too, is smiling. They are both determined to dismiss a blatant fact as a simple misunderstanding. I turn back to William.

"Is it because I ask uncomfortable questions?"

"There's nothing uncomfortable about your questions, Miss Hale. Sorry I haven't got better answers to meet up with them. As for the absence of eligible young men, might I suggest a trip to Lethbridge or Macleod? You'll find herds of them there.

Depending on what exactly it is you're looking for, you'll fare much better there than here, I'm afraid."

I try to laugh away the fact that he has caught me out, but end up sputtering more in frustrated embarrassment.

"Thank you for the session," he says as he dons his hat and walks towards the door.

"Oh Mr. Snow?" I say.

He turns back. "Ma'am?"

"Don't be so sure I'm not the Devil come into your peaceful little world."

"Never said I wasn't." He spits out the toothpick into his hand, smiles broadly at me - the kind of smile that can knock the wind out of your lungs - and runs off out the door.

"William's right, you know," his mother offers as I set about cleaning my brushes. "The young men in this town do behave in considerable contrast to the young women. Same as anywhere else, I imagine. However, you are also right. They are all keeping too much to themselves of late, and this needs to be addressed. I'll tell Charles of what was discussed today, and ask him to issue a stern reminder to the young men of the ward."

She squeezes my hand in a show of genuine appreciation.

"Thank you for having the courage to bring it up," she tells me. "I'm sure it's not easy to ask the uncomfortable questions."

21

OCTOBER THE 10TH. ANOTHER SESSION CANCELLED THIS MORNING. I should have been finished the commission by now, had my subject attended all the sittings we had agreed upon. The two young Owens girls have been pestering me to paint them, and so I finally concede.

I can use the practice, if I'm totally honest with myself, as I find I am obsessing now about the portrait. William, at first, was simply a beautiful young man that I wanted to paint. Now, as is becoming more and more clear, he is a young man with a heavy future before him. The town, for reasons unexplained, has weeded out the other young men, and all focus and attention is directed entirely upon him. I feel compelled to include something of the undeniable strangeness of him and his world. After all, it is part of the artist's job: to help others see what is hidden, to reconnect that which has been split apart.

The painting practice *would* be helpful, but my two models are never still enough to allow for any real substance. I grow frustrated with them, and just as I am about to lose my patience altogether, a knock sounds at the door. It is Mrs. Owens.

"Sorry to bother you, Miss Hale, but I'm looking for Eileen."

She turns to the children, who have suddenly frozen like statues before their mother. "Are these two behaving for you?"

I glare at the two girls, whose faces silently plead for clemency.

"Modelling is a very exhausting profession," I explain with tremendous diplomacy. "I think they've earned a break. As for Eileen, I believe she might be in the barn."

I know for a fact that she's there. It's milking time and William has been taking over the chores for Mr. Owens as he helps the farmers around town streamline their production to supply the cheese factory. Eileen slips away and visits with William every afternoon, as per my instructions, and I cover for her while gone. The more time she can spend around him, the more her nerves settle. Normally I would honour my promise to keep her secret, but I cannot bear to be around these two imps any longer.

I make my way outside, and Millie jumps to her feet and chortles with anticipatory joy thinking I'm here to take her for a walk. Many jackrabbits run free out here, and the chases that follow find Millie in her glory. Never have I seen a dog run so fast, her ears pinned down as she slices through space. Thankfully, for the rabbits, she never catches up, and I do believe those tiny animals know she can't catch them, and exploit their speed and Millie's desire for pure sport.

"Not this time, girl," I say as I give Millie a consolatory scratch behind the ears.

The barn smells funky and damp as I step inside. An orange tabby cat growls mildly upon seeing me, a grey mouse frozen between its jaws. I stand and watch, and the cat soon comes to the conclusion that I'm not here to steal or rescue the poor rodent. He drops the creature down to the dirt floor, blades of straw scattered serve as his serving table.

The mouse's eyes are wide with terror, like tiny ebony balls stuck to a slab of grey soapstone. It soon snaps out of its frozen stasis and attempts an escape. The cat's paw lands like a guillotine blade, pinning his prey who emits a squeaky plea for mercy. He won't find it anywhere near his captor.

I've heard the metaphor of cat and mouse many times, but this is the first I've ever seen the natural mother of the expression. Were I the mouse, I would soon give up the fight and resign myself to the fate awaiting me, but this tiny creature - its heart pounding like a bass drum in a marching band, pushing the saliva-slicked fur in and out - refuses to accept its destiny. The inherent cruelty of the cat is almost too much to bear, but I can't pull my eyes away from the scene. Nature is brilliantly cold and ruthless, and I fight the urge to save a life by removing the predator. Human compassion is a flawed emotion when applied to the food chain of the animal kingdom. Darwin be damned, but what place does sympathy have in this barnyard opera?

As spectator, I find I cannot be entirely passive, so I treat the event as sport and begin to cheer the mouse on, willing it to find the speed to break free. The tabby's curiosity is driving him as much as hunger, perhaps more so, as evinced by the writhing of his tail. The appendage is a snake, undulating with excitement and pleasure (so unlike the tail of a dog), an image that is purely feminine in the most sensual way, encompassing the basic survival instincts of hunting, procreation, and feeding in its pendular sweep.

My focus leaves the tail and sharpens on the jaws when I hear the sound of teeth cracking the tiny bones of the mouse's skull. The cat drops the headless corpse as he quickly and efficiently chews the eyes and whiskers and teeth of his victim. A paw carelessly rests on the motionless body, knowing there is no longer a commander to send the tiny feet scurrying away to safety.

"Atta boy." William's voice startles me and I let out a little squeak of a cry. "Oh, Miss Hale. I didn't see you there."

Flushed, I quickly stand and brush the bits of straw and dirt and manure from the knees of my skirts and then retreat into a shadowed corner of the barn.

"Sister Owens is looking for Eileen. I've come to fetch her."

William whispers a 'thank the Lord' under his breath and calls loudly over his shoulder.

"Eileen! Your ma is hunting for you. Needs you at the house."

A pause, and then a small voice responds from further in the barn.

"Oh... Uh... Okay."

William reaches down and picks up what's left of the mouse by the tail, just as young Eileen comes into view.

"Your ma says to take this up for dessert."

Eileen wrinkles her nose at William's offering.

"That's disgusting," she says, and exits the barn without seeing me.

The cat leaps up to a shelf above William's shoulder and sets about to walk the length of his arm to the dinner dangling at the end of it.

"Git off," he says, throwing the little carcass across the barn to one of the stalls, the tabby voicing his disapproval as he leaps after it. William turns to me with a shrug. "We all have to eat, I guess."

"I guess."

He lifts a bucket off a nail on the wall, and fills it with some water from the pump. He returns to the barn and wraps his hand around the leg of a three-legged stool in the corner.

"Ever milk a cow before, Miss Hale?"

"Never."

"Come on, then," he says, "I'll show you how."

Two large cows stand side by side, their faces buried in a pile of shared hay laid out before them. William puts the stool in between them, waving the flies and mosquitoes out of his face as he does so.

"Grab that other stool and bucket there, and sit yourself down on the other side of this heifer."

The large barn doors are open, offering a picture-window

view of blue sky and golden wheat fields beyond. I set the stool beside the large animal as instructed.

"You want to place the stool at a right angle like so," he instructs, "and rest your head on her flank. Like this."

He positions my stool and sits down, his head against the flank and his hands ready underneath. He freezes the pose for a moment, as if caught in a photograph, and then breaks and stands up.

"Now you try."

I assume the position.

"You may want to roll up your sleeves some," he suggests.

The cow's tail swats around like a whip, aiming lazily for the flies that land on her hide. William returns to his stool in the middle, and then sticks his head underneath, his deep brown eyes popping out at me from below.

"Hello," he playfully says. "Fancy meeting you here."

I laugh and greet him back. The animal shifts its weight and nearly knocks me off the stool. I stand and back away.

"Aww, don't let her scare you. She's just a dumb ole' cow, wanting her milk out as much as we want to get it. She won't hurt you."

I set the stool back and pat her on the flank as I take my seat, reassuring her that I'm not afraid. If only I was so easily assured.

"She's awfully large, isn't she?" I say. "You don't realize how big they are until you're sitting right next to one."

"First thing is we want to do is wash the teats off with a bit of water and a rag. Like so."

I bend low to watch him work, his large hands remarkably gentle on the animal.

"Just go slow. It feels good for her, but is also a sensitive spot."

"I've got a couple myself," I remind him. "I know all about it." I see his face redden with a blush as he shoots back up to sitting.

"Fair enough."

I slowly wash off the two teats, freeing them of dirt and manure, revealing a sweet pink flesh, swollen and tender. I hear the tails whip around, both towards the centre.

"Damn it all," William cries out.

"You all right?"

"Pardon my language, but both of them just caught me in the face at the same time. One of them tails wasn't particularly clean neither." He reaches down and steals the washing pail away. "Hand me that cloth, please and thank you."

I throw him the cloth I've just used on the teats. I can hear him slosh it in the water and then scrub it on his face.

"Tasty?" I ask.

"Better than cow dung."

There is another whip of a tail, this time to me. I cry out as it lashes the side of my head, the sting of it lingering for a moment or two. William laughs at my cry.

"Stings, doesn't it? Here. I've got an idea." He stands and takes the tails, one in each hand, and ties them together in a simple bow knot. "That ought to hold them long enough."

"Doesn't it hurt them?" I ask.

"Doesn't seem to," he shrugs. "I've seen it done a thousand times."

He then explains how to take a teat into my palm and squeeze it at the top with my thumb and forefinger.

"Follow up with the rest of your fingers, down to the bottom of the teat and force the milk out in a stream like so. Then release and repeat."

I watch his effortless grace at extracting the creamy white liquid, and conclude that it's a simple enough task. When I try the first time, however, nothing comes out except a low moaning low from the cow. William laughs.

"Keep trying. You'll get the hang of it."

He's right. After a few more attempts, I'm squirting milk consistently from the teat, giddy and pleased with myself.

"Ah! William! Look at me. I'm doing it. I'm milking a cow."

He glances down at the wet stain forming on the barn floor.

"You may want to consider aiming into the bucket a bit more," he says. "We've a baby cheese factory to feed and nourish."

I appreciate his ease with me. Such playfulness in his gestures, his tone, as if life wouldn't dare overload him with a burden or a care. He pokes his head beneath the cow.

"Thanks for rescuing me from Miss *Eileen-on-you* Owens. It's hard to get any work done with her around gawking at me all afternoon."

"I know all about that," I jab with my words, "the challenge of getting work done when your work partner doesn't live up to their agreement."

William smiles in recognition.

"Sorry about all that," he says. "If it were up to me, I'd be sitting with you four hours a day, every day. Father and Mother, I'm afraid, can't always make themselves available as chaperones."

"And yet, here we are alone, and the world has not ended."

"Not yet, anyway."

"I won't tell if you don't."

He continues to pull on the cow's teats, the sound of milk squirting into the pail underscoring our deviant time together.

"Mother's growing very fond of you, by the way. She's been aching for someone to fill the void left behind when my sister got married and moved down to Cherry Creek."

"Cherry Creek," I say, boasting of some knowledge I've picked up in town. "Headquarters for the church."

"Yes, ma'am," William affirms. "One of the most beautiful places on Earth. She's there with her husband and their baby boy, who turns two in November."

"She must be happy," I say, "to be so close to the centre of things."

"She is," he says, "but she also misses it up here. She misses Mother and Father."

"And you, no doubt."

"No doubt," he repeats with sarcasm, but then adds in a genuine tone, "I miss her too. But we'll all see her soon, for the baby's Induction Ceremony."

Silence rolls in like a fog, augmented by the rhythmic sounds of milk squirting into the two pails.

"Induction Ceremony?" I ask. "I've not heard of that before."

He stops, pokes his head beneath the belly of my cow, and looks at me for an instant. He seems to be searching my face to determine what I know and what I don't. Suddenly he laughs and rolls his eyes in some manufactured embarrassment.

"Induction, Baptism, Acceptance, Marriage," he recites, as if listing the ingredients of a recipe for pound cake. "The four rites of passage for every member of the church."

"Only four?" I ask. "I would have thought that last right of passage would be repeated a few times over."

William laughs that knife-less laugh of his.

"Only for us boys," he says. "We get Induction, Baptism, Acceptance, Marriage, Marriage, Marriage, Marriage. Well, the two of us left here in Emmett, that is. Since our deadly secret has been discovered by the inimitable *Sherlock Hale*."

I aim a teat at his face and pull. Bull's eye, right in the mouth. He spits and sputters, and then pulls his head back from underneath my cow and returns to his own.

We both milk quietly for a few moments, the rhythmic squirts splashing against metal acting as a metronome to our shared silence. I play with the timing of my pulls, coming in on '1' and '3' to his '2' and '4'. I start to whistle the church hymn Sister Snow sang to me while I was laid up, but lose the tune after a few bars.

"You know this song," I say, inviting by way of assertion. "How does it go again?"

He continues to milk and says nothing.

"Oh come now, William, pouting doesn't become you. It was just a little milk."

Still quiet.

I stop what I'm doing and lean underneath to see just how upset he is.

A shot of milk - warm and sticky - instantly hits me in the eye.

"Now we're even," William says with a laugh. "We best get back to work, or we'll have both of these girls drained with nothing to show for our efforts."

I sit back up and pick up the tempo of my milking, which he matches with a speeding up of his own.

"Baptism I understand. Eileen has told me about acceptance and the missions. Marriage, of course is practiced in places other than Emmett, but the other…"

"Induction."

"Induction," I repeat. "I know what the word means, but have no idea what it means in this context. Who is being inducted? And into what?"

"It's particular to our faith," he says. "I'm not surprised you haven't heard of it before."

"There are no communities like yours in Nova Scotia, as far as I know. And the prairies are still considered a wild, savage wasteland of Indians, dust bowls, and bible tents. It's all the same until Victoria, which the rest of the country thinks of as a civilized colony of Great Britain."

"I wouldn't know about any of that," he says. "Ain't been so far east as to shake the dust off my wild boots nor so far west that I could see out from under the tent roof. What I do know is that around these parts, folks only know of us as law-breaking polygamists who don't take spirits or tobacco. And that's all they ever care to know."

We continue milking.

1, 3, 2, 4.

I wait patiently for him to tell me of this induction ritual.

"Here." William's hands come over top of mine, soft as his voice, and I suddenly feel how tense and rigid my fingers are around the teats. "Ease up a bit," he says, "the udder is nearly empty."

I look down and see the volume of milk in the bucket has risen considerably. His hands remain on mine, calming them with their touch. Blood rushes to my middle, and I can feel the flush of heat in my cheeks.

"Listen," he whispers, "if I tell you something, can you promise to keep it a secret?"

"Yes, of course," I mumble, my lips close to his ear.

"I'm not officially allowed to tell you about the Induction," he whispers, "or I'll have to answer to Father's wrath. So if you promise not breathe a word of it, I'll fill you in. It's really the most beautiful of all the rites. You must have sensed that when you singled out the passage from scripture. Chapter 26, verse 14."

My mind races back. It was Eileen who singled it out, not I, but I don't correct him.

"The children? Speaking of marvellous things?"

William nods and smiles, gently patting the back of the cow with his open hand, causing clouds of dust to take flight and dance in the late afternoon light.

"Thanks for your help with the milking," he says. "You're a natural with it. Let's finish up and I'll fill you in as we haul this milk up to Mr. Ibey."

The two of us reach down and remove the stools and buckets, then William slaps the side of his cow with a loud 'GIT' and the two of them run out of the wide, open doors into the field.

It's only when they've cleared the barn threshold that William suddenly looks up in horrific remembrance and drops the stool from his hand.

"Sweet Jesus!"

The cows - relieved of their milky loads - run in opposite directions once clear of the door, forgetting the makeshift bow knot that their tales were tied up in. William's cow - the smaller of the two - rips the opposing tail out of its neighbour's hind end, snapping it free like a dried wishbone after a roasted chicken dinner. The losing cow lets out a ferocious cry of pain, unearthly in its agony, and spins in a demonic circle like a beast possessed. Blood soon stains the hind legs and flows down to the freshly emptied udder and drips from the teats that only seconds ago I held in my hands. William tries to approach the suffering beast, but can't get anywhere near it for all the flaying and kicking and unpredictability set loose with fifteen hundred pounds of a wild animal in pain. He turns and calls to me.

"Run to my house and fetch my father!"

I turn to go, and in my haste I inadvertently kick over a bucket of milk. Bending to set it aright, I hear William's voice shout once more.

"Leave that and fetch my father. Quickly, please!"

I run out of the barn, and set towards the Snow house, my thoughts quickly turning from the unanswered mystery of Induction to the unpleasant image of a bloodied milking cow.

22

THE LATE INDIAN SUMMER YIELDS TO A VIOLENT AUTUMN thunderstorm. I'm awoken by the sound of the wind in the dark, and I can feel the windows rattle in their frames.

Today is the 15th, albeit only a few hours in. Back home, the sun is coming up, and I imagine my father rising with it. I'm overcome with heart wrenching sorrow and a deep yearning to see him. The two girls sleep blissfully through both storms. The howling one outside, and the stifled howls of the one within. I choke back tears and bury my face in the pillow to silence my uncontrollable sobs.

I was dreaming of him. I try to pull the memory of the dream out of the sticky web of sleep, but cannot. Instead, I call to mind a memory from about ten years ago, when I was eight or nine.

Every weekend morning my father and I share our dreams, he with his cup of creamy coffee, and me with my glass of milk, or – in the summer months – orange juice. He starts by telling me what he dreamt, which usually revolves around books he is reading or lectures he is piecing together. One morning, he's a bit more pale than usual, and discloses a dream about finding me in a bathtub, drowned, due to his own negligence.

He holds me on his lap, hugging me while he speaks. I can see tears in his eyes, though he never cries them out.

"I don't like bad dreams," I say.

"They aren't as easily defined as that, Tara," he tells me. "They can give you good feelings or bad ones, but the dreams themselves are far more neutral than we give them credit for. They are teachers, speaking a language that is very hard to understand, but not impossible to decipher. The more you try, the easier it becomes. In time, you will be able to read the lessons like you would any other. Keep this in mind: dreams that stay with you for whatever reason are the big lessons. There's something so important in them that they haunt you while you're awake. They may even repeat themselves until you've gotten the point they were trying to make."

"Here was a big lesson," he tells me, "one that will haunt me for many days. And it has little to do with you and much to do with me. That is how dreams communicate. I am telling myself that I need to pay more attention to the child-like aspects of my life: recreation, nurturing, play, or they will die. My dream used an image powerful enough to get through to me. It used my love for you."

The memory provides cold comfort. Since nothing will substitute the aching in me born out of being apart from him on this day of days. I fall in and out of sleep. More dreams I can't recall. More memories whose weight I struggle to bear.

By mid-morning, I rise from bed. There is no sign of the sun this day. Five degrees cooler and it would be a snowstorm, and I am assured it will turn to snow later this evening and overnight. Millie takes shelter on her blanket in a corner of the porch, curled up like a cat against the wind, rain, and deafening noise.

By late afternoon, I am a wreck. I've spoken to no one, cancelled my portrait session, and watch the storm descend. I feel one with this sky, both of us dark and caring little about the endless tears we let fly. I sit under the awning of the Owens barn, away from the house. Nobody is around, as they've all gone to help other families batten down the hatches, so to speak, in preparation of the storm.

The irony being that their own house is left vulnerable in their absence. Which is why Charles Snow is here with his son, trying to put the storm windows up.

I see William's arms wet and rigid with muscle, his hair falling into his eyes and sticking there. I see his face laugh and smile and laugh again in spite of or because of the deplorable conditions he is forced to work in. Trying to prepare for a storm while in the middle of it is a comic exercise in futility.

He yells something to me as he lifts a window into place on his own; his father has run off to close a gate that has blown open. He is fighting the force of the wind against the sail of wood and glass and the wind is winning. I can barely hear his voice and make him repeat himself.

"Could you lend me a hand?!" he bellows.

I am in no mood to assist or be around anyone, but he is helpless. I run out into the yard and am nearly knocked over. The sting of each rain droplet is sharp and cold against my face, and still palpable through my jacket against my back.

"What kind of pioneers are you?" I shout, as I help William lift the window. "Didn't you see this coming?"

His laugh is child-like, a grown-up giggle, as he nails the window into place.

"There was no warning on this one," he howls. "It came out of nowhere!"

"An act of God?" My hands are already starting to freeze. He fails to see the irony.

"Mysterious are His ways, Miss Hale," he yells and then yelps with wild, cowboy exuberance into the heavens, the way I heard so many do in September. "PRAISE THE LORD!!! AMEN!!! I SAY AMEN!!!"

"You're mad!" I yell with chattering teeth. I'm angry at him and my own uselessness, trying to hold the window in place.

William knocks his jar of nails over while bellowing, and they are now scattered in the mud and grass.

"I figure I have two choices," he barks. "Resist and be miserable, or accept it and praise the Lord. Either way, I'm gonna be wet and frozen and standing in mud up to my balls."

No blush, no awareness of what he has just said.

"I'll take the path of misery and resistance, thank-you very much."

"Hey?" he yells.

The wind and rain are stealing and drowning our words like pitiless mercenaries.

"I said that I prefer the resistance and misery option," I yell back, "if it's all the same to you."

"I know," he replies. "That's your problem! You can't fight God, Tara. You'll always lose."

"We'll see about that," I yell.

"What?" William points to his ear and shakes his head, grinning madly at the sky.

I gesture a 'never mind' with my frozen hand.

He stares at me with his wild grin, betraying no sign of having heard me, nor giving any indication that he hasn't. I can hardly hear myself, and the cold makes it nearly impossible to get another lung full of air to repeat it.

William positions the final nail into the wood of the frame, struggling with numb fingers to hold it steady. The hammer is difficult to wield, and a half-hearted swing slips from the nail head and lands on his thumb.

"Son-of-a-" he cries, winces and sticks his wounded hand into the opposing arm pit. He looks up with eyes red from the involuntary tears of sudden pain, but still with that crazed smile.

I suddenly put my frozen hands on his cheeks and kiss him hard on the mouth for half a dozen seconds. I don't know why, but I count it out.

After the count of six I pull back. He looks stunned and completely terrified. I imagine I look the same.

Where the hell did that come from? We both ask with our expressions.

Neither of us has an answer. Me especially.

The window, which is holding on by two nails, cries out for help as the wind creaks it out of place. Before either of us can respond, his father appears, pushes it back into place, and is nailing it down with the efficiency and precision of a master carpenter working in ideal conditions.

"Your hand is bleeding, son!" He barks this observation, and William holds up his bloodied paw as if seeing the colour red for the first time in his life.

Mr. Snow turns to me with instructions to take him inside, get him cleaned up and warmed. We both stand frozen, awaiting some other instruction or worse.

"There's nothing else to be done out here but ride out the storm," he shouts. "I'll be along shortly with a night's supply of wood from the shed. Go!"

Whether or not he has seen me kiss his son, I cannot tell. He doesn't mention it later that night, and I dare not ask.

23

MY BEHAVIOUR ON TUESDAY WAS ERRATIC, EMOTIONAL, AND entirely selfish. I should not have kissed him. How could I be so careless? I was more desolate by nightfall than I had been all day. I shudder to think what my father would have made of my actions.

Who am I kidding? He would have laughed it off as a romantic impulse and said nothing more about it.

I need to get out of here. If there was ever an ideal moment to pack up and head west, this is it. The pull to Vancouver is almost visceral, like a tiny tug-boat is fastened to my organs, my very life and vitality, pulling for all it's worth.

The portrait is nearly finished. I require only one more session for the eyes, and it will be ready for framing.

That session should be happening this morning, but when the designated hour arrives, it is Charles Snow alone who darkens the door of the chapel, no son to be seen.

"I'm sorry, but William will be delayed somewhat," is all he says, and pulls out that little book of his to scribble in.

I take it the kiss was witnessed after all. Or confessed. Either way, I sense William's presence in my company has been curtailed on purpose. So be it. Today is Friday. The next train out is Sunday night. I plan to be on it.

I will work on the eyes using the father in place of the son. I need this man to raise his focus from his book and allow me a chance to capture his eyes.

"Another report to your superiors?" I ask.

"Hmm? Oh, yes. Three times a week now," he says, with only the slightest glance up. "Mostly cheese related, I'm afraid. All terribly dull."

Think, Tara.

"How is Chloe?" I venture.

"Who?" He asks, without looking up.

"The Owens cow?"

This will be harder than I thought. I'll need to draw him into conversation more stimulating than the reporting of cheese production.

"Ah. Much better. Thankfully, a cow's tail is not a vital part of her anatomy, nor does it affect the output of milk. She's a bit gun-shy, of course, and the flies are sure to drive her mad, but all in all, there was no great harm done."

"I'm glad she'll pull through," I say.

He looks up as he lets loose a laugh and speaks, more to himself than to me.

"Whatever possessed that boy to send them out tied together? I can well imagine his reaction. Young William has never weathered blood trauma well. He hasn't the stomach for farming."

"And you, Brother Snow?"

He finishes scrawling out a sentence in his book, dots the end of it with a gentle stab of the pencil, sets it down, then settles those magnificent eyes on me as he answers. I sketch without explaining why. Perhaps he has guessed, but most likely he couldn't be bothered to care.

"I was born and raised on a farm, Miss Hale, in New York

State. When I was ten years old, I crossed over the great wagon trail to Zion, hunting and skinning buffalo to feed my family as we rode for hundreds of miles with an ox and simple cart. At the age of twenty, I built a log cabin with my own two hands, then lived and worked as a farmer until my marriage. Ten years ago, I traveled from my home in Cherry Creek to the northern frontier, all the while eating only what I was able to trap, hunt, or fish. I have spent my life with God's creatures, great and small; herding, hunting, butchering, eating, and healing them whenever merited."

He stops there, blinks once or twice, and then picks up his pencil once again and resumes penning his annoying little missive.

I require more, and must work harder to get it.

"May I ask you a strange and somewhat personal question?"

"You may," he answers.

"Do you consider yourself happy?" I hear the tone my query tries so hard to mask: vulnerable, hungry, almost desperate. The question surprises me, I must confess, but hits him exactly how I hoped it would. His eyes ignite.

"I believe, Miss Hale, that you are the first and only person to truly ask that question of me, a question I have never thought to ask of myself. You must understand the context in which I was raised, and the role happiness played with my parents. Those were very early days for the church, and my father was a prominent member. Advisor to the Prophet, leader, and public figure."

A question rides across my mind, and clearly leaves its tracks on my face as Brother Snow reads it instantly.

"And yes, I had more than one mother. I know of the conversations you've been having with William and the young women. I don't mean to imply that there is surveillance at play here in Emmett. It's just a small town and, as such, secrets are seldom kept with any success. My father lived during the early days of the Principle, and followed its tenets. And let me say that I loved all four of my mothers equally and was blessed to have been loved by all in return. In those days, sunlight was dominated by work, twilight by prayer and meetings, and night by sleep. Sundays, of course, were set aside for services and social gatherings, and for promoting the message of our Lord."

"And what was that message exactly?" I ask.

"Not *was*, Miss Hale. *Is*. That ours is the one true church as founded by Jesus Christ in the New World, and that our founding Prophet was visited by God and His son, instructed on restoring the church to its original and holy character, and that all who hear the word and follow the gospel will forever be the children of God."

"Happy children?" I add.

"If happiness is at all attainable in this world," he answers, "then I know of no other way to find it save through the gospel. Just stepping into the fold brings eternal happiness for many of our brothers and sisters. It brought it for my mothers. My father would speak of it in service, passionately and, for the most part, convincingly."

"So he was happy," I conclude. "Your father."

"I can't say with any surety that I know the answer to that question. He appeared happy, he invited others to the feast at the banquet of happiness, and he never spoke out of character."

"But?" I ask, suspecting a qualifier in his answer. My hand captures the light show in his eyes with furious accuracy.

"Who knows what lives in another man's heart," Mr. Snow answers. "The original question, however, pertained not to my father's happiness – or lack thereof – but to my own."

"Or lack thereof," I add.

"No lack, none at all. I have more than my share of happiness and have faith that I will enjoy more happiness in whatever time the good Lord allows me on this earth. Until the next life, which I assure you will be the true measure of happiness. There, I will be reunited with my family; my mothers and father, my siblings, cousins, grandparents… all those who have passed on before me."

He says this last line with great solemnity, as if someone near to him had only died a few days ago.

It stands out for me because as he speaks it, he slowly brings his eyelids down for a lengthy blink (perhaps it was more of a wince), and when he opens them again there shines a crystallized brightness. All the gold in El Dorado would not glitter more than this.

"It is my belief, Miss Hale, that when we experience happiness, we are tasting bliss; we are granted a foreshadowing of the eternal existence promised to those who have embraced Jesus Christ and are the true children of God. This is our inheritance. The more we devote ourselves to our Father in heaven, the more we follow His plan for us, the deeper we can drink from this bottomless cup of bliss. Earthly happiness is insignificant compared to this, and I admit that I experience little of it. There is a continual dissatisfaction with it that I find difficult to shake. My life has been spent in the discovery and execution of my Heavenly Father's plan, His wishes, and His business. I will never rest until I have completed this business, nor will I find pure happiness before I rest. But I drink from His holy cup often, and for that I am grateful. And fulfilled."

"And for today," I persist, "here on Earth, the now? Are you happy?"

I dig around the haystack of his sermonizing for the needle of an answer, to fuel the fire in his eyes.

"How can I be happy until I see my beloved family once again?" he replies, stretching out his arms as if to embrace an invisible brood of relatives, closing his eyes a second time in a similar fashion as before, keeping them closed for considerably longer, swaying to his own bittersweet lullaby, holding tight all those he loves.

When he comes out of it, he glances around as if unsure of where he is, unaware of and unapologetic of the tears staining his cheeks and beard. The look in his eyes makes every other moment dull in comparison. I mix blues with greys with white on my pallet and try once more to find what's right before me. There's not much time.

I'm so close to capturing them perfectly when there is a light knock at the door. I cry out a 'not now' but it's too late. Mr. Snow and I both turn to see William standing there, and a tall, deeply tanned man in a North West Mounted Police uniform beside him.

"Father?" William quietly interrupts. "Sergeant Parks would like a word."

Mr. Snow excuses himself and stands behind the door with the constable, leaving William and I alone together in my makeshift atelier. We share an awkward smile, and I proceed to wash my brushes out and clean up the area. Every so often, a glance towards William reveals a curious - perhaps the word I want is 'confused' - expression on his face.

"Your portrait is all but complete," I tell him.

It's the first time we've spoken since the storm window episode. His thumb is bandaged from the hammer blow at the window, but he makes no mention of the other assault that befell him there.

He simply nods, then backs up a foot or two in an attempt to catch some of the conversation in the foyer. I assume it has to do with church or Emmett business, until a lightning bolt of a question splits me in half: *why are they talking here? It must have something to do with --*

"Miss Hale?" Mr. Snow says as he steps back into the room. "Robert - er, Sergeant Parks would like a moment of your time."

The Sergeant steps forward, his scarlet Norfolk jacket hitting the room like a brilliant sunrise. He is in his late thirties, taller than William, with his wide-brimmed Stetson hat sitting straight upon his head. There is some mud above the soles of his long brown boots, but otherwise every aspect of his appearance is clean, pressed, and impressive.

"You're Miss Tara Hale of Nova Scotia?" he asks.

"I am."

My stomach tightens and buckles immediately as the words echo in my head. 'Of Nova Scotia'? Something has happened back home. Something to do with my father. My breathing suddenly shortens as I anticipate whatever news is about to fall on my ears.

"Tell me!" I cry.

I grip the back of the chair, the chair Mr. Snow was only moments ago sitting in, speaking of his happiness, answering my frivolous questions, anticipating the happiness to come. A cold block of ice presses upon my chest at the thought of the word 'happiness', for any that I have in this world, I feel, is about to be ransomed.

"You are the same Tara Hale who was in Calgary during the early days of September of this year?"

"Yes."

"And you boarded in the home of a Mrs. Peter Ness, widow, for the duration of your stay?"

"Yes, but..."

"But?" he asks as he raises his eyebrows.

"What does this have to do with my father?" I desperately ask.

"Nothing, Miss. I have no news of your father or your family. This is a matter concerning a complaint filed by Mrs. Ness that you fled the residence in the middle of the night without paying your boarding fee."

The sudden emotional deflation fizzles out of me, by way of a manic burst of laughter. The Sergeant steps forward and assumes a tone of judicious importance.

"Miss Hale, you are accused of breaking the law, which I assure you is no laughing matter in these parts."

"No sir," I say, breathing myself down. "You're right. Please explain again what the problem is."

He sighs, and flips back one page in his notebook.

"Mrs. Ness claims you owe her upwards of fifteen dollars."

"Fifteen?" I screech. "I was only there four nights. Even at *half* fifteen it would be robbery. I would never have agreed to such a charge, and even if -"

Sergeant Parks raises his hand to silence me, and I comply.

"Robert," Mr. Snow uses the silence to pose a question, "this seems to be a rather petty offence to involve the police. Two detachments, a visit from a sergeant to a remote village such as this, all over a mere peccadillo?"

Parks removes his hat and relaxes his stance as he listens to Brother Snow speak.

"I agree," he says. "We have better things to do, I'll be honest, but it seems Miss..." he checks his notebook, "*Mrs.* Ness has maintained some of her late husband's influence with friends, including our staff sergeant in Calgary. It would appear that she's a woman who gets what she wants."

I recall the night in her room, and her attempts to get what she wanted from me. The dormant embarrassment wakens in me and I suddenly smell the tent city fires all over again, oil from the lamp, the perfumed skin, port, whiskey. With weakened voice, I exhale a response.

"It's been six weeks," I say. "Why is this only coming up now?"

"Who can say, ma'am?" Sergeant Parks answers me. "She had to convince the staff sergeant to investigate a case he'd rather not be bothered with, and from what I know of him, that takes some doing. If she was unsure of your whereabouts, it would take some time to track you down. Who knows? What I do need to know, Miss Hale, is this: did you pay for the room or not?"

"Yes and no."

"Could I trouble you to narrow that down to one answer for me?"

"It's complicated, officer."

"Sergeant," he says, correcting me.

There is a long silence in the room as the men stand around me, waiting for my reticence to yield. Throats are cleared, eyes wander to the window and are followed by the long brown boots of Sergeant Parks. He spins his hat in his hands like a wheel, skilled at balancing the Stetson as it turns, all the while looking out the window at the blue sky and sunshine.

"Quite the storm we had, Robert," Mr. Snow comments.

"That it was, Charles."

The silence resumes for another half a minute, then is suddenly broken by an abrupt about-face on the heels of Sergeant Parks.

"Mr. Snow assures me that you are a woman of good repute and character. If he's willing to stake his impeccable reputation of twenty years on that statement, then I'm willing to report that I've not found you, Miss Hale. *Not yet.* But I'm getting awfully close. Understand?"

"I do, sir. Yes. I understand."

"Good. I'm at the St. Mary's detachment."

I turn to William with a look to ask if he knows where that is.

"Northeast of town," he tells me. "About three or four miles. An easy enough ride."

"As soon as your answer becomes less complicated, Miss Hale," Sergeant Parks continues, "please come see me there."

"I will, Sergeant," I assure him. "Thank-you."

"Good day, Miss. Charles. William."

He shakes both of their hands, places his hat upon his head, and takes his leave. Brother Snow follows him out and their voices trail off in conversation. William stays. I can see in his face that he wants - perhaps expects - to be told everything.

"So," he exhales the word slowly, "who's the renegade from the law *now*?"

"Hardly," I say.

"A bona-fide criminal."

"Accused," I say, "but I've committed no crime. This is all a horrible misunderstanding that I'd rather forget about."

I turn away and go back to the maintenance of my brushes,

trying to still the shaking in my hands. William persists with his questions.

"Is this why you arrived here with an injured foot?" There is tenderness and concern in his voice, but still a sense of entitlement that I'd rather not play into right now.

"Yes, it's part of what happened," I say.

"Who's this Ness character?" he asks.

I turn to him, my face red with shame.

"Quite all right," he says, "You don't owe me or anybody an explanation about anything."

I nod in agreement, and watch him silently withdraw from the room.

I leave the portrait on its easel to dry, and make my way back to the Owens'.

24

SATURDAY AFTERNOON, AND THE ENTIRE TOWN IS STANDING ON THE banks of Lee's Creek for the baptism of Mr. Ibey, the cheese maker from Ontario. I stand along with them, as my absence would require far more explanation than my attendance. Killing time, killing space.

Winter has settled into Emmett, though today has offered a cloudless, sunny sky as its baptismal gift. Earlier this morning, before the crowd gathered, I held my hand in the creek bed for as long as I could. It remained numb with cold for a considerable time afterwards.

Now Mr. Snow is standing waist-deep in a pool of the creek, dressed entirely in white. He looks impressive; much more so than the skinny and slightly stooped Mr. Ibey before him, also dressed in white. Neither wears insulating material to stave off the cold water. Ibey shivers and shudders like a dog shitting razors, but Mr. Snow is still and calm as if immersed in a warm bath.

There is some quiet discussion between the two of them that the rest of us can't hear, some nodding of the heads and shared laughter. The entire exchange strikes me as unexpectedly informal given the sacred nature of the act before them. The men and crowd quiet down, and Mr. Snow takes Ibey's left hand in his own, holds up his right hand and declares in a loud voice:

"Having the authority given me by Jesus Christ, I baptize you, Ronald Robert Ibey, in the name of the Father, the Son, and the Holy Ghost."

Ronald Robert is then fully immersed in the creek, head to foot, and a round of applause greets him as he surfaces. Mr. Snow leads him out of the water, where one of the sisters stands with a blanket to wrap him in.

I expected more of a service, but given the cold water and Saturday chores that everyone needs to get back to, it makes sense to keep it brief. Some of the women in attendance weep with joy, as if they had just witnessed the most romantic of wedding ceremonies or funeral speeches. Anything but the uneventful dunking of the local cheese maker.

I walk to Eileen who stands by herself near the back, tilt my head in the direction of the weeping women, and raise my eyebrows.

"They always do that," she says.

We watch them, but not one approaches, congratulates, or shakes the hand of the newly minted member of their fold.

It is then that I notice Charles Snow talking with a man I've not seen before. For better or worse, I can descry an outsider immediately, the way I was once easily spotted when I arrived in town. He is easily a full head taller than Mr. Snow, thin as reed, and entirely bald.

William is close by as well, shading his eyes from the mid-day sun as he listens to the stranger. Laughter erupts from all three.

"Eileen, who is that speaking with William and his father?"

"Don't know," she says. "Never seen him before."

William turns and starts walking towards us.

"Miss Hale," he starts, "there's a gentleman up from Cherry Creek. One of the Quorum of the Twelve. He'd like to meet you."

Before either of us can answer, Mr. Snow and the visitor also make their way towards us. I look to Eileen who stands with friendly anticipation and smiles in the bright, harsh light of the sun.

"Good morning, ladies," his father says upon approach. "I was just telling Brother Harris of the incident with your milk cow, Sister Owens."

"If you're worried that I'll repeat the story down south, Brother Snow," the stranger says with a sardonic tone to William "you have good cause. The Tale of Chloe's Tail will be told and cherished for generations."

"Wonderful," William acknowledges with an embarrassed red rubbing into his cheeks. "But be sure to include my accomplice in the story, Miss Tara Hale. Miss Hale, Brother Oliver Harris."

I see Eileen's face react as if it has just been slapped. She had heard about the tail - everyone had by now - but did not know I was alone with William when it happened.

"A pleasure, sir," I manage to say as he shakes my hand.

"The pleasure is mine, Miss Hale. May I be the first of the brethren to welcome you on behalf of the Prophet of the Church."

His gentle grip is almost non-existent, and I as I shake his hand, I afford myself a quick study of his face. He's in his mid-thirties, with deep set green eyes which bristle with a mixture of satisfied knowledge and child-like curiosity. His complexion is clear beneath a clean-shaven jaw, and his traveling suit is well cut and properly fitted, as would befit a successful businessman. He appears healthy and strong with a mild gaze that quickly surveys my entire person as I study his.

"Though the air is cold," he says to Charles, "and the water colder, your Mr. Ibey could not have picked a finer day for a baptism, Charles. I'm happy to be here to witness it."

"Do you attend all baptisms, Mr. Harris?" I ask.

"Brother Harris's presence here is twofold," Mr. Snow informs me.

"Someone from the Twelve tries to attend every baptism in the ever-growing community of God's children," Harris says, "but I'm also here to meet the artist responsible for William's portrait. It's not every day we have one so gifted as yourself pay a visit to the fold."

"How long will you be here?" I ask. Though the portrait is more or less done, I'm not ready to unveil it quite yet. Touch ups are required. I'm suddenly anxious at the thought of anyone outside of the Snow family seeing the painting.

"I've been here two days already," he replies, "staying in your old room at Sister Talbot's, as a matter of fact. Unfortunately, however, I must take the next train home. We're all very proud of William down in Cherry Creek, and very excited about his mission." He leans over to Brother Snow, adding "not to mention very excited about his inevitable return."

I steal another look to Eileen, as a blush loosens and escapes from her cheeks.

"An excitement," I offer, "shared by many of us, I'm sure."

Silence elbows its way into our gathering like a child, clutching a happy secret in her hands. Mrs. Snow approaches and gives a gentle tap on her husband's shoulder.

"Yes," he nods, "of course. William, would you be so kind as to transport Brother Harris to the train station? I'm afraid we've kept him longer than scheduled."

"A pleasure to meet you, Miss Hale," Mr. Harris says as he shakes my hand once more. "And enjoy William's Acceptance Dinner. I've tasted Sister Snow's cooking before. Believe me when I say you're in for an exquisite treat."

I blanch at his words, and can feel the blood rush out of Eileen's face beside me. I don't even need to look.

"I'm afraid you're mistaken, Mr. Harris," I try to explain. "I've not been invited to William's Acceptance Dinner. That unique privilege belongs to Miss Owens here."

Oliver Harris stops, and looks quickly to Charles Snow, and then back to me, regaining his composure instantly.

"I apologise for my mistake, Miss Hale," he says. "And to you, Sister Owens. I…"

Whatever he's about to say next will only serve to make an awful moment worse. He wisely claps his mouth closed, turns on his heels, and walks off.

William keeps his focus on the ground as he follows Mr. Harris away. Charles clears his throat, and walks away with his wife. Again, without a word spoken.

I turn to Eileen, but she too makes a hasty exit.

I'm left alone on the banks of the creek, foolishly carrying the blame and guilt for someone else's slip of the tongue.

I am done with this place. Tomorrow evening cannot come soon enough.

25

It is Sunday morning. My favourite time of the week, as I have the house - indeed the town, if I want it - to myself.

The portrait stands beside me, bathed in the soft light coming in through the south facing window. I am happy with it, particularly the eyes. It captures William's beauty today, and whatever power may be coming to him tomorrow. Like a child I've created and reared, this painting will be hard to part with. I'll drop it at the Snow household this afternoon, before my departure.

The sense of closure is comforting, and I capture my mood in a sketch for home. My final one, I assume, before arriving at long last in Vancouver.

It is an image from the perspective of a painted subject, looking out from an unfinished canvas with those eyes, seeing me as the artist. I wield a paint brush drawn like a sword, dripping with paint that could be mistaken for blood.

It is silly and obvious and over the top. And perfect. I inscribe it with the following verse:

> *The Vision — pondered long —*
> *So plausible becomes*
> *That I esteem the fiction — real —*

The Real — fictitious seems —

I fold it into an envelope and no sooner do I address it home, when I am startled by a knock at the front door.

"I'm sorry to disturb you, Miss Hale, but I wonder if I might have a moment of your time."

Charles Emmett Snow stands in the doorway, his frame casting a lengthy shadow into the room.

I invite him in, and we sit at the long kitchen table.

"Something tells me, Mr. Snow, that you don't easily skip out on church," I say after a moment's silence. "You must be here for something terribly important."

"I am indeed," he confirms. "William would very much like for you to attend his Acceptance Dinner this Thursday evening. As would his mother." He looks up to me with those eyes of his. "And I."

This is a surprise. That he would take the morning away from church to ask me this?

"I'm honored to be asked, Mr. Snow," I begin to reply, "but I am leaving -"

"Yes, you are planning to leave tonight. Which is the reason for the urgency of my request."

He stands from the table, clearly struggling to choose his words carefully.

"William is my son, and though I try to raise him with firmness and as little indulgence as I can manage, I can see he is very taken with you, Miss Hale. Since that afternoon in Calgary, when first he met you. You're all he speaks of, all he thinks about."

Can this be true? If so, he has hidden it well. Well enough, anyway. My eyes widen in surprise.

"And judging by your actions the day of the storm, I assume you return his affections somewhat. Enough to merit a stolen kiss at least."

"He told you of that?"

"He did not, Miss Hale. I saw it. William is open with his

mother and I, yes, but not with matters of the heart, apparently. He doesn't know I'm here, asking you to forestall your departure a few more days. I would appreciate it that he never know, regardless of your response."

"Of course," I say. I am embarrassed anew by my reckless behaviour.

"The Acceptance Dinner is typically open to members of the church only. A young man, on his 19th birthday, celebrates the acceptance of his mission, with those most precious to him. His family, of course, and, if he so chooses, one guest. It could be a close friend, a mentor, or a young woman he cares for. Sometimes, yes, they wed upon the young man's return, but certainly not always. I've asked for a special dispensation from the President of our church, by way of Brother Harris, to allow a non-member to attend the dinner. A rare exception has been made for an exceptional young woman. And nothing would bring our son greater joy than to share his final meal here with you, Miss Hale."

I try to process all of this. A special dispensation from the president of the church? Their prophet and revelator need be consulted for this? And Brother Harris? Surely he didn't come all this way to deliver an answer in person. And what about Eileen?

"And what of Miss Owens?" I ask. "Is she not invited and expected at William's Acceptance Dinner already?"

Mr. Snow pulls back in confusion. "Eileen?" He then laughs and shakes his head as he sits back down. "Whatever gave you that idea?"

"She confided in me," I say, surprised at his reaction. "She told me that her and William have been promised to each other since they were children. Having seen the close connection between the two families, I'm inclined to believe her."

"Oh dear," he says, still with a laugh and shake of the head. "I… I don't know what to say. That certainly explains the awkward moment yesterday with Brother Harris."

He contains his mirth, and assumes a tone of officiousness once more.

"No," he says emphatically. "I assure you, there is no promise between William and young Eileen. Whatever she has told you exists solely in her imagination."

"Imagined or not, she believes it to be true. She'll be crushed to not be there. And devastated if I am."

"Yes, I see," Mr. Snow concedes. "A tricky situation, and perhaps best sorted out with Sarah and Sister Owens. But I understand. You harbour some loyalty towards her."

"We are friends, and confidantes, Mr. Snow. I could never betray her like this."

"I see," he says, standing once again. "I cannot condone betrayal in any form. You should know, however, that young Miss Owens is not, nor will she be, invited on Thursday night. William simply has no interest. She is sweet on him, but so is nearly every young woman in town."

"Shame there is such a dearth of young men in town," I say, watching his reaction carefully, "to lighten the load."

"Indeed," he agrees, without making excuses. "Such is the way of things for us."

For us?

He rises, thanks me for my time, and makes his way to the door.

"One final thought, Miss Hale, if I may be so bold as to speak entirely selfishly. As a father who won't see his child again for two years, I would love nothing more than my final night with him to be as happy as possible. As a child close so obviously close to her own father, and yet so far away from him…"

Seeing the sting of his words on me, he nods and dons his hat.

"Well. I'm sure you can understand. I hope you will reconsider."

·   ·   ·

EILEEN DOES NOT COME BACK from church right away. It is she who has been wrangled into taking me and my trunk to the train station, so I'm anxious for her return.

By late afternoon, I have finished packing everything away, and come into the kitchen for some food. And there she is, sitting silently at the table. In the same chair that Charles Snow sat in a few hours earlier.

"Are you going to marry him?" she fires at me, with desperation strangling her words as she speaks them.

"What? Who?" I cannot stifle my laugh.

"You know well enough who. Just answer yes or no," she instructs, like an interrogator new to the job.

"Oh my god, Eileen. *No.* I have no interest in marrying William. Or anyone for that matter. No, no, no."

She smooths her hands across the table, like she's attempting to flatten out some imagined dough.

"Then you should go to his Acceptance dinner. He wants you there. Not me."

I see now that the conversation threatened between Charles and Sarah has happened. As well as words between Sarah and Mrs. Owens, perhaps Mr. Owens as well. Poor Eileen must now bear the weight of changing my mind.

"Thank you, but I'm not interested in delaying my trip any longer."

"Please," she says, her eyes pleading now. "Do it for me."

For her? She *wants* me to go? How is this possible?

"It is primarily for you that I am *refusing* to go, Eileen. I'm sorry, but this is all far too confusing. How could you want me to attend?"

"If you don't go," she cries, "he'll blame me. He will. Long after you're gone, I'll be the one who prevented him from getting what he wants."

"And what does he want?"

"He wants you there. If you're not going to marry him, then there's no harm in attending, is there? If you don't go, he'll be miserable. And he'll leave for his mission miserable. And he'll blame me for his misery. But if you go, he'll be happy, and he'll leave for his mission happy. It makes sense, Tara."

Does it?

"Then, in two years, you'll be long gone and I'll be here. Please. I've asked nothing of you since you've arrived. Do this one thing for me, I beg you."

Between her pleading and the thought of my father so skillfully planted in the garden of my mind by Mr. Snow this morning, I find my artillery of excuses are running dreadfully low.

"The dinner is Thursday, correct?"

"Yes," Eileen says, excitedly. "It promises to be a fine meal. The Acceptance Dinner is -"

"I've had more than my share of fine dinners," I stop her with my hand and voice. "Besides, with no wine to pair anything with, how great can it be? Believe me, I would not go for the food."

Eileen nods her understanding.

"There's a north-bound train on Friday night, that will take me to Calgary, correct?"

"Yes, yes," she replies, "I'll take you to the station myself. If you miss the train, I'll carry you to Calgary on my back."

I shake my head, trying to dislodge the trilogy of images. Charles' pleading eyes, my father's pleading eyes, and now hers. I blow through my lips like a horse, broken at last, ready for saddle.

"Very well," I say, "but please know I'm doing this for you, Eileen, and for Mr. Snow. Not for William. And not in any way for myself."

She suddenly jumps up from the table and throws her arms around me, squeezing me half to death in her jubilance.

She *could* carry me to Calgary on her back.

26

I ARRIVE AT THE SNOW HOUSEHOLD FOR DINNER AT SIX O'CLOCK sharp, dressed in the finest fineries I can find. Well, that Eileen could find. She scoured the town, begging, borrowing, what she could, and likely stealing what she could not. A mountain of discarded options lay on my bed. The choices were all variations on modest plain, but I was instructed to dress as formally as I could, and she immediately rose to the occasion.

It is hard for Eileen, that I cannot deny. Yet I've come to accept that I'm here by proxy for her. This was never stated, but knowing she would not be invited, the next best thing was having someone attend with little interest in attending. I am her spy; these borrowed clothes my thin disguise.

The sun has recently set, and the night, barely old enough to be out on its own, is warm. I set the portrait of William by the door, wrapped in brown butcher paper. I'll await a suitable moment to unveil it.

Normally the table resides in the large country kitchen, I assume, like the Owens household, with meals taken by the same wood stove where they are cooked. Tonight, it's more of an altar – freshly oiled and adorned with fine linens and white Belgian lace – boldly positioned in the centre of the room.

Candles pour a soft honey light across the walls, and a Victrola in the corner sings with the bittersweet whisper of a Chopin nocturne.

Seconds after my arrival, William and his father come to the door. Have they been banned from the house all day? Were they forced to bathe and dress at a neighbour's place? I assume this is the case, as their silence upon entering their own home speaks to their surpassed expectations and surprise.

Sarah Snow stands regal and radiant at the head of the table upon our arrival, showing no sign at all of the hours she has most likely spent in preparation for the dinner. The evening is ostensibly about William and his Acceptance Dinner, but I anticipate it will be his mother who will shine brightest tonight. Walls and floorboards have been scrubbed, oiled, lemon-scented, and the upholstery on the chairs and settee appear to have been dusted and adorned with freshly laundered throws and covers.

Mrs. Snow appears to be in her crowning glory of pride; not in herself or her accomplishments, but in her family, her place within that family, and her dear, darling, ferociously handsome son.

"Mother, I..."

He is as much at a loss for words as a northern warbler must be, arriving for the first time at its southern winter home. His mother comes to him and removes his overcoat, folding it over her arm with the grace and aplomb of a veteran *maître d.*

"Welcome, my son," she whispers, standing on her toes and kissing him on the cheek. "Happy nineteenth."

Here is a family not easily given to demonstrative affection with one another, and to see the softness of her gesture, a hand laid so tenderly upon his one reddened cheek, and the slow press of her lips upon the other, moves me very much. It is a picture I will not soon forget: a mother's kiss to her adult son.

"Miss Hale?" Mr. Snow says.

He is poised to remove my loaner cape, the hood of which catches upon a ringlet curl of my hair. The clumsiness of the two of us trying to detach the shawl from my locks contrasts quickly and sharply with the puissant grace of the scene immediately prior. So much so that the sweet, suspended tension of magic breaks with laughter, as always happens when a love scene is punctured by the farcical entrance of the clown. Yet still the spell sustains, as Mrs. Snow takes her son by the arm and leads him to the table. An equally proud and speechless father escorts me. Once seated, all eyes turn to the head of the family and head of the table.

"Our dear Heavenly Father, it is with humbled hearts that we gather round this table for thy sacred offering to us. Just as thy son sat with loved ones before accepting his divine mission, so too does our William sit with his mother, his father, and his beloved friend Tara…"

I steal a glance at William, who smiles and winks at me through the soft glow of candlelight as the grace concludes.

Mrs. Snow rises to start the meal, but when she gets to the door, there is a pause. She then returns to the table, reddened from some embarrassment unknown, and procures a small brass bell from the side table and gives it a ring. Immediately the kitchen door swings open and two ladies emerge in full black and white server's aprons, brandishing a large porcelain tureen of soup, which they commence to serve. First to William, then myself, then his mother, and ending with Mr. Snow.

"Thank-you, Sister Taggart, Sister Godfrey," he utters.

The two women hold back their giggles as best they can, equally nervous and exhilarated to be playing their parts in the evening's pageant. After soup is served, they quietly and efficiently return to the kitchen. Having been fortunate enough to attend formal president's dinners at the university with my father, I must say that these two were given instruction on how to serve (albeit quickly and under-rehearsed). Another hint of the thorough planning on the part of the matriarch of the house.

"Servants, mother?" William quietly acknowledges.

"Nothing but the best for my little boy," she says.

"Well," William replies, "at least the best that Emmett has to offer."

His father laughs, and then stifles his laughter at his son's humour.

The first course - a wild mushroom soup with fresh cream, tomatoes, pork rind, and a hint of lemon, accompanied by fresh hot bread made in the French style - is superb. When the course is finished, the bell is rung again, and in swoop the *Sisters* to clear away the bowls and set down a selection of cheeses to nibble between courses.

"I cannot get over the extravagance with which you have handled every detail of the evening, my dear," Mr. Snow comments. "It must have taken weeks to plan."

"A true labour of love," she replies, receiving the compliment with grace and poise as she rises to crank the Victrola and change up the music selection. "But yes, you're right, a great labour nevertheless."

She returns to the table, dancing slightly to the Bach cello suite now playing, and lays her hand upon William's shoulder.

"I laboured extensively when I brought you into the world, and have laboured with equal intensity to send you back out into it."

"Ah, but I'm worth it, Mother," he responds. "Don't you agree, Miss Hale?"

"If you convert a few hundred souls to the church over the next twenty-four months," I quip, "then perhaps you will have earned a dinner like this."

It's the first mention about the impending mission. Despite the painful toll that this two-year separation is going to take on his parents, my little joke is met with warm laughter and acknowledgement. Mr. Snow – ever the bishop and leader of the flock – cannot resist a response.

"There is only one conversion William will be capable of on his mission," he says, "and that is all that will be expected of him."

I look to the birthday boy for further explanation.

"Myself," he acknowledges. His answer is met with his father's glass raised in approbation. "But I'll *baptize* – how many courses tonight, mother?"

"Five," she tells him. "Including dessert."

"Then I'll baptize five souls for every course," he boasts, popping a piece of cheese into his mouth. "Plus one more for this morsel of cheddar." Bits of white crumble on his teeth as he speaks.

His mother rings the bell again, and the third course is brought in, beautifully presented on four bone-china plates. A salad, with carrot, pickled beets (thinly sliced), and green beans, topped with a delicious honey vinaigrette dressing.

"Mr. Snow," I say, turning to William's father at the head of the table, "how does this compare with your own Acceptance Dinner so far?"

He finishes his mouthful of food, chewing slowly and with great savour, clears his throat with a mouthful of water, and dabs his lips with all the decorum of a practiced diplomat.

"Acceptance Dinners were not practiced when I came of age, Miss Hale," he replies.

"The year of our lord, 1743," William adds.

"But as leader of the church here in Emmett, and, prior to that, as bishop and councillor back in the old country," he says, colouring 'old country' with suitable irony and we all share a laugh at this reference to the very young, very new America, relative to a real old country, "I have had the good fortune to sit at numerous Acceptance Dinners, as a represented official, sometimes as a welcome guest. Many of them were simple, charming affairs, some attempting a grace and formality similar to what your mother has so adroitly achieved tonight. I always considered it lack of means that forestalled the realization of such goals, but now I understand it was lack of resourcefulness. For as we all know, our means are no better – indeed, in so many ways, much more humble – than many of the families back home."

"And you, Mrs. Snow?" I ask as I turn to the other end of the table. "Have you attended an Acceptance Dinner before this?"

"Sisters *give* Acceptance Dinners," she calmly replies with a slight nod, "we don't attend them."

"What about when a young woman celebrates her nineteenth birthday?" I ask. "Is there no dinner for them?"

"We serve our fathers, our sons, and our husbands," she answers. "That is what we do, and there is no greater honour than to be of service to the Lord."

"Service to the Lord is one thing," I say unable to stop myself from stirring things up, "service to the brethren is something else."

"One and the same," she smiles to me. "There is great peace to be found in service, my dear."

"Miss Hale," William interjects, "is there ever a time in the day and night when you don't seek to ask uncomfortable questions?"

"First of all," I say, smiling at him in response, "I'm asking a simple question, not an uncomfortable one. And second of all, no, there isn't much of a window in my day when I passively accept the status quo, whatever it may be. Don't you think customs and norms and values should be poked and prodded every once in a while?"

"To what end?" he quickly replies, enjoying the repartee. "Why not just accept the things you cannot change?"

"If everyone followed such a tenet," his father intercedes, "we would all be living under the pagan sun worshippers or Judaic law. Imagine if our founding Prophet let sleeping dogs lie when he went praying in the woods that fateful afternoon? The frustration one feels with a status quo should always be explored, William. I agree with Miss Hale emphatically. It should be voiced and acted upon, for that is how God's work is manifested on earth. If the Lord sees fit to have a custom destroyed and a new one rise from its ashes, He will choose the instrument for the task. If a true need for change is at work, then change will happen. The temple will be cleansed, the hypocrisy of leadership will be overthrown, and the dead will rise up and speak. If change is not in the plan, then all the resistance and challenges will be mere wind, and eventually blow away without leaving a mark. But one cannot know without beginning."

I raise my crystal glass of water to Mr. Snow in acknowledgment of his endorsement, and he bows his head slightly to me.

"But Father, what if those questions," William asks, "be they from the mouth of Miss Hale or anyone else for that matter, what if such questions carry in them the seeds of destruction which eventually lead to the demise of our way of life? Your way of life, Father. The church you have dedicated yourself to for your entire existence? What then?"

His father lets fly a hearty guffaw, covering his mouth in the process, and shakes his head at his son as the laugh slowly subsides.

"If such a catastrophic demise is inevitable, William my boy, then there is little I or anyone else can do to stop it. If it is the Lord's wish, then I can only help it to fulfillment. If not, then such questions will be mere words with little more than awkward discomfort to endure as a result."

I can see that the evening is on the verge of revolving around me and my provocative question, which is the last thing I want. Such insensitivity on my part would be unforgivable.

"My thanks, *Brother* Snow, *Brother* Snow," I say, with a nod to both of them. "There is, however, a more pressing question burning inside that I must honour with immediate release."

Charles Snow pulls the bottom of his vest down as he sits upright, then opens his hands in a gesture to say 'proceed, please, I am fully attentive and ready'. I turn to his wife.

"What was William like as a child?"

Mrs. Snow radiates at the chance to speak of William, and speaks at length of the early days here, and the concomitant challenges of setting up not only a home but also an entire town.

"William was the first church member born in this country,"

she says as she reaches over to grip her son's hand. We are very proud of him, but as a boy, he was a terror and a half."

I listen to stories of his boyhood. All the anecdotes are heart-felt and filled with a mother's pride, but as common and indistinguishable from any other mother talking about any other boy with one exception.

"And then there was the time he went missing for exactly forty hours," she slows, her delivery down to accentuate the saga to come, "and we couldn't find him anywhere."

"Mother," William groans in protest, "don't tell that story."

"Hush now, William, your mother's speaking," I admonish playfully. "Go ahead, Mrs. Snow."

She tells of how, in the summer following his eighth birthday, William ran away after his baptism.

"It was about four o'clock in the afternoon, and the baptismal celebration was just winding down. I was saying goodbye to the few guests that were still there and beginning to tidy when I called to William saying there was a final piece of lemon pound cake remaining and it was his for the taking."

"I love lemon pound cake," William confesses as he blushes with vivid alacrity. "It's my all-time favourite."

"So you can imagine my concern when he didn't come running," his mother continues. "I only made it on special occasions and never offered a second piece. Well, I searched through the house, the closets and cupboards, through the store and any compartments he could be hiding in, and then out in the surrounds and various outbuildings. I even carried the plate of pound cake with me, hoping that the smell or sight of it would prove an effective lure, but I could not find him anywhere."

William stabs a small block of cheese with his fork, deposits it into his mouth, and then buries his head in his hands upon the table as he chews.

"It was late July," she describes, "in the middle of a nasty bout of heat, with long summer nights where it only cools down but a little."

"I've come to know those days well," I tell her.

"So I was not too concerned about him at that point," she explains, then turns to her husband. "Remember I asked you if we should go out searching for him?"

"He had just been baptized," Mr. Snow explains to me, "and so I told Sarah that he was filled with a not-altogether false sense of having grown up a little bit. I figured he was out on an adventure of some sort and told my wife not to worry, that he'd be back when he was hungry."

At this juncture in the story, the two servants appear at the door to the kitchen. "Sister Snow?"

"Oh yes, of course," Sister Snow nods, snapping out of her reverie. "Please bring in the entrée, Sisters."

"Son," his father says, "would you honour your mother, your guest, and myself by serving?"

"We'll finish the story of William's mysterious disappearance over dessert," his mother assures me as William dishes out first to me and then to his parents.

The aroma wafting up from the dark stew is promising, with potatoes, carrots, onions, and chunks of lamb and ground veal (or chunks of veal with ground lamb, I'm not entirely sure) comprising the ingredients. The sauce is thick and dark, the spices reminiscent of a Middle Eastern origin, almost like a curry, but not quite, as if one were being served Irish stew from Calcutta. I find it tremendously savoury, and the meat is especially succulent and tender (if a bit fatty); a dish silently screaming out for a nice Beaujolais.

"Exquisite, my dear," Mr. Snow proclaims after his first mouthful.

"Thank-you, Charles."

"Yes, it's very good, mother," William says, finishing up his first serving instantly, and as he reaches for the spoon, his mother gently admonishes him about waiting for the entire table to finish their first plate before indulging in a second helping.

I offer my complements as well as I involuntary reach for a non-existent wine glass after every mouthful.

"Would it be out of place," I ask, "to enquire as to the ingredients or even the recipe? I've never encountered these flavours together in one dish before. Is it Indian? A Bombay collection of spices?"

"The ingredients and instructions came from down south," Mr. Snow interjects. "Hand delivered by Brother Harris himself."

"All I did was put it together," Mrs. Snow humbly admits.

"If I may," I say, laying down my fork to give her my full attention, "I have had the good fortune to indulge in many meals of exceptional quality, and though am I no chef myself, I can fully appreciate the talent and gifts of one. Any monkey can follow instructions, whether it be in cooking a meal or painting a picture. The gifted craftsmen and artists leave their mark, and the results are unmistakable. Such is the case with this meal."

She blushes slightly, but gracefully acknowledges my words with a slight bow of her head.

We enjoy the rest of the dish in relative silence, all of us adhering to an unspoken solemnity around the food. I begin to wonder if there isn't some port or other heavy spirit involved in its creation, for I can feel an intoxication taking over; not only in myself, but around the table. Perhaps we have been hoodwinked all this time as hedonistic gourmands; it is the eclectic assemblage of tastes and meats that bring on inebriation and not the wine at all.

"Ah, William, I almost forgot," his father says, removing an envelope from his jacket. "This letter arrived from your sister earlier in the week. I meant to have you read it before, but was sidetracked by the story of your eight-year-old escapades."

"Which I still want to hear the end of," I insist.

"And you shall," his father assures me. "But first, a message from your sister Clara."

He hands the envelop to his son, who is feasting on his

second helping, as are we all. William opens it and begins to read it silently to himself.

"Oh William, don't keep it all to yourself," I protest, lightly pounding the table with the bottom of my fork. "I would love to hear what your sister has to say. Read it out loud, for all of us."

William smiles, and touches my foot under the table with his. I am unsure if this is an acceptance of my suggestion or a dismissal. Either way, the clandestine physical conduct sends a ripple of energy up my leg.

"Or not," I quickly add. "I'm sure it's none of my business."

"I only hesitate," he responds, "because it's likely to be dull and boring and not worth reading out to everyone present. My sister leads a decidedly uninteresting life. However, since you asked." He takes a drink of water and begins to read aloud.

"My dear brother William..." His voice is high-pitched and feminine.

"Does she really sound like that?" I ask with a laugh. We all enjoy his impersonation of his sister.

"Worse," he tells me. "Now don't interrupt."

"As the eldest of the family, it is my duty to wish you a happy birthday and, more importantly, the happiest and most rewarding of Acceptance Dinners that I can offer. I was present at your Induction and your Baptism ceremonies. Not a huge achievement, as I was a young girl at both. I'm sorry I can't be with you at your dinner tonight. What a wonderful adventure you are embarking on. As for me, I've only had but one serious adventure in the last month, aside from raising little Jacob: getting a nail in my foot from walking around old floorboards without shoes or slippers. Daniel was kind enough to pull it out..."

William stops reading for a moment and informs me that Daniel is her husband. "His voice is even higher than Clara's," he says.

"Oh William," his mother admonishes, "be nice."

"It only kept me awake one night, and the coyotes insisted on sitting up, so it became a noisy occasion rather than a silent misfor-

tune. All is well now, and I watch where I step with much more clarity and caution. Mother wrote and told me of a certain lady-friend in your life…"

"Whoever could you have been referring to?" he queries his mother.

I kick him – hard – underneath the table.

"Very unlady-like behaviour," he yelps, rubbing his foot, "from my lady-friend," and then continues reading.

"… about whom I expect a full and detailed account from you either in person or by post. She must be pretty remarkable if she has managed to make you sit still long enough for a portrait to be painted."

"You hear that, Miss Hale?" William interrupts his reading. "Your reputation has now officially spread south of the 49th parallel. You're famous."

"I'm sure she has stolen not only your heart but Mother and Father's as well. She sounds exquisite."

The way he colours 'exquisite' leads me to believe he is fabricating this particular part of the letter.

"She never said that," I protest.

"I swear it's right here," he defends, then looks back down at the letter. *Exquisite*."

"Please," I say with a blush, "don't tease."

"See for yourself."

He hands the letter over the table and I scan the document, noticing first his sister's lovely penmanship. All the familiar words from top to middle catch my eye: *'eldest', 'adventure', 'nail', 'coyotes'*. Then I find the sentence in question. *'Exquisite'* is the word indeed. I smile, but cannot help my nosey eyes from reading on to the next line. It reads *"I miss you very much, as I miss all four of my brothers. Though I do not wish it…"* I stop and hand the letter back to him without mentioning what I had found written there.

"Well, was I right?" he asks.

"Right you were," I say. "It seems there's a first time for everything."

He tries to kick me back under the table, but I move my foot away with split second reflexes. He ends up kicking the table itself, upsetting two glasses of water and one of milk. His mother quickly mops up the mess as William finishes reading the letter.

"I miss you very much…"

He pauses here, and I feign ignorance in my expression expecting him to steal a glance at me. He never looks up, but pretends to cough and takes the opportunity to rub his foot under the table.

"That really hurt," he says rubbing his foot once again, before returning to the letter.

"I miss you very much, and can't wait to see everyone again for Jacob's Induction on the sixth. I'll sign off now. Great work lies ahead of you. We are so fortunate to be living at this time. With love, Clara."

The pregnant silence hovering around after the reading of the letter could claim as its parents any or all of the following: the absence of Clara now profoundly felt; the mention in the letter of me as William's 'lady-friend'; the result of gorging ourselves on rich food and the ineluctable drain of energy from the body as it sets to work on the task of digestion. Whatever the source, William takes it upon himself to run the silence through with the quick blade of a question.

"So, where were you in the telling of the most embarrassing moment in my life?" He addresses the question to his mother, but it's his father who takes up the mantle.

"Once we realized that our boy was cunningly, deliberately staying away from us," he regales, "we made the shift from worry to patience, and waited for him to come home."

The story continues, but without the sense of play in William that accompanied it before.

Dessert soon arrives. Plates of cheese and apples and bread pudding and – of course – lemon pound cake are laid upon the table. I drop in and out of the remainder of the story, unable to shake the fact that nowhere in the story is there any mention made of the brothers.

If it were one unmentioned brother, I could understand. But three? As I've felt before in this town and around this family, something is clearly amiss.

WE RETIRE to the parlour after dinner, and talk about William's upcoming mission abroad. He and his father will take the morning train south to Cherry Creek, where William will undergo a month's worth of training. He will then join a group of missionaries bound for the British Isles.

By the end of the evening, the moon is near to full and serves to illuminate the snow that begins to lightly fall. Large, soft flakes float down upon the small town and the paths surrounding it.

"Such a picture outside," William comments. "Mother. Father. May I walk Miss Hale home?"

His parents look at one another, and his father gives a quick nod to Mrs. Snow.

"Unchaperoned?" she asks. "And at night?"

"Come along if you like," William offers. "But it's been such a wonderful night. I'd like to wish Miss Hale a fond farewell in some semblance of privacy."

"The Owens house is close enough," Mr. Snow decides. "We can watch you from the window here, and no doubt curious eyes will be keeping watch from their window there. Between us all, you'll be well observed, especially with the bright moon lighting your way."

My exhaustion, disinterest, and eagerness for my bed will be chaperone enough, I want to assure them, but turn my focus to the painting instead.

"Before we go," I say, handing the wrapped portrait to William, "please accept this and my thanks for sitting so patiently for me."

"Ahh," William sighs with excitement. "May I?"

I nod, and he delicately unwraps the brown butcher paper.

His mother clears a place on the mantle, and he rests the painting on top against the wall. Everyone stands and beholds the picture in silence, the soft light of candles giving it a flattering debut.

"Extraordinary," Mr. Snow is the first to speak. "An extraordinary likeness. Don't you think, my dear?"

"Beautiful," she replies. "Especially the eyes. Incredible. You've done a remarkable job, Miss Hale."

"The light is very kind this evening," I say, "so please hold your accolades until the morning sun has had its way with things. You may not be so complimentary in the hard light of day."

They both mutter 'nonsense', and I agree. I know how exceptional it is.

Though William remains quiet, his eyes betray how moved he is by seeing his portrait at last.

"Thank-you for an extraordinary dinner," I say, holding out my hand to his mother. She steps forward instead and wraps her arms around me in a sudden and tender hug. I am instantly reminded of the care and attention she administered to me upon my arrival here. "It's an evening I will cherish for all my days," I add.

Mr. Snow also offers a hug, but seemingly more out of duty then genuine affection.

"Thank you," he whispers.

I am glad to have been able to grant a father's simple wish.

27

It's warm and bright from the moon and snow, as if a muted summer's day is trying to muscle its way into a dark autumn night. I untie Millie from her post outside the house, and she runs free and happy.

"They love the painting," William says after a few moments. "I can tell."

"And you?" I ask.

"I'm a bit overwhelmed, I must admit," he begins. "I don't see myself very often. Never had a photograph taken, don't spend a great deal of time in front of a mirror. So it's a little unnerving to suddenly see one's face, especially as it is seen through the eyes of someone else."

He stops and takes a deep breath. "I love the painting very much. However, I must confess to loving the painter even more."

I have no idea how to react to his declaration. We walk in silence for quite some time. William has a shameless smile spread across his face. I see the Owens house glowing in the distance.

"I can't believe how perfect a night this is," he exclaims. "The warm air, the moonlight, the snow."

"It is lovely," I add, trying to hurry my pace without appearing to.

"You know," he begins to say, "an Acceptance Dinner is seen, by some, to be an engagement dinner as well."

"Yes, Eileen has mentioned that more than once," I remark, trying to shimmy her into the conversation. "You know how sweet she is on you, don't you?"

"Stop the presses," he exclaims. "She's been sweet on me since I was baptized eleven years ago. Every girl within forty miles is sweet on me."

"That sure is a heap of sweetness coming your way."

"Can't say that I blame any of them. What with being my father's son and all. And the fact that there ain't a pile of boys to choose from. That's all I'm saying."

"Gives you the pick of the litter, doesn't it?" I tell him. "You've a pretty high opinion of yourself, William Snow."

"Just speaking God's truth is all," he shrugs. "No harm intended."

"I take it then that you're not so sweet back on her."

"The Holy Spirit ain't said nothing about me and Eileen so it doesn't matter whether I'm sweet on her or no."

"Ah! The Holy Spirit" I repeat. "How terribly convenient."

"I have heard many whisperings about you, however," he says, blissfully ignoring my criticism. "I do believe we are meant to be together, Tara Hale. I plan to follow through on that in two years' time."

A white jackrabbit runs across the field, which catches my eye only because of the shadow cast from his ears and tail. I lose my train of thought for a second as I register the fascinating paradox of seeing something first by shadow and not by light. I walk slowly forward, inch by inch, and take the opportunity to think and prepare a response rather than simply react. This is a skill I learned from my father, who would always act and force a reaction; rarely did he react to others.

"So, we'll get married then, in two years' time? Is that what you imagine?"

"Sounds good to me," he replies with disarming confidence.

"And I am to wait, am I, with a candle in the window for my soldier to return from his tour of duty?"

"I should hope so," he said, "but you're welcome to wait wherever you like. Vancouver. Halifax. It need not be here."

I laugh at his bravado, his outrageous impudence. "How magnanimous of you, Mr. Snow."

He bows extravagantly, like a royal prince, which he probably thinks he is.

"And then what? We have a dozen children together, and raise them to be obedient little church members?"

He is nodding vigorously, either ignoring my sarcastic tone or missing it all together.

"Some," he says. "Maybe not a dozen. Lots. A big family to be sure."

"Like yours?"

"Hmm?" he responds, laughing in surprise.

"Your family," I repeat. "I never knew you had so many siblings. You've only mentioned your sister."

"What do you mean?" he asks, a quizzical expression spreading across his face.

"The letter you read at dinner tonight," I remind him. "From Clara."

"Yes…" he responds, stretching the word out slowly, expressing his continued bout of confusion.

"I saw what was written there," I simply say. "She made reference to *all four of her brothers*."

"What are you talking about?" he says. "I never read that."

"I know, you skipped over it. But when you handed the letter to me, I saw the words there. I didn't bring it up then, and wouldn't have thought much of it if you hadn't left it out in your reading. Now I'm very curious."

"You must have imagined it," he dismisses. "I don't recall anything like that in the letter."

"Read it again, and I'll show you where."

By the ample light of the moon, I see his expression change before my very eyes. The way it does when one who has been in control is suddenly - and surprisingly - relieved of their power.

"First thing in the morning," he says. "Let's keep walking. Get you home."

"No, read it now," I challenge him. "I hate going to bed knowing I'm right but not having proved it."

"I left the letter at home, so let's keep –"

"No you didn't. You folded it up, slipped it back into the envelope, and tucked it into the inside pocket of your dinner jacket," I say as I quickly reach into his jacket and pull out the note in question. "See?"

"Oh. So I did."

He makes no move to open the letter and read it. He just stands there as if the argument was about whether or not he had it on his person, not the content contained therein.

"Well?" I urge.

"Well what?"

"Read it again," I insist. "Otherwise give it to me and I'll read it."

Reluctantly, and with slow moving hands, he opens the letter again and re-reads the passage confirming that I was right. His sister makes mention of four brothers.

"I'm awfully sorry, Tara," he concedes. "You were right."

He folds the stationery back into his pocket, pulls the collar of his jacket higher up around the back of his neck, and comments that it's getting a bit chilly.

"Let's continue on, shall we?" he suggests and takes a few steps while I stand stock-still. He turns back. "Are you coming?"

"When you finished reading the letter at dinner," I say, "the entire mood changed. Before the letter, you couldn't wait for the story about your escapades to be finished. After the letter, you worked very hard redirecting the conversation back to it."

"Do you mind if we walk and talk?" he asks, leaning his body towards the house, trying to coax me along.

"Now you're acting the same way," I say without moving, "trying to take my mind off something you don't want to talk about."

"That's right," he quickly replies. "I don't want to talk about it. I want to go home. It's late and I have an early morning and a long train ride ahead of me."

"And I will have two years of silence ahead of me," I return with anger in my tone. "Waiting, of course, for your triumphant return as my lawfully wedded husband."

"It's very complicated, Tara," he starts to explain, his body manifesting the discomfort caused by my defiance. He is so young, so transparent, so unlike his father. "I'm not the one to explain it to you, my father is the only—"

"Gee, William," I say cutting him off, "you were so convincing a moment ago about marrying me, I thought for sure a ring was going to suddenly appear and you would be down on one knee. Now, you can't wait to dump me off and run home to your father. What's changed all of a sudden?"

"Please," he implores me, "I'll explain everything in the morning. I'm tired and so full of excitement. Can't this wait?"

"Where are they?" I demand, standing my ground.

William may be short on his father's qualities but I'm filled to the brim with mine.

"Tara…"

"Down in Cherry Creek? Elsewhere? Did they refuse to move up here? Was there a falling out with your father?"

"Let's just go."

"Tell me where they are."

"I can't!" he barks, like a cornered dog.

Now the fight is rising up in him. He squares himself off to me as the fire ignites in his cheeks and eyes.

"I can't tell you."

"What do you mean you *can't* tell me? Who's stopping you?"

"It's not my place to tell you of such things," he says with finality, "so drop it."

"You better make it your place," I shoot back. I'm not easily silenced when I know I have the upper hand. The ceremony may be a couple years away, but let's pretend that as of this moment, you're my husband and I am your wife."

"Then as my wife," he says, pushing back harder, "you must respect my wishes and do as I…"

"Don't you dare finish that sentence!" I bellow.

"Tara," he says, righting himself after being slightly bowled over by my threat, "there is a tradition and a way of doing things that…"

"Not for me, understand? I may not know everything about your church, but I know enough to see that it's a mighty adhesive that holds families and communities together, and it brings a great deal of peace and joy to its members. But don't think for a moment that I'll do what I'm told just because I'm somebody's wife."

His face betrays the shock of my words.

"Just as I thought," I say. "You have no idea what you want wishing me to be your spouse. Goodnight and goodbye, William Snow."

I turn and walk towards my room at the Owens, Millie running circles in the snow with excitement that I'm finally free of my escort home.

"They're with Heavenly Father," he announces.

I stop and turn.

Tears flow from his eyes, but his breath and voice betray no sign of crying. He is releasing completely and giving over to me. I feel the bittersweet taste of victory.

"Oh my lord," I say, guilty for my behaviour. "I am so sorry. How terrible for you. For your parents."

I stand beside him, filled now with compassion and sympathy. I can be a vicious ass when I want to be.

I'm shocked to see a smile float to the surface in the water of his tears.

"It's not terrible," he assures me. "They're with our Father in Heaven. How could that be anything other than glorious?"

It is a miraculous stroke of genius that religion achieves over and over again: the recycling of the morbid horror surrounding death into the greatest joy and cause for celebration. How I wish I could share in it.

"How did it happen?" I ask.

"The Induction Ceremony," he answers. "I guess I never got a chance to tell you all about it."

"So tell me now."

He begins.

"Every child in the church, at the age of two, is inducted into the faith."

He goes on to describe the importance of the ceremony, how the family gathers around the child for days before its second birthday, offering prayers, supporting the parents, and the extent of the celebration around it.

"It's a very beautiful time for our families," he tells me. "My nephew in Cherry Creek has his in a couple of weeks. We'll all be down there for it."

He goes on to tell me that the ceremony takes place inside a special room of the temple. No parents, no family, just the child and the prophet of the church.

"President Wooley," I say.

He describes how it's "a very sacred and important meeting between our Heavenly Father and His child. Can you imagine such a scene?"

He is aglow with divine strength, speaking with the support of what he must take to be his Holy Ghost. I feel powerless against such an imagined ally. It's so much easier to break him when he is merely stubborn and evasive.

"An innocent babe, incapable of forming sentences moments

before, speaking coherently, intelligently, with their Father in heaven?"

"Marvelous and wondrous things," I quietly say. "Chapter 26, verse 14."

"Yes! Oh, how I wish I could be the Prophet for just one of those miraculous ceremonies."

He then goes quiet, and, still with his confidence and authority, adds the following. "But it is different for boys than it is for girls."

"Different how?" I ask, a slight pinch taking hold in the pit of my over-stuffed stomach.

"I know you are an independent woman, Miss Hale, and quite unlike any other I've met. The ways of the church, no doubt, must seem primitive to you, but you can hardly fault us for that. Men and women play different roles in this world, and have different expectations placed upon them. The Induction Ceremony acknowledges this fact early in a child's life."

"How is it different, William?" I urge him to continue.

I should walk away. I know it. I should walk away and lock my door until my train leaves tomorrow, but I cannot go without piecing everything together. I sense the entire puzzle of Emmett and its founding family is about to be completed, and William stands before me holding the final piece.

"Not every boy comes away from that meeting," he says, beginning to tremble with his words.

"What do you mean?" I can no more walk away now than I can pull myself out of a nightmare.

"Tara," he says, stalling again, "it is so difficult for us to understand the ways of God and His plan for us."

"Answer the question, William," I bite my words out. "What happens to the boys?"

"Heavenly Father chooses who is to stay with Him as the blessed children of God, and who among them are returned to their parents."

Stay? Returned? My mind trips over itself as a picture starts to form.

I feel a cold wind, and can taste the sea on it. I'm back at the curling rink. Death is all around, unkindly stopping for me once again.

"I'm sorry," William entreats me. "I should not have said anything."

My mind is spinning with the stars above. My knees suddenly give out. I fall to the ground.

"Tara," William calls, as he reaches down for me. "Please. Come back with me to my house. Let Mother care for you. This is too much for you to bear on your own."

In the distance, the distance in the silence, I can hear Millie barking.

Like a parent knowing their child's cry, I understand the message of each bark, and can decipher whether it is the call to play, the call of neglect, or the call of adventure upon seeing a rabbit or a ground squirrel or a butterfly. I know the call of danger, the call of hunger, and the plain, comforting, everyday call of hello. In the distant silence now, as I kneel in the snow, I hear the call of something new, something I cannot understand. It chills me, and makes me fearful not for Millie, or myself, but for some other thing that I have no way of knowing how to define. The chill unleashes words, and I slap William's hands away as I speak them.

"Father in Heaven…" I say, pitifully.

I somehow manage to pull myself up and march towards the Owens house. William starts to follow but I shoot him so horrific a look that he stops in his tracks and does not take another step.

"Hallowed be thy name…"

My whispered words mingle with the snowflakes and the moonlight, and as I speak, I can no longer hear my dog's call.

"Thy kingdom come, thy will be done…"

I forget entirely about Millie in the execution of the prayer, hearing only the words that are not my own. The Father in Heaven does not speak back.

28

I return to my room in a state of shock, unable to settle my mind sufficiently for sleep to come. I go over William's explanation again and again as I curl myself up in the tightest possible ball on my bed.

Heavenly Father chooses who is to stay with Him, who is to return.

He did not explicitly say what *staying* means, but it does not require a terrific leap of the imagination to guess. His three brothers, all with their Father in heaven. All the young men who should be here in Emmett, being ogled and dreamt about by Eileen and the young woman here, all with their Father in Heaven.

What else could it mean? *Father in Heaven?*

Oh how I wish I had not pressed him so. That I had never seen the letter. That I had not attended that damn dinner. That I had left last week. That I had never arrived here. That I had never left my father.

My father.

Finally, it is he who keeps me up all night.

In dreamy states of semi-consciousness, his face never leaves my sight, his voice rings in my ears every time I close my eyes, his hands reach out to me in desperate supplication. This continues for hours, until the first traces of dawn caress my weary thoughts and afford me an hour or two of uninterrupted rest.

By the time I give in to sleep, there is a knock at my door.

"Sister Snow is here to see you," Mrs. Owens announces.

I emerge, still in my dress from last night, and catch a glimpse of myself in the reflection from the looking glass that hangs over the washing basin. I look a fright.

"The kettle is on, and there's some dried chamomile in the canister by the flour," Mrs. Owens exclaims as she hastily gathers things to leave the house. "The girls and I will be out for a couple of hours, and Brother Owens is at the Stringhams. Please make yourselves at home."

"Thank you, Sister Owens," Mrs. Snow replies, satisfied that orders have been followed.

She quietly waits for the family to close the door behind themselves, before speaking.

"Charles has decided to delay William's mission departure for a day," she begins. "The two of them left before dawn to the Stringhams as well, to help raise a barn."

"I see," I say, and set about making a pot of chamomile tea. What I would not give for some genuine Assam tea leaves right now?

"How is he?" I ask as I pour the hot water into a pot with the flowers. "How's William?"

"He seemed very distraught this morning," Sister Snow answers, "but he has his father's stoicism about him when he needs it, and so left quietly. To be honest with you, he was a right mess last night when he came in. What on earth happened between the two of you?"

"He told me of the Induction Ceremony," I say, surprisingly cool with my delivery, almost challenging her to hear me. "All of it."

"And what of it, my dear?" she asks, unmoved by my words, betraying not a hint of awkwardness or dismay.

I just stare at her, waiting for her to acknowledge my evident disbelief. She continues to smile, awaiting some further elaboration from me.

"I'm sorry, Miss Hale, I'm not understanding you. Why don't you tell me exactly what William said, and maybe then I can get a handle on what was so upsetting for the two of you?"

I feel the surge of contempt in my stomach rise up, and taste the acidic announcement of vomit, but hold it back as I speak. I unfold the events of my exchange with William as if they were fragments of glass, broken and sharp and wrapped in burlap.

"Yes, that's all correct," Mrs. Snow assures me. "The Induction Ceremony is a very sacred event for our families. It all sounds correct, what William spoke of. Is there something upsetting in of all that for you?"

"Not every boy comes away from that meeting," I say, trembling with the words. "Do they?"

I emphasize the last as a challenge for her to respond, as if she herself was responsible for it all. She remains very calm and collected.

"Miss Hale," she begins, "it is very difficult for us to understand the ways of God and His plan for us."

William's exact words. The repetition of a script breaks me, and I bang the table with my fists.

"Are children being killed?" I explode. "Two-year-old boys sacrificed? Is this God's plan for us?"

I am up and pacing now, the words finally out of my body, demanding an explanation with my actions.

"Oh heavens," she says, shaking her head, "no no no. This is not the case at all, my dear. Did William tell you this? I can't imagine he said these things. You misunderstand. Now please, my dear, come sit down and try to relax."

I stand my ground at the end of the table.

"He said that Heavenly Father chooses who is to stay and who is returned to their parents. What else could it possibly mean?"

"Please," she entreats me, "look past your judgment and your fear and try to see the beauty of it all: a pure moment between Heavenly Father and His beloved children. Tara, please."

She stands up and holds her arms out to me.

"We are talking as friends," she patiently asserts herself. "You need not fear me. Please, let me help you. Such knowledge is a heavy, heavy burden for you to carry on your own. How can you?"

I listen as I stand still, my mind spinning with the room. They are right, of course. I cannot bear the weight of this on my own. I am overloaded and feeling crushed by it. She offers some analogy of a young peasant girl who carries water to her village every morning from the well. The water is essential to the life of her family and village, but it is so heavy for her she curses it every time she is forced to haul it.

"You can't blame your cargo for your own limitations," she explains. "The Induction Ceremony is not wrong, my dear, but it is nearly impossible to carry alone. We have husbands and elders and sisters to help us share the burden of it. And we have our undying faith in the Father giving us wings to lift this most leaden of weights. Come my dear, let me take some of it off your shoulders. Come."

I find myself wrapping my arms around her waist. I bury my face in her bosom, and unload my sorrow. I can no longer feel the floor beneath my feet, nor can I hear a sound other than my own heart racing, pounding thick and heavy in my ears. The room is no longer real but a crystallized portrayal of a room, and a lightness fills my chest and brings with it a sense of peace and elation. I sink down into the soft cushion of a settee, still holding onto Mrs. Snow, who says nothing at all.

When finally I sit up and look into her eyes, I find them incandescent.

"It has been so long since I have witnessed such earthly sorrow in another," she confides. "I have lived with order and duty and the heavenly joy that results in such a life. Your pain, Tara, is great, and I understand it fully, but it is radiant and magnificent and beautiful to witness. I feel blessed to be called upon to share it with you. And most importantly, I understand. Believe me I understand."

"Did you…"

"Yes?"

"When you were told of this…" I stumble, unsure of how to form the question.

"Of the Induction Ceremony? Yes, go on."

"How did you react?

"It is a very complicated thing," she explains, "and very difficult to understand. Some never do and resist it altogether. They are the sad ones in our faith, and I feel greatly for them."

"How could you?" I ask. "Your own children. Your *children*."

I watch as her eyes enlarge slightly, and the colour drains from her face. The hand holding the teacup and saucer begin to tremble ever so faintly, so I take it from her and set it down upon the table.

"Oh my," she softly says, as she stands up from the settee.

My eyes follow her to the window, then to the door, which she opens to let in some air. The bright, mid-morning sun stands alone in a cloudless blue sky. The air is crisp, and as a breeze blows into her eyes, I see the glassy presence of regret.

"Excuse me for a moment," she says. "I was hit with a wave of dizziness there. I'll be all right in a moment. In just a moment."

Her composure is finally breaking apart as distant recollections – silent as they have been for so long – awake within her.

"These feelings," she quietly speaks, barely a whisper… "I've not felt them… for so long… so, so long… I thought they were gone, dealt with… I'm just…" She grips my arm suddenly for support, as though she is going to fall over at any moment.

I lead her back into the front room. Her complexion, her eyes, even her bone structure appears to have changed dramatically.

She is fighting to keep her emotions in check, but they are taking over, like hungry ants on a discarded piece of bread. She paces the floor, restless and energized, emitting a power potent as electricity.

"I'm fine," she assures me, "and you deserve to know more about this. Secrets are often necessary, but not within a family. They can tear a family apart. You deserve to know that your feelings are not uncommon. Not in the slightest."

Then, suddenly, the fuse ignites the powder and she detonates with a pent-up combination of rage, resentment, and relief as she tells me how the Induction ceremony was explained to her.

"I was eighteen," she begins, "and had just given birth to my first son."

I feel that at any moment she might beat her chest with her fist and cry out 'my son, my son, my son' three or four times, transfixed by an angry sorrow worthy of an opera score, but she only turns away and suppresses the tears she has more than earned.

"I attended a church conference at the time," she says, "with about half a dozen other new mothers. Each of us was escorted to a small, private room without being told why. Sister Emma Jane, she was one of Charles' mothers, the one I felt closest to and trusted the most, was there waiting for me. She, Charles, and Brother Cannon were all gathered there waiting for me. This was the same for each of the young mothers: an authority, their husband, and a trusted sister; one who was older, had children of her own, and had been initiated into the Induction Ceremony already. I've played that role myself on occasion since. Most often it's the mother-in-law, unless that relationship is strained for whatever reason. It's imperative that the woman present is a true and trusted friend.

"When I arrived in the room, I was showered with love and praise and congratulations on bringing a child – especially a male child – into this world. It showed how selfless I was, and that I was a true instrument of God, doing His will with such grace and beauty. Charles wept as he held my hands. The authority wept, I wept, Emma Jane wept… we were all weeping and open and vulnerable. There was also a great deal of activity throughout the day, and so I was considerably exhausted by the time of our little meeting. Exhausted, yes, but also elated high above the clouds. I had it all: a loving husband, a beautiful child, supportive friends, and was in favour with my Lord. I was never happier."

I watch as she transforms again, into the young and vibrant new mother she once was.

"In my euphoric state," she continues, "they tell me how the ancient traditions and practices of the church have built it into what it is today, and that it is constructed upon the capable shoulders of women like myself. Loving, selfless, and ready to do the will of their Heavenly Father. That His ways are often hard to understand, that they require some hardship at times, some great sacrifices. That in the end, the rewards far outweigh the trials. That such minor demands on us, His children, made today, will seem inconsequential later. It is repeated over and over to me, that we are so fortunate and blessed to be the true children of God. How we must have sympathy and love for all the other lost children in the world; those who are of different beliefs, with their weak and flimsy Sunday morning faiths; and those infidels who have no presence of Christ in their lives at all; and those who have rejected Christ and are in the clutches of Satan. But *we*. We are fortunate and blessed, ready to do God's bidding, just as a child is called upon to do her chores, with no idea of the great benefit, the lessons learned, the achievements gained. Just as we expect our children to obey and not grumble and complain, so too does our Heavenly Father expect it of us."

"How do you remember all this so clearly?" I ask, amazed at her ability to paint so vivid a picture.

"I had buried it all away," she explains, "just as every mother must in order to survive. But I find as I open it up again, it's all there, perfectly preserved without the corrosion of time. Indeed, hardly without even the dust of time, as if it were a memory of a few days ago."

"I'm so sorry," I say as I embrace her, "that you were forced to endure such a thing."

"You don't understand," she says as she slips out of my attempts to console her, "I *chose* to participate in the Induction Ceremony. Five times, I chose it. And my children - all five of them - are beloved and protected by their Heavenly Father because of it. It is not anything that I was *forced* to endure. As children of God, we act on the principle of free agency. The Induction Ceremony - like everything else in our faith - is a choice for each family to make, and not enforced by the church in any way whatsoever. It is an offer extended by God to His children; the church is simply there to facilitate and administer by way of our Prophet."

"How could you choose this?" I demand. "How could anyone choose such a horrific ordeal?"

The thought comes to me that I am dreaming all of this. If so, I cannot force myself awake. If not, I am unable to tear myself away from the light that is finally hitting a dark and terrible secret. Either way, I must endure until it is over.

"Goodness," she sighs as the colour drains from her face, "to deny such an offer from our Heavenly Father. I would find that unacceptable. Consider how the Lord would feel if He wanted to see His child, just once, and have a talk with him or her, only to be refused? Think of your father. If you could arrange to see him, to talk with him, for a few minutes, how would you feel if someone refused you such a simple request?"

Hurt. Confused. Devastated.

"Our Father in Heaven was once a human being," she continues, "like you and I, with the same capacity for love and anguish."

My eyebrows raise in skepticism. I knew Jesus was regarded as a person - demi-God to be precise - but the Almighty Himself?

"Yes, he was a person, just like you and I." Mrs. Snow says in answer to my unspoken thoughts. "With free agency, the capacity to love, to doubt. I could never think to deny Him anything. He that gives us so very much. He gave us His only Son, sacrificed him for us. The least we could do is afford a few minutes from our children's lives to spend alone with Him."

She holds my eyes with hers for a moment. I search her face for some sign of doubt in what she has just told me, some tiny fracture of incredulity, but there is nothing. She solidly believes what she is saying.

"By the time they told me of the actual Induction Ceremony," she explains, reading the trouble in my own expression, "I was ready to accept it. They wouldn't have told me if I wasn't."

"But how?" I say, shaking my head vehemently. "How could anyone accept such a thing? What does it possibly offer you?"

"The heavenly bliss of seeing my sons again in the next world," she answers, beaming with pride. "The opportunity to raise my children in the Celestial Kingdom, after this life is over, at the side of God, is an incredible offer. I have raised two children here, in this dispensation, and will raise three more there in that one. Every mother dreams of having more children, raising them again, reliving the memory of when they were babies. As children of God, it is a dream come true. The earthly sorrow we feel is temporary, but the heavenly joy is eternal. There is really no choice but to accept it as the greatest gift we could ever be given."

"No!" I cry. "This is outrageous! To carry a child inside you for nine months, to give birth, raise that child, love him for two years. How could you even consider such a proposal, let alone go through with it again and again?"

"One learns to accept the things one must in order to live," she replies. "You could ask the same about giving birth, being with child and in labour. 'How could one knowingly endure such hardship, such intense pain?' The answer is the same. The hardship is minimal when weighed against the gains."

"You're a liar!" I lash out. "Shame on you. Hiding your heart behind empty rhetoric and clichéd platitudes."

I call her out on her nonsense with unrestrained anger. Self-delusion is far less forgivable than stupidity, but when the two are so intricately combined, it is infuriating.

"Tell the truth!" I demand. "You can't have felt so cavalier about it, not deep down in your heart. Tell me you were outraged, disgusted. Show me that you're human, that you have feelings. These were your children, for God's sake! Your children! Three beautiful, defenceless baby boys."

I watch her face change a third time, as if my words have shattered another layer of mask and the pieces fall like shards of glass. Years of buried rage erupt from her.

"Yes," she cries, "I did give in to the sorrow, the anger, the pain. For weeks - months! - I cried silently in my pillow whenever I could, but they were always there to comfort me, to ease me through the darkness, never leaving me alone. I cried without tears, without sobs, without breath. I grieved my choices, regretted them, and hated Charles for it. I hated my husband, I hated this church, I hated God! My stomach turned at the very thought of it all. I wanted to run, to drown myself, to rip my womb into shreds so as to never endure such anguish again."

The strength of her anger is overpowering, and I sit stupefied as I listen, fearing someone outside will hear it and start banging on the door. There is no consolation I can offer her. I half doubt she is even aware of my presence in the room. She's a mansion on fire, and no amount of water can threaten such a blaze. The only recourse is to let her burn herself out, and do my best to keep the flames from spreading. I cannot imagine a scene more difficult to watch, nor a creature more deserving of the full extent of compassion.

"But I didn't, do you see? I found strength where I never thought it existed. Through prayer, through fasting, through the intercession of the Holy Ghost, I was able to accept it as divine.

Throughout my time of grief, my hatred and anger reaching its highest pitch, Heavenly Father never once left my side. He understood my sorrow just as He understands yours now. That's what it means to be a parent: you stand by your children in times of darkness as well as times of light."

After she has spent herself, she speaks in a choked, raspy voice.

"And I would do it all again," she confides. "I would have a hundred children if I could and I would be the first in line at the temple to see them all through the Induction Ceremony."

I turn away at her words, utterly defeated. I am no match against the potency of one twisted by toxic, foolish faith.

"But if I can spare my children, I will," she quietly says, and I turn back to her. "It's too late for Clara. Her son's Induction Ceremony is a fortnight away. But it's not too late for William."

She grabs me by my shoulders, and pulls me close to her face.

"Take him away from all of this," she whispers, as if there are ears hidden in the walls. "If there's any chance for him to escape the path that lay before him, it's you. He loves you. I think he would follow you away from here. Since you arrived, it has been my and Charles greatest fear. That we would lose him to you."

For the first time this morning, perhaps forever, she cries. Tears are streaming down her face, and I cannot help but join her.

"Now it is my greatest hope. Please. Take my son with you tonight. I beseech you."

It is now she who buries her face in my bosom, sobbing like a parent who has lost her child.

29

MILLIE AND I RETURN TO THE SNOW HOUSE IN THE AFTERNOON, with an hour to spare before my train departs. I considered leaving without doing this, but I could not deny his mother's wish. She saved me, after all, and if there is a chance to repay my debt to her in this way, I'll happily take it. I can take William to Calgary with me tonight, and sort out what to do from there. How does one extricate an adult from his religion? From his family?

I have no answers, but I must try.

As I approach the house, William appears at the front door. A good sign, as he is obviously expecting me and watching for my arrival. This anticipated act on his part relaxes me a great deal. We stand apart from one another, each waiting for the other to speak. His hands are blistered and red, and he smells of freshly powdered perspiration.

"I'm sorry about last night," he whispers, "I should never have spoken such things."

"I'm glad you did," I tell him. "Besides, it was I who asked. You never forced anything on me."

"I know, it's just... I wish I hadn't said anything. I wish... I don't know. I just wish that this was all simpler. That we could just be together and share the same beliefs, the same life. I wish there was nothing secret between us. Ever."

Millie lets out a whimper for attention. William reaches down and scratches her behind her ears.

"I want the same things," I tell him. Whatever it takes to break him free.

William presses his forehead into Millie's neck. "How? How can we do this?"

"Come with me, William. Tonight. Leave this behind and start a new life, unhindered by ceremonies and obligations and regrets. Maybe we can find God together. Who knows? In a way that we both can accept. Through art, perhaps. Or nature. Service. As adults, not children." I pull him close and add in a whisper "get your bag. The train leaves in an hour."

It is then that I notice the doorway to his house is open, and filled with the imposing presence of Charles Emmett Snow. He and Sarah have been there all along, listening to our every word.

"Good evening, Miss Hale," he says with practiced cordiality

I steal a glance at Sarah, who catches then avoids my eyes. I look to William for an answer, and hear his father's voice behind me.

"Yes, Son, you have a big decision facing you."

William looks me in the eyes again, his back to his parents, and mouths without sound that he'll be right back.

Without a word to his parents, he walks past them into the house. His father maintains his composure while his mother clings to her husband's coat sleeve.

The two or three minutes of William's absence is a complete suspension of breath, and though we stand outside with miles of space around us, the lack of oxygen seems as palpable as if we are locked inside a wardrobe together. The longer he is gone, the more convinced I become that he is packing his bags and gathering whatever valuables he can in short notice, as if a fire is burning and he needs to make quick decisions about what to carry out on his back and what to leave behind forever.

My heart races, and when he finally appears in the doorway, it stops altogether. He carries no bags, no packs, no traveling hat upon his head. Nothing.

"You should have this back," he says as he extends his arm to me, a piece of parchment rolled up in his hand.

I unroll it. It is the charcoal sketch from that summer afternoon in Calgary. It seems so long ago now. Such a different time and space. I look to his mother.

I feel the fool standing here in the snow, with my bags and dog at my side, trying one last time to bring about change, to do the right thing.

"Help me," I say.

"With all due respect, Miss Hale, I would ask that you not attempt to use my wife for your manipulative purposes. She –"

"It's all right, Charles," she tells him, "I can speak for myself."

He looks to her in protestation, but she repeats again that it will be all right, and steps forward to address me directly.

"I was under the impression, Miss Hale, that private conversations between friends – sisters, if you will – were not intended to be made public. However, since you have so brazenly called upon me to speak, before my husband and my son, I shall not deny them an answer out of pettiness and propriety. Our visit this morning, though perhaps a balm to you, was troublesome for me, and left me feeling tremendously unsettled. Upon reflection and prayer and silence, I realized the source of my discomfort: I had been coerced into saying things contrary to my true belief and feelings. The words came not from me, but from a force outside of me."

"What?" I say in utter disbelief. Can this actually be happening?

She holds up her hand to me. "Please. Allow me to speak. I blamed you, of course, for my descent into falsity and betrayal, but soon realized that you were only an agent of darkness, not the darkness itself."

I continue to protest but she cuts me off once more.

"The Induction Ceremony is a gift from God," she proudly proclaims, "and I stand by it. I stand by my husband and my Heavenly Father, and ask both for their mercy and forgiveness. I spoke against them today, and cursed their strength out of my own weakness."

She turns to her husband momentarily, and he nods to her, slowly, acknowledging her contrition. She turns back to me.

"As women," she continues, "we are subject to emotion, and can lose ourselves in the ocean of it and quickly drown. I should have seen it coming, but Satan played upon my weakness like a virtuoso, and I was powerless against it."

She takes a step closer, away from her husband and son.

"Tara, you are loved by all of us here. You can overcome your fears and the power of darkness, but you must give in to the love that is available to you."

I can see, out of the corner of my eye, William's body language in hopeful anticipation of this, as well as that of his father.

"Stay with us," she pleads. "Stay with me and Charles and give yourself some peace."

"Peace?" I cry. "How can you have any peace knowing what you know, doing what you do?"

Mr. Snow comes forward and puts his arm around his wife, and leads her back to the house.

"Come, Sarah," he says, "just leave her be."

"Your own children!" I say, my anger finding voice. "Flesh of your flesh, fruit of your loins."

"We do nothing with our children," Charles responds, "but love them and guide them according to the laws of God. That generous offer has been extended to you twice, from the loving nature of my son, and now out of the compassion of my wife. I offer it to you a third time, here and now, as a father who cares for you as his own, and wants only what is best for you. You sat with us at William's Acceptance Dinner. Ate at our table. To tear yourself away will hurt me as much as it will hurt William and Sarah, but to try and take our child away from us? For shame! You are like family to us."

"You are," his wife repeats, "and we will love you as fully and completely as if you were our own."

William stands with them for a moment. Is he seriously waiting for me to come forward? I can hardly feel my legs, let alone walk on them. After a moment, he turns and walks slowly into the house. His mother follows him.

"Sister Owens will transport you to the train station," Charles says to me, sadness in his words. "She is waiting for you at the Owens barn. Goodbye, Miss Hale." His voice cracks as he bids farewell and disappears into the house.

I start to walk away from the Snow's yard when I notice an aching in my lower arms. To my surprise, I see that both of my hands are closed in tight fists and the knuckles are a bloodless white. I force them open and see that I've crushed the end of the rolled-up sketch.

A white jackrabbit runs across the road. Could it be the same one from last night? I am ready to scream at Millie to stay put, but she doesn't budge. I walk forward three paces and stop, and she follows me, stopping as I do, remaining dutifully by my side. We both watch the rabbit who has now stopped and is watching us.

"Good girl." I crouch down and spread my arms around her neck. "How have I survived this long without you?"

She licks my face in reply. The rabbit, having decided that there is no immediate threat to its life from these two sources of heat, lightly makes its way towards the Owens place. I follow it with my eyes, watching it disappear behind the barn and see a warm light glowing in the small barn window.

"Come on, girl."

30

EILEEN IS INSIDE WITH HER SISTERS. THE TWO GIRLS ARE JUMPING into a pile of fresh straw, burying one another in it, while Eileen readies the harness. I enter silently, and after standing for a few seconds without making a sound, Eileen suddenly senses my presence and turns around with a sharp gasp.

"Miss Hale."

I can only imagine the sight I must be to her at this moment - tear-stained, sleepless, and seething with rage.

"You're to take me to the train station, I understand."

She orders the two younger ones back into the house. Normally they would argue such an abrupt end to their play-time, but they too can feel the disturbance I have caused in the air, and quickly disperse.

"You look an awful fright, Tara"

"Have we time to stop at the police detachment on our way?"

"St. Mary's?"

I nod. Without another word, she lifts some blankets down into the buggy.

"Let's fetch your trunk and be off," she says. "There's time for a short stop if we hurry."

· · ·

MY FACE CREASES into the wind as we race the carriage out of town, Millie running behind. We arrive at the river, and follow it northward. As I try to prepare some kind of statement to say, my mind becomes muddled by seeing both sides of the issue simultaneously. To pull William out of his world would be just as horrific for him as my entering his would be for me. If I could have managed to cut him loose from this madness, however would I have stopped the bleeding?

I notice that we have slowed down to a trot, and ask how much further the detachment is.

"Just up ahead," she says, "on the other side of the river. You'll have to walk across the foot bridge from here."

"You are the kindest soul I've ever met, Eileen Owens," I blurt out.

She freezes while holding the reins, not looking at me but listening to my voice with taut muscles and breathless silence.

"I fear I've done irreparable damage to you by stepping foot into this town," I confess, "and for that I am terribly sorry."

Indecision threatens to take hold, and I look out across the blue-lit surrounds, the banks of the St. Mary river shining with snow and ice, the water surging forward. Stars are beginning to awaken for the night, and they yawn brilliantly as they come to life. I turn my head around to look backwards, and there's my Millie in the distance, running to keep up with me, to stay by my side.

I recognize the beauty of all things, and it rises up in waves, crowding me forever, 'till I die. The beauty of colours, the beauty of shapes, the beauty of the beating heart of the animal behind me, far more human than any of us.

The beauty of my father washes over me, and I taste its brine on my lips. Beauty I've tasted, beauty I've squandered. The beauty of a face posing for a sketch in a tent, the beauty of a kiss.

I look at Eileen. The beauty of falling in love, the promise of marriage, the beautiful possibility of children.

Children.

My stomach becomes a fist and tightens as we arrive at the small outpost on the river.

"I'll be back soon," I tell Eileen. "Please keep Millie with you."

I dismount and walk across the bridge towards the door.

Beauty, mercy have on me.

A FIRE quietly burns in a pot belly stove which stands in the centre of the room. The smell of beans and coffee emanates from the small closet kitchen opposite the entrance, where a smaller box wood stove plays host to a pan and kettle. These aromas mix with pipe tobacco, animal hide, and shoe polish.

Sergeant Parks sits on the edge of single cot mattress pressed into the corner of the building, a large union Jack flag hanging on the wall directly above. He holds one of his boots in his hand, the other rests on the floor beside a tin of opened polish. I stand at the door and announce myself. He stands and steps forward.

"Good evening, Miss Hale."

"Good evening."

"I'm afraid you caught me during my dinner hour," he says. "You don't mind if I eat, do you?"

"No. Not at all."

He sets down the boot, wipes his hands on a large polishing cloth, and scoops the beans and franks onto metal plate. He sets this on a table and then lifts the pot off the stove.

"Will you have a cup of coffee?"

"No," I reply. "Thank-you."

He smiles and winks as he pours himself one. "Don't tell me they've converted you to a coffee-free existence over there in Emmett?"

"Officer Parks, I -"

"Sergeant."

"Sergeant. Sorry. I -"

"One moment, please," he interrupts again, "let me collect my notebook." He sips his coffee and winces. "You made the right choice about the coffee. It's terrible. Still haven't quite figured out how to make it right." He fishes through his Norfolk jacket for his notebook and pencil, and brings a second chair to the table. "Have a seat, Miss Hale."

I sit down and loosen my cloak, draping it on the back of the chair behind me.

"You're here about the matter of those unpaid boarding fees in Calgary, I presume?"

"Something far more serious, Sergeant," I say, trembling at the words, "involving the Snows and the people of Emmett." I let loose a large sigh after breaching the subject at last. There is no turning back now.

"I see." He blows a spoonful of beans, cooling it before eating, and chews noisily as he writes the date and time into his notebook.

"Friday, November the first," he speaks as he writes, then stops and looks up at me. "November already? Where does the time go?" I offer nothing back, and he continues to annoyingly announce what he writes *as* he writes. "5:20 pm. Very well, Miss Hale. What is it you've come to report?"

Two possible voices compete to speak first, and I find myself allowing the lighter of the pair to proceed.

"Let me say at the outset that the people of Emmett - Charles and Sarah Snow, William, and the Owens family especially - have shown me nothing but kindness and hospitality since my arrival there seven weeks ago. It is not my intention to demean or discredit them with what I am about to say."

"Understood." He makes a few notes in his book and then takes another bite of his dinner. A dollop of bean sauce falls from his mouth onto the pages below. He procures a hanky from his trousers pocket, wipes his book, and then his mouth. "Excuse me. Go on, please."

"Last evening I was invited to attend dinner at the Snow household. A very special dinner for William, his Acceptance Dinner. Are you familiar with this custom?"

Sergeant Parks shakes his head as he eats.

"Yesterday was William's nineteenth birthday. Traditionally in their church it is the young men's time of acceptance of the faith, followed by his mission abroad. The dinner is a very formal affair -"

"Miss Hale, please," he says as he lifts his large hand, palm-forward, and holds it there in silence. "I have a long evening of paperwork ahead of me as it is. If you wouldn't mind getting to the heart of the matter, I would appreciate it very much."

"A letter was read at dinner. Are you aware, Sergeant, that William is not an only child?"

"Yes, he has a sister down south, I believe. What of it?"

"And three brothers."

"Miss Hale..."

"All of whom are deceased."

Sergeant Parks runs his tongue over his top and bottom teeth, savouring the taste of his dinner one last time before laying his spoon atop his plate and pushing it aside. He makes a couple more scratches in his book and then opens his hand in a gesture for me to continue, finally gracing me with his undivided attention. Emboldened by this, I allow my guard to weaken and choke out the next chapter of my delivery.

"I fear..." I choke on my words. "I fear that they were killed. All of them. They call it the Induction Ceremony. Every one of them sacrificed - with their parents' knowledge and consent - on the second anniversary of their births."

I feel my knuckles tense up and whiten again as I grip the edges of the table. When it starts to tremble, Sergeant Parks reaches over and unclasps my fingers.

"Miss Hale, I need you to take a deep breath and try to calm yourself, do you understand?"

"Yes, yes, yes."

I nod furiously and breathe through my tears, wiping my eyes with the handkerchief offered me, the same one that a moment ago was used to wipe the pages of the notebook and the corners of his mouth. The smell of beans and coffee leaves its trace around my eyes.

"How have you come to know these things?" Sergeant Parks asks.

"William."

"He told you this?"

"In a manner of speaking."

"Please, Miss Hale, either he told you or he didn't. It's a simple question?"

"He confessed to me that he has three brothers living with, and I quote, *their Father in Heaven.*"

"He told you that they were killed?"

"Well no. Not exactly."

"What were his exact words, Miss Hale?"

I do not have to think hard to call the scene to mind. I fear I'll never forget these words as long as I live.

"Heavenly Father chooses who is to stay with Him as the blessed children of God, and who among them are returned to their parents."

"So he never said they were killed? Or, what was the word you used? He consults his notes. '*Sacrificed*?'"

"No, not directly," I say, and then feel my voice rise in pitch. "Oh, what does it matter? I learned a cruel truth that I wish to God I'd never heard tell of. Never in a hundred years."

He writes in his book again, and then asks if anyone else has told me - directly or otherwise - the same information.

"Yes. Mrs. Snow. William's mother."

"Sarah Snow?"

"Correct."

"And she would corroborate this now if I asked her?"

"No, I highly doubt that."

I lift my fists to my eyes and press them in. The sergeant's voice remains steady and calm.

"And why not?" he asks.

"She..." I try to breathe, to catch my breath, but only press my fists harder into my eyes, trying to push the tears, the anguish, back from whence they come.

"Miss Hale?"

"She confessed it to me this morning. That she agreed to it, that she hated it. But by this evening..." I feel his hands on my arms, but snatch myself back, continuing to bury my fists into my eyes. "She went back on her words and said..."

"Yes?" he asks, impatient for me to continue. "She said what? Miss Hale, please, however difficult this is for you to recount, you must get hold of yourself and continue."

I force my arms down and blink my sore eyes into focus on the man across the table. His eyes are narrow, fixed on me, and I see the tiredness behind them.

"She said that she had been coerced into speaking falsely to me by the forces of darkness."

"Darkness, Miss Hale?"

"Satan."

"Satan," he repeats, and then squints in silent stillness at me for a moment. "So she denied whatever it was she told you earlier in the day."

"Yes, that's right."

"I see."

He points his pencil lead upon the notebook, pauses before writing anything, and then sets it down, abruptly closes the book, and gulps back the rest of his coffee. Dumping the dregs out on his plate of half-eaten beans, he crosses over to the kitchen stove to refill his mug.

"I understand, Miss Hale, that you and young William have been engaged in a courtship of sorts. Is that correct?"

"No, not at all," I protest.

"You didn't steal a kiss from him?" He flips back a page or two in his notebook. "On the 15th of October?"

I feel the air press out of my lungs. I take a deep, sharp inhalation to restore it.

"How do you know this?" I ask.

"Charles and William stopped here this morning for a visit," he explains. "Mr. Snow was good enough to bring me up to date on things in Emmett. I inquired as to your well-being, Miss Hale, as I do need to keep an eye on you, I'm afraid, due to the outstanding charges against you from Calgary. If you were to skip town..."

"*Skip town*, Sergeant Parks?" I ask, offended at the implication that I was somehow a prisoner of Emmett.

"Apologies for my frontier vocabulary, Miss Hale," he says. "I'm usually dealing with renegade Americans and outlawed Indians, not sophisticated ladies. Please believe me when I say that your personal affairs are of little concern to me, and how you choose to embark on a courtship is entirely your business. However..."

"There was no - *is* no - courtship," I say, but he ignores me completely as tobacco is pulled from a pouch and stuffed into a small pipe.

"... when personal details become pertinent to a crime or, in this case, a complaint, then I am beholden to delve into matters otherwise personal and private. And to that end, I understand that the nascent courtship between yourself and young Mr. Snow has recently - how shall I say this? - gone off the rails?"

"I beg your pardon?" I feel the impulse to stand up and leave, but he fires another question my way.

"How old are you, Miss Hale?"

"I fail to see what difference -"

"Seventeen? Eighteen?"

"I'm eighteen, but that's-"

"And your religious persuasion? Catholic? Protestant?"

"I was raised Catholic, but that has no bearing on -"

"Right."

He finishes packing his bowl full of pipe tobacco, and strikes a match against the flue. I watch him suck the flame into the bowl, pulling on the pipe to ignite the tobacco. Such a simple, common sight, but one which I've not seen for several months, just as I've not inhaled the aroma of pipe smoke or coffee for the same amount of time.

These otherwise piffling events serve to remind me of a world outside Emmett. Even the sergeant - as much as I loathe his demeaning stab at playing Sherlock Holmes - is an emissary from the world outside. The first and only one I've encountered. His crude manner is in sharp contrast to the formality of the Snows.

"To each his own, Miss Hale."

"What?" I nearly scream. "Haven't you heard a word of what I've been saying?"

"Charles Snow has been living here longer than you've been alive, ma'am. I've personally known him for ten years, and I can honestly say that he is a fine, upstanding, law-abiding citizen of this country, this province, and this area. Say what you will against their church, but I hold him and his kind in the highest regard."

"But Sergeant Parks -"

"When he and William stopped in this morning, I noticed the young man was hanging his head pretty low, so I asked Charles about it. He said his son was nursing a bout of heartache. That was all. He had every opportunity to disparage the source of the heartache - and from what I can see he wouldn't have been far off wrong in doing so - but Charles Snow is above such petty mudslinging."

I feel my heart begin to race. Steadying myself against the table, I make a great effort to stand up, but the force of the sergeant's judgement presses hard down on me.

"You said yourself, Miss Hale, that they've shown you nothing but kindness, and here you are espousing ridiculous claims against them. I see this as nothing more than religious prejudice mixed in with the vengeful actions of a jilted lover. And so, I repeat: to each his own."

I stand and take a number of steps towards the door, and then realize I have left my cloak on the chair. I walk back to retrieve it and Sergeant Parks meets me there to help me into my cloak. I snatch it out of his hands. He dismisses me with a laugh.

"Sorry if I've angered you, Miss Hale, but frankly your opinion of me is a matter of little importance. I will brook no slander of the Snows by you or anyone, especially a story so spurious and unfounded as this."

He holds the door open, and I see Millie rise from her spot across the river and wag her tail.

"I will, however, be sending a wire to the detachment in Calgary with regards to the outstanding claim by Mrs. Ness. If you do not report to the staff sergeant there within 48 hours, a warrant shall be issued for your arrest. Good evening, Miss Hale."

I am utterly humiliated and defeated as I climb back up to the carriage, my tears freezing to my cheeks and my nose running icy mucus onto my lips. Millie continues to walk behind, her tongue hanging along the way. She'll sleep soundly on the train ride tonight. I can only hope to do the same.

We arrive at the train station with ten minutes to spare, and Eileen unloads my trunk for me.

"I should have listened to you," I quietly say at the end of a silent ride.

"Sorry?" Eileen asks.

"You told me to forsake this place. I should have listened."

She is gracious enough to not deny my words this time.

As she carries my trunk to the platform, I whisper a choked goodbye.

She hugs me one last time. Soft and strong, but says nothing. I watch as she rides away back to Emmett.

I send a telegram to Jennifer Ness from the station, telling her that I will arrive later tonight and be around first thing in the morning to clear up the matter of unpaid boarding fees.

The jarring sound of the train door latching closed, amplified in my head, plays over and over as I sit awaiting departure. I don't know how many times I look out the window in the hopes of seeing William there. Millie is curled obediently at my feet, sound asleep.

31

I⒯ ɪs ᴠᴇʀʏ ʟᴀᴛᴇ ᴡʜᴇɴ ᴡᴇ ᴀʀʀɪᴠᴇ ɪɴ Cᴀʟɢᴀʀʏ. Tʜᴇ ᴄɪᴛʏ ɪs collectively asleep. To my absolute shock, there is a horse and carriage awaiting me at the station, compliments of Mrs. Jennifer Ness, with instructions to deliver me to her residence upon arrival.

In light of recent discoveries, I realize that no one is the sum total of our impressions of them. Positive or otherwise. Considering the late hour and paucity of accommodation options, I quickly decide to take my chances with her invitation. Besides, better the devil you know than the one disguised behind a costume of kindness. I am eager to clear up the matter of payment as soon as possible, and I'd rather do this with her directly than subject myself further to the services of the North West Mounted Police.

The warm chinook air that was merely visiting Emmett earlier seems to have moved in here tonight, and the ride is pleasant. Millie and I turn the corner and the house comes into view. A light glimmers from the main floor drawing room window and my shoulders ease down with the promise of a warm bed.

Mrs. Ness appears at the door after only a couple of knocks, wearing the same green silk dressing gown as worn on the night I left.

"Well, I'll be," she smiles. "Come in, Miss Hale."

"You remember Millie?"

"Yes, of course. Do come in, both of you."

The soft light in the foyer gives us both a chance to see each other properly, and I fill the silence with awkward words about my surprise to be met at the station by a driver.

"I wouldn't hear of it otherwise," she comments. "You look hungry. Let me get you something to eat."

"Don't go to any trouble, please."

"No trouble at all, my dear."

There is a softness to her that I did not notice before. Not simply kindness, that was always there, but a nurturing tone to her voice, her eyes.

I hear the sounds of plates and cutlery being assembled in the kitchen. She calls from within.

"I've some cold chicken left over from dinner, and plenty of scraps for Millie. Have a seat in the front room and make yourself at home."

All is as I remember it, and I sink gratefully into the velvet chez lounge and close my tired, puffy eyes. I hear Millie's name called and a bowl set upon the floor, followed by the lapping din of a thirsty dog drinking her fill.

"You must tell me where you've been," she calls from the kitchen, still with that tone, "and what you've been up to all this time."

I open my eyes to see her brandishing a wooden tray with a quarter chicken, boiled potatoes, a dinner roll, and a glass of milk, warmed on the stove and served in crystal. She sits across from me, close enough to be of comfort, but not so close as to be invasive

"First things first, Mrs. Ness," I say.

"Call me Jennie, please."

"I owe you for the room and board from September." I

fumble into my bag for my money purse, and she waves my words away with a single sweep of her hand, fingernails beautifully manicured.

"We can discuss all that in the morning. Just eat and fill me in on your adventures. I've been so curious."

I ask her about the complaint filed with the police.

"Oh heavens. That was months ago. They've only found you now?"

"The first I'd heard of it was three or four weeks ago, but was afforded some grace to officially report in. I spoke again to the same sergeant earlier today, and was told that I had forty-eight hours to clear the matter up or I would be facing arrest."

"Damn them and their cowboy bravado," she says, shaking her head in disgust. "I'll pay a visit to Staff Sergeant Bagley first thing in the morning and settle the matter once and for all. How terrible for you to have endured such unpleasantness on my account."

Jennie pours herself a cup of tea.

"When I rose that September morning and found that you had gone," she explains, "I felt sick inside. I acted terribly. My behaviour was unacceptable. In the light of a new day - and sober temperament - I went in search of you to offer my apologies. You were nowhere to be found in the city, and believe me I am well enough connected to have searched high and low for you. I remember you had mentioned something about Banff, so I set about tracking you down there. Staff Sergeant Bagley is an old friend of my late husband's, so I went straight to him. When he asked the nature of my request, I had to think quickly. I said you had skipped out on paying my boarding fee and I demanded that you be notified of the charge at once. He was terribly reluctant to involve the force on such a trifling matter, but I insisted, saying a crime was a crime."

The potatoes are buttery and cold, but are easily washed down with the warm milk.

"Things move slowly in that inefficient organization, and it was the better part of a fortnight before I received a message that you were not found in Banff. Bagley asked where else you could be, and I considered dropping the entire affair then and there. Obviously you had no interest in returning to Calgary and resuming our acquaintance - and who could blame you? - but I had my reputation to consider. I had raised such a stink initially that I could not very well turn my back on it, and told Bagley to search south: Macleod, Lethbridge, and surrounds."

Jennie sits back in her chair and lifts the teacup to her lips. She holds her gaze on me as she sips.

"Miss Hale, let us not mince our words. I made a play for you that night and was rejected. Although I regret the manner in which the play was made, I do not regret making it. I was hurt, perhaps angry, yes, and so acted accordingly. A cooler head prevailed on me over time, and though I wanted very much to see you again, I took pains to ensure the message was delivered with the least amount of risk to either of us."

"Risk?" I ask.

"A woman in my position, with my... preferences... must exercise caution, as I'm sure you can appreciate. All I wanted was for you to return, and here you are. I am sorry if the communication of my desire to see you once again was unpleasant for you, as this was not my intent. I only wanted a chance to explain myself, apologize, and purge the air for both of us."

This is a welcome relief. I was unaware how much the burden of this was weighing on me until it was lifted.

"Thank you," I say. "I am sorry as well for-"

"You have nothing to be sorry for, my dear child. Nothing at all."

There is a sadness in her eyes. She is trying to hide it, but I sense it all the same. Surely she can't be that upset by a misunderstanding from seven weeks ago? Had I not just come away from a dreadful matriarchal experience, I would almost say Mrs. Ness was acting *motherly* towards me.

I finish my dinner and drink the last of the milk. Its warmth makes a fast track to my head and I feel my eyelids heavy as barn doors, hanging half closed. I'm about to drop the glass, when I feel Jennie take it from my hands. My eyes snap open.

"I can ill afford to break a glass of fine crystal every time you visit me," she says with a smile. "By the way, how is your foot? All healed, I trust?"

I toy with telling her how close I came to dying on account of my foot injury, but balk at the saga that would inevitably unfold with such a disclosure. I haven't the stomach nor the energy to tell all tonight, so instead I say my foot turned out fine.

"Thank god for that," Jennie says. "I knew I did a poor job on your injury that night, and was well aware that it was not as clean as it should have been. Truth be told, I was far too eager to resume other activities and leave the nurse duties until the morning. I'm glad there was no harm done."

I smile knowingly to myself, sighing a deep breath of relief as she opens the door to the lower floor bedroom.

"Your room is made up," she says, "so I'll fetch some fresh towels and bid you good night. Tomorrow all will be set right, and you can tell me as much or as little about your time down south as you like. Judging by the lines on your face, I expect it was nothing less than an ordeal of epic proportion."

She reaches over and brushes my hand with the most delicate touch of her own. There is no trace of desire or lust this time. I look into her eyes, filled with what I can only discern as worry for me.

"Is everything all right, Jennie?" I ask. "You seem so terribly sad."

She smiles warmly, tells me not to worry, and assures me that we will discuss all tomorrow.

Millie stretches out on a rug in the foyer and I retire to my room, so exhausted that I am only able to mumble a simple thank-you. The large, down pillow accepts my head with ease, and within minutes I sink into a deep, deep sleep.

· · ·

I AWAKE at noon and find a note on the bureau outside my room:

> *Tara,*
>
> *I've gone to meet with Staff Sergeant Bagley and run some errands. Help yourself to anything you find to eat (I've put out some food for Millie already)*
>
> *See you this afternoon.*
> *Jennie*

There are some fresh smelling tea leaves in a golden tin, and I can hardly contain my excitement as I set about making myself a long overdue pot. I boil extra water for porridge, and load my bowl with nuts and dried fruit, topping it off with some syrup and a dollop of cream.

Millie has long since emptied whatever bowl of scraps were left for her, and she only sniffs at my offer of porridge. Either she's full or fussy. I assume the former.

The spring-like warmth of the night before has blown over, and the nascent face of winter bares his teeth today. I bundle up and take Millie for a walk, exploring the grounds where the Stampede was held. It is a barren stubble of snow and brown grass, the rivers meeting in a confluence of broken ice.

We return to find Jennie home and at work on dinner preparations. She is making a rabbit pie with cabbage, carrots, beef barley soup, and small pastries for dessert.

"Welcome back to the land of the living," she says. "I peeked in on you at half-ten this morning, and you were still out to the world, so I let you be."

"I was more exhausted than I realized," I confess. "Thanks for allowing me the chance to catch up on sleep."

"I spoke with Bagley and all is settled. A wire had arrived today from the St. Mary's detachment near Emmett, regarding the situation. Staff Sergeant Bagley had little good to say about the sender of it."

"Sergeant Parks," I tell her.

"In any event, the matter is now closed. Bagley was happy to toss the entire file into the stove, so don't give it another thought."

"Thank-you," I say as I reach again for my money purse, but she offers another proposal.

"We have much to discuss, Tara, and I hope you will stay here as long as you wish. My home is your home, for however many days and nights you need it. I gather you've spent time in Emmett, some or all of the weeks since your last night here. As I said, they're a strange bunch there. Good customers, yes, but terribly aggressive when it comes to converting outsiders to the fold. I can't imagine what you've been through, but it will take some time to recover."

I swallow hard, and bite the inside of my cheek, but there's no hiding how close to the bone of truth Jennifer's words are scratching.

"My poor little bird," she whispers, soft and matronly "everything is all right now. I'll look after you."

I feel safe here, and whisper my thanks.

"When you're ready, we can talk about everything. I've some things to share with you as well. But no rush. Eat. Rest. Drink oceans of wine. When time serves, and you feel up to it, I'll happily accept a piece of art from you in exchange for your stay. *Stays*. Both then and now. Whatever subject you choose. In whatever medium you choose. That is all."

I search myself for any indication of manipulation or dishonesty in her words, and find none. There is no threat, no hidden agenda. On the contrary, the offer to create a piece of art of my own choosing lifts me a little bit out of myself.

"I'd be honored."

THE NEXT MORNING, Sunday morning, I sit with a pot of tea, allowing my mind to wander back. I'm at the church service in Emmett seven weeks ago to the hour, recalling the sermon

Charles Snow delivered that morning. How he had asked everyone to close their eyes and imagine their loved ones no longer with them. I remember noticing the lack of young men. How did I not put it together?

"Are you ready to tell me what happened down south?" Jennifer asks, snapping me out of my disturbed reverie. "And explain what's changed you?"

"Changed me?" I nervously ask, unaware that I'm reaching down to Millie for support.

"Travel changes us," she explains, "otherwise why bother? If you're not changed, you're simply a mobile consumer, touring through different scenery, eating it up like fire as you go. I can see that something's happened to you, some profound change has taken place."

"I'm afraid I've undergone a metamorphosis worthy of Ovid," I laugh, feeling completely caught out. "How much time do you have?"

I vomit my story out to her, beginning with the moment I walked, or rather tried to walk, out of here, wounded and limping, in the early hours that September morning. I tell her everything: the train ride, seeing William at the end of the line, the cellulitis infection. How Sarah Snow saved me.

I tell her of my convalescence, reading their book of scripture, attending church. Eileen's kindness, William's charm, his father's control and penetrating eyes. The cat, the mouse, the loss of a cow's tail, a kiss. The discovery of the Induction Ceremony, and the unbearable weight of learning something I wish I hadn't. How Sarah Snow betrayed me.

"And tell me, what are your feelings around this William boy? You kissed him, and invited him to come with you. Do you love him?"

I open my mouth to respond, but find I cannot dig up the words. I don't love him, that's certain, but maybe I love him.

"I ask only because if he or his family *thinks* that you do, then your story with them is far from over. They will come for you. He will for sure."

She pours more tea.

"And what of your art? Did you create anything at all while there?"

I tell her of the portrait, and how good it was, how proud I was with the eyes.

"Then you have not lost who you are," she concludes. "Some things change, that is life, but who we are never alters. Even Ovid's Proserpine, regardless of whether she's in the land of the living or land of the dead. She's still Persephone. A daughter. A queen."

Comfort comes with her words.

"You're still Tara Hale, the artist," Jennifer affirms. "They didn't take that away from you. They never will."

The conviction of her words sinks deeply into me, settling my nerves and reminding me of why I am even here in the first place.

"Thank you, Jennifer," I say. "I needed to hear that more than I knew."

"There is something I need to broach with you," she announces, quietly, with that unmistakable loving, parental tone I suspected earlier. "It will be a difficult conversation, so I want to give you some advance warning."

"I see…" I stretch the words out, wondering what she could be referring to. "What, may I ask, is the nature of the conversation?"

"When I reported you to Bagley, I told him you were from Halifax. I did not suspect that you went all the way back home. However, he did make some enquiries with the detachment out there."

My heart, so suddenly filled with strength and confidence, is just as suddenly punctured. I can feel the blood drain from my face. She obviously sees my reaction, and lifts the tea pot.

"I'm going to refill this, and when I come back, we can talk about what Bagley discovered."

I start to breathe quickly as panic rises within.

"Or we can talk about something else," she offers with a gentle smile. "Or talk about nothing at all. There's no rush, my dear. No rush whatsoever."

As she is walking into the kitchen to refill the teapot with water, I notice Millie's tail begin to wag as her ears perk up and she looks towards the door. I'm turning my head in the same direction when I hear the knocker tap three times. Listening as Jennifer opens the door, my stomach tightens involuntarily before I hear the all too familiar voice.

"Begging your pardon, ma'am, but is there a Miss Tara Hale currently residing here?"

Millie runs to the door before I'm up from the table, and as I turn the corner to the front vestibule, I see the young man come to standing after crouching down to greet my dog. A lock of golden straw hair falls down from his head as he removes his hat. My knees lose all their tension as I gasp in astonishment.

"Good morning, Miss Hale."

32

THE THREE OF US STAND AWKWARDLY IN THE FRONT HALL OF THE house, and I catch Jennifer's eyes as William turns to admire the furnishings of her home. She silently mouths "he *is* beautiful" and smiles broadly, as he proceeds to indulge her with endless questions about her house - much to Jennifer's delight - and I silently become spectator.

Mrs. Ness knows that the discussion is born more out of eagerness to make a good first impression than genuine curiosity, and she is gracious with her answers.

"I thought you would have set sail for England by now," I say, broaching for the first time the reason behind his presence here, and then turn to Jennifer. "His mission for the church."

"Ah yes," she replies, curious as well to know the plot.

"I'm supposed to start my training tomorrow in Cherry Creek," William explains. "Then board a train to New York after four weeks, and cross the Atlantic by mid-December. However, I've bucked all convention and have chosen to begin my mission here in Calgary."

"How does this decision sit with your father?" I ask. "I can't imagine he accepted it easily."

"He's somewhere between livid and resigned," William

answers. "Mother, on the other hand, was all for it. Both, despite their opposing positions, send their love."

"Cherry Creek?" Jennifer asks. "That's a lengthy train ride, I imagine."

"About nine hundred miles, due south," William answers. "We wired a request to our church president, asking for his dispensation on the matter, and so I'm here with the blessing of the church. I'll have a bit of catching up to do down there, but I believe it's worth it."

"Quite the missionary gamble over one soul," Jennifer observes, nodding in my direction.

"I'm motivated by quality, ma'am, not quantity."

William looks at me and immediately blushes. I too feel a surge of blood to my cheeks, and steal a glance at Jennifer, asking her to stay close with my look.

"Please, come in and have a seat, Mr. Snow," Jennifer offers, picking up my request effortlessly. "You'll surely join us for dinner this evening?"

"Thank-you, ma'am, but I'm afraid I must be back on the train this afternoon. My father is waiting for me at the station. We'll head straight through to Cherry Creek."

"How did you know I would still be here in Calgary?" I ask him as we all take a seat. "Had I continued straight on to Vancouver, you would have missed me altogether, and your travels would have been for naught."

"This is true," William says, "but I knew I'd find you. The Holy Ghost was on my side in this."

"A worthy ally to be sure," Jennifer says.

"Yes, ma'am," William nods, and then turns back to me. "Father took a big risk with asking President Wooley about this. The church takes the missionary rules very seriously. It could have caused a great deal of strife for all of us."

"Of all the church's transgressions," I reply, "I would think a violation of missionary rules would rank pitifully low."

He ignores my jab, as I suspected he would.

"The point of my mission is to bring souls to the church. Yours is the only one I care about saving, and I want it for myself."

"My soul is fine exactly how it is," I quickly shoot back. "It is not in danger, and thus need not be saved."

"I could not live with myself," he tells me, "if I felt that I hadn't done everything I could to win you back, and to show you the glorious truth of the gospel. I was at fault the other night, not the church. You must give it another chance, Tara, or else you'll spend eternity outside the garden. I could never forgive myself knowing that. I can accept your dismissal of me, hard as that is, but I can't accept your dismissal of the gospel on account of my stupidity."

Jennifer quietly listens. I look over to her and can see the smile of one resisting the urge to say *I told you so.*

"I'm going to leave for Vancouver soon," I say, "and finish what I started so long ago. I can't go back to Emmett, William. Not now. Not ever."

"I'm not asking you to come back to Emmett," he croaks. "Nor do I want to keep you from Vancouver and your life out there. I want you to go there."

"What then? What are you offering that I could possibly want?" I would have thought being blunt would feel triumphant, but I only feel like a common bully.

"Little Jacob will have his Induction Ceremony on the sixth," he says. "Three days from now. I'm asking you to come to Cherry Creek and be a part of it."

A loud gasp explodes from my mouth.

"You must be kidding!" I cry. "I reported that barbaric practice to the authorities."

"Yes, Father had a visit from Sergeant Parks, and Mother told me of your talk with her. You've jumped to a horrendous conclusion, Tara, that couldn't be more wrong. And it is my fault."

He hands me an envelope of bills, crumpled with folds from being stuffed into the front pocket of his trousers.

"Mother insisted that we pay for your train fair, and she'll skin me alive if I come back with the money."

"William, I can't accept this," I say, pushing the bills back to him. "Besides, that's not the point."

"Hear me out, Tara, and then I'll be gone. You can decide then what you want to do. Everything in the world was right before I told you of the Induction Ceremony. Now everything is wrong. We are not what you think we are. Please. Come to Cherry Creek, and see for yourself. I swear on the lives of my father, my mother, my sister, on the souls of my brothers. Should you decide to sever ties with me, with my family, and with the church, I'll not bother you again. I believe you care for me a little bit, somewhere inside of you. Give me this chance to correct the wrong I've done you, my family, and my church. Heavenly Father wants you back so much, almost as much as I do. Perhaps just as much. It can't be more, so great is my love for you. I've done nothing but pray and fast over this since you left Emmett. Please, Tara. Give me one more chance."

He holds the envelope out to me once more.

"There is enough for train fare from Calgary to Cherry Creek, and from Cherry Creek to Seattle and up to Vancouver. Mother says that if you decide not to come, you're to use the money for your studies. Either way, you must accept it."

I keep my hands at my sides.

"You were never paid properly for the portrait, or the lessons for the young women," he adds. "Take it for those reasons if you like."

William places the money in my hand and presses the other around it. He holds his hands on mine in a moment of silent farewell. He then rises from the table, utters a small goodbye to Jennifer, and sees himself out the door.

Millie runs after him, and I must call her back.

William does not turn around.

. . .

I'M STILL STANDING at the door when Jennifer comes up behind me.

"You're considering his offer," she speaks. "Aren't you?"

I turn to her for some direction. If she is to be my mother temporarily, then I'm curious to know what she would advise.

"Is that wrong?"

"There is no right and wrong when it comes to these things," she says. "That type of thinking is what forms religions like theirs in the first place. I've never bought into it, and I'm not about to start now."

She's right. God and the Devil, Heavenly Fathers and Earthly Children. Light and Shadow. Right and Wrong. I too am far more interested in the world between these opposites.

"What would you do?" I ask her. "If you were in my shoes right now?"

"Run like hell," she quickly responds.

"Towards something or away from something?" I ask, echoing her question from our night at the King George. A smile slithers from the nest, and rests on her face.

"I'm not a curious artist, in pursuit of truth. But you are, Tara. If going to Cherry Creek will bring you peace of mind and some closure, then you should go. If you go with eyes open and a trusty second by your side, you can withstand whatever they will throw you. But you'll find, my dear, that it becomes increasingly difficult to serve more than one God at a time."

I laugh when she says this.

"You don't believe in God," I say, lowering my voice.

"True. But I do believe in *gods*," she explains, "and we can only serve one at a time. There is the God of Beauty whom you followed out west seven months ago, or rather the Goddess. She of beauty, of art, of discovery. You began your worship of Her when first you touched pencil to paper. Now there are other deities competing for your allegiance: the God of this church you have no time for; the God that is this young man who is in love with you; the God of Truth, driving you with an endless rage to know. They aren't overly jealous divinities, and will allow you to visit the temples of their competitors whenever you like. But they will demand your allegiance, finally, in the end, and shower you with gifts in exchange for it."

I wait for her to continue, trying not to betray the confusion I feel at her words.

"And there's the God that is your father," she concludes. "Which, I think, is the one you have been following more than all of the others. It is that one you must release, Tara. You will never come into who you truly are until you let him go."

The heave in my chest catches me off guard. I wrap my arms around my heart, trying to squeeze everything back in.

"If you shun the battle you have been called to, you run the risk of wearing the albatross named *What If?* around your neck for the rest of your days."

"You think a trip to Cherry Creek is akin to going into battle?"

"It's the final leg of an adventure that you've been called to," she says with a smile. "And you must decide how to respond to that call. To go or not to go to battle is not, alas, the question."

"What, then, is?"

"Which God's crest you'll wear on your shield when you ride into it."

33

OUR TRAIN PULLS INTO CHERRY CREEK ON TUESDAY AFTERNOON. Mrs. Ness immediately goes off to arrange a hotel room, while Millie and I explore. The late afternoon sun casts its intoxicating wintry light over the town centre, and one can barely detect the farming hinterland that surrounds the wide streets and well-defined blocks that make up the large town. Two sawmills, a flour mill, three large hotels, a tool factory, a foundry, a chinaware factory - all well maintained - thrive in the townsite and its outskirts, while the white limestone temple stands impressive and imposing on the bluff, visible from every corner.

I realize in the sudden whirlwind of arrival that William never told me his sister's last name or address. Perhaps I expected the town to be much smaller and easily navigated. To be honest, I expected an exact copy of Emmett, which is clearly not the case. I consider asking around, but find the idea of confronting complete strangers with incomplete questions far too onerous.

I sit with warm chocolate in the town centre, feeding on some nuts and dried fruit (being sure to share with Millie), and try to find an easy road out of my dilemma. Memories of experiences and conversations begin to take shape, and in the half-formed images coming to mind, I see a tall, balding man laughing with Charles Snow by the creek.

I stop the next person to pass and ask if he knows where Brother Oliver Harris resides. The stranger's easy kindness flickers for a moment, as if my question were a miniature lightning bolt that struck him unawares. He quickly recovers and points out a grand mansion at the end of the next street, watching Millie and I with mild suspicion as we head towards it.

The door is answered by a young girl, about thirteen or so, who eyes me rudely for a number of seconds before speaking.

"Yes?" she finally asks, as if she's asked it three times already and I've not bothered to answer yet.

"Hello," I say. "I'm wondering if Mr. Harris is at home?"

"Who are you?"

"Tara Hale," I tell her, "from Canada."

"Where?" she asks, obviously having no clue about the nation that sits atop her own.

"Canada," I repeat with waning patience. "It's a country not far from here. I met your father there about ten days ago, in a little town called Emmett."

"I should have known," she says with a roll of her eyes, "Emmett. You're from the Church," and abruptly closes the door.

I stand on the porch, the large white columns running along the length of it, unable to move due to the shock of what just happened. Millie, who has been exploring the snow-covered rose bushes at the front of the house, comes to my side, sensing the peculiarity of the moment.

Concluding that I've been given directions to the wrong house, I knock once more to ask if this rude child could set me straight. The door swings open quickly, revealing Brother Harris himself, the young girl at his side. He wears an apron that is far too small for his tall frame, and he is wiping his hands on a towel.

"Mr. Harris?" I ask.

"Yes?" He squints at me, trying to place the familiar face before him, as he wraps a protective arm around his daughter.

"I'm Tara Hale. We met at Mr. Ibey's baptism. In Emmett."

"Yes, of course, I remember," he says without showing any sign of it being a pleasant memory or not. "What can I do for you, Miss Hale?"

"I've arrived in town rather unprepared," I say, feeling terribly uncomfortable on his porch, "and have lost the address for William's sister, Clara Snow."

"Clara Glenn," he corrects me. "Yes, she's a few blocks away back towards the centre of town. Amanda will show you the way."

His daughter steps forward, the same expression of disrespect on her face as when she greeted me here a few moments ago. She lights up when she sees Millie.

"Please walk Miss Hale and her companion to the Glenn house and then straight back home for dinner."

"Yes, Father."

"Good day, Miss Hale," he says, and closes the door before I can even get a *thank-you* out.

We walk the first two blocks in silence. I spot Jennifer outside the hotel, and wave her over to us.

"I see you've made a friend already," she teases, as Amanda makes no effort to cloak her abhorrence of me. "Where are we off to?"

"Battle preparations," I tell her, with no effect whatsoever on the child's silence. She laughs easily with Millie, however, throwing a broken elm branch repeatedly for her.

"Thank-you for the escort, Amanda," I say, when we arrive at our designated spot.

"Ma'am," she responds, and takes her leave.

I have to call Millie back three or four times to prevent her from following the girl home.

"I thought I recognized that voice," someone calls from the front door. "Praise be!"

Sarah Snow, holding her skirts in both hands, comes across the yard towards me. She slows her pace when she sees Jennifer at my side, but still extends her hands, taking mine in hers, as if nothing unpleasant had ever passed between us at all.

"Miss Hale," she says, "how wonderful it is to see you."

"This is a dear friend from Calgary," I proudly announce. "Mrs. Jennifer Ness, may I introduce you to William's mother, Sarah Snow."

"A pleasure, Mrs. Snow." Jennifer extends her hand, the perfect picture of diplomacy.

"Mine as well," Mrs. Snow replies.

She opens us up towards the house where a woman is emerging with a toddler in her arms.

"Ah! There they are. This is William's sister, Clara," she announces with a flourish, "and my adorable little grandson, Jacob."

"I've heard so much about you, Miss Hale," Clara says. "Welcome to Cherry Creek, and to my home."

I observe both Clara and her mother interact with Jennifer, all the ladies cooing and smiling in the presence of the child. Not a single crack in the armour can be detected in the mother or grandmother, despite both being fully aware of the ceremony tomorrow. I am equally disgusted and in awe of such powers.

"This must be little Jacob," I offer, attempting to equal them in my ability to mask emotions.

The child's hair is blonde and wispy, curling atop his head as if trying to find its way in the world. His eyes widen when I smile at him, and he smiles back before turning away and clutching his mother's neck.

"Yes," Clara playfully groans, "but little Jacob is not so little anymore."

"He's not too heavy for Grandma," Mrs. Snow declares, as she reaches for him.

He holds on to his mother with a smiling loyalty, clutching

her thin, dark hair in his chubby hand, pulling strands out of a carefully set bun atop her head.

"Come here, you little rascal," his grandmother urges as she pries his fingers free. "Can you show Miss Hale peek-a-boo?"

The boy covers his eyes with his tiny hands, then opens them as both mother and grandmother say 'peek' in high-pitched voices. The entire routine is repeated twice then thrice with much merriment and hugs.

"He's beautiful," Jennifer says to Clara as we walk towards the house.

"Yes," she replies. "Heavenly Father has blessed Daniel and I with a healthy, happy angel. Everyone just loves him to pieces."

"I can see why," Jennifer says with a nod. She reaches over and clasps my hand as I try to breathe through this. It is much more difficult than I ever could have imagined.

"Some say he looks like William," Clara tells me. "Mother seems to think he's the spitting image of his uncle at the age of Induction."

I stop walking. Millie nudges her head between the two of us. For the first time in our lives together, she's not the focal point of attention and knows it. Even Mrs. Snow fails to greet her, occupied as she is with her grandson.

Clara suggests we confine her to the back yard, and walks me around the side of the modest little house. She lays out an old blanket, and sets down a bowl of water. Millie's subdued whimpering falls on deaf ears as we all head inside.

Charles and Daniel are in the front room, leaning over some rough sketches outlining plans for an addition to the house. Mr. Snow smiles broadly as he extends his hand to me in greeting. Again, as if the showdown we shared four nights ago was a figment of my imagination only.

He asks about my time in Calgary. I answer, simply, that it was 'full'.

"William is still at the missionary training centre," he tells me. "I'm afraid you won't see much of him until tomorrow's ceremony, and even then he'll have scant time for visiting."

"I expected as much. He told me his detour to Calgary would cost him some overtime here."

"He'll catch up," Daniel says. "It's not like he has to learn a foreign language or anything, although I don't envy him trying to understand the English and their nonsensical way of speaking. He's pretty quick at scripture studies and will pick up the proselytizing technique in no time."

The fabricated normality of this scene strikes me as entirely absurd. I continually steal glances to Jennifer, who is as skilled at maintaining appearances as they are. Perhaps more so. I am the amateur here, and find the effort exhausting.

"Was that the Harris girl walking towards the house with you?" Clara asks.

"Yes," I say. "I had to pay a visit to Mr. Harris as I didn't know where you lived or even your last name. His was the only recognizable name I remotely knew in town. Amanda was kind enough to show me where you lived."

Silence reigns over the room for a moment, broken by Daniel.

"My nieces keep asking their mom why they can't play with the Harris girls," he says.

"Ach!" Mrs. Snow remarks. "Those poor children."

"Did you visit with Brother Harris at all?" Mr. Snow asks me.

"Hardly," I say. "It was a strange reception, to say the least. I could see he recognized me from Emmett, but I found both him and his daughter to be disarmingly unemotional, almost rude. Not what I was expecting at all, and certainly not the same person I met ten days ago."

"He happened to be up in Canada on the day of Mr. Ibey's baptism," Mrs. Snow adds, "a few days before he..."

"Ah," Clara nods, "I see."

Mr. Snow reads the confusion on my face and turns to his daughter.

"Forgive me, Clara, but perhaps we should fill our guest in on the course of events regarding Brother Harris."

"Yes, of course," Clara replies.

Jennifer and I look to each other, both of us curious to know what is afoot.

"Brother Harris has renounced his faith," Mr. Snow explains, "and resigned his position in the Church."

"What?" I respond with genuine shock.

"Not only that," Clara adds, "but he seems bent on tainting everyone he meets with his crazy notions."

"He spreads the most ridiculous rumours about church policy and history," her husband adds.

"It's as if he's gone mad," Clara declares. "And frankly, I think he has. Such a horrible shame, too, as he and Sister Harris were such a vital part of our community here in Cherry Creek."

"How is she taking all this?" Mrs. Snow asks.

"She's moved back to her parents' home, but the girls still spend time at the house. I can't imagine how she could bear to allow her children to be around such a man, but there it is."

"What could have happened?" Jennifer asks the question that I, in my stunned silence, have not voiced.

"He seemed quite happy," I add, "and sure of himself when I met him."

"No doubt he was then," Mr. Snow tells me, "but at some point betwixt then and now, he became blackened by Satan and seems determined to be blacklisted by our Father in Heaven. I've tried talking to him, as has almost everyone else, but to no avail. He is diseased with anger and hatred, eager to infect anyone he can with his curdled views and outrageous ideas."

"It's simply awful," his wife interjects. "He's in our prayers, of course, and we all wish him nothing but peace."

Everyone in the room agrees, as the focus shifts to Jacob who squeals and coos for attention.

I wait for an opportunity to learn more about Oliver Harris, but such an opportunity never arises. Jennifer and I are offered seats at the table for dinner, and it takes a great deal of repeated refusal before we are able to leave.

"Well isn't that an interesting development," she offers as we walk with Millie back to the hotel. "I suggest we seek out the company of *Brother* Harris at some point tomorrow. Get him to shed some light on this."

34

WE ENJOY A LATE SLEEP-IN ON WEDNESDAY MORNING, AND AFTER much searching in this abstaining town, find a small diner that offers coffee and tea with our breakfast.

I can hardly eat, and afraid anything I do manage to put down will not last there. The Induction Ceremony is scheduled for noon, and I suggest that Jennie and I stop by at Oliver Harris's on our way to the temple grounds.

There is no answer when we knock upon the door.

Clara offered their back yard for Millie for the day, and so we drop her there. The entire family, save Daniel, left over an hour ago, and he alone is there to help Millie into the yard. He is dressed entirely in white, like an angel late for a business meeting.

"The immediate family gathers in the Celestial room of the temple," he explains when we ask what the procedure for the day is, "while Jacob is alone with Heavenly Father and the Prophet. Hence the whites."

Again, he is calm and at ease with his explanation.

"But you're both invited to join us beforehand in the church and hear a talk from President Wooley. He's a marvellous speaker, and any chance to hear him is a grand occasion."

·   ·   ·

J<small>ENNIFER</small> and I sit well towards the back of the chapel. We can see William, sitting up front with what I assume are the other young men preparing for their missions. He is beaming with joy, and when his eyes catch mine, it seems he will boil over with happiness. I offer a smile in greeting back, and then turn away.

Jennifer appears equally at home here as she does in the Grill Room at the King George as she does posing nude upon her bed. A chameleon of a woman.

The Prophet's address is preceded by a couple of short talks from various members, including a testimony from Clara and Daniel. Both stand before us all, holding their angelic child at the front of the church, extolling the truth of the gospel, the love of Heavenly Father, and their gratitude at having so many brothers and sisters gathered to celebrate the Induction of their son.

Jennifer's hand is on my lap, in response to the trembling in my legs that will soon spread to my entire body.

Charles Snow offers a short testimony, as does Daniel's father. Brother Glenn is a quiet, shy man, not at ease with public speaking.

Flowers adorn the chapel, and an unmistakable air of euphoria permeates the celebration. I cannot take my eyes off little Jacob, who is joyfully oblivious to the attention being showered on him.

Leonard C. Wooley - Prophet and Revelator - takes the podium. He too is dressed entirely in white, and the silver halo of hair that circles his head lends him an air of seraphic authenticity. He is considerably older than everyone else in Cherry Creek, clean shaven, bespectacled, and short in stature. He looks for all the world like a clerk, retired from some respectable firm. If you found him sitting behind the telegraph window at the train station, you would not give him a second look. Until he speaks.

"My dear brothers and sisters," he begins, "how wonderful it is to look out and behold all of you gathered here on this beautiful winter day. How grateful we are to have the supreme beings of an eternal Father, his son Jesus Christ, and the Holy Ghost ruling over us, watching over us, loving us, caring for us, as we rule and watch over, love, and care for own children. We are the children of God, and how fortunate for us all to gather together as a family."

He pauses for a moment to acknowledge the family gathered at the front with him - Clara and Daniel in particular - and then turns back to us.

"The Lord is with me now," he says, "even as I speak to you."

He pauses again, and I judge from the reactions of the people around him that this is not standard practice. Something is different today.

"We are here today," he resumes, "to celebrate the Induction of Jacob Joseph Glenn into the bosom of his Heavenly Father. Like the Acceptance Dinner afforded to the young men among us, it is a rite of passage unique to our faith, revealed to me by our Father in Heaven so many years ago. Many of you here today have undergone your own Induction Ceremony, have had your tongues unlocked by the Holy Ghost at the age of two, and have spoken wondrous things, more wondrous even than words spoken by our saviour Jesus Christ. I have heard these things. I have seen it happen with my own eyes. I will see it again today with little Jacob. There is not a single aspect of my calling as your President that I cherish more than to bear witness to the miracle of the Induction Ceremony. I am indeed... most blessed... amongst men."

He says the last with what appears to be failing breath, waving away the two or three men - including Charles Snow - who step to the podium in his aid. I watch as he takes on an incandescent glow. His voice deepens, and he appears to grow in stature right before my eyes.

Jennifer and I exchange looks. She wears a skeptical expression upon her face, which puts me at ease. However, everyone else in the chapel appears to be holding their breath.

"*Behold my servant, Leonard Wooley,*" he says, though in a voice different from his own, "*who stands before you now in the latter days of his office. He that shall succeed is one with whom I have spoken upon his second birthday, and will speak with again. He has also served his heavenly Father well, and will be called by me as Prophet in due time. Verily I say unto you, my children, that soon the presidency of my Church will bear the verdant signs of new life, and all the keys will be held by those with whom I have spoken, those whom I have inducted into my church. When such a time has come to pass, then will all the principles and ordinances be restored, and you, my children, will live once more as fully as I have intended for you to live. Fear not, my children, for it is your father who tells of these things. Amen.*"

The speaker falters, slightly, but holds firm to the podium. Others gather round him and attempt to lead him back to his seat. Again he refuses their aid, and summons a secretary who brings the book into which the proclamation has been recorded. Wooley quickly reads over it all, and dismisses the small group that has clustered around him. He clears his throat and addresses the congregation once more.

"Thus sayeth the Lord," he quickly murmurs, his original voice and stature restored to him now. "We live in remarkable times, my brothers and sisters, when the almighty Father speaks directly to His beloved children on Earth. We are truly -" but his voice cracks.

Pausing to regain some composure, he summons the breath to support his words:

"I look forward to seeing all of you after the ceremony for a reception in the main hall. Go in peace."

THE CONGREGATION from the chapel has relocated to the hall - with the exception of the immediate family - and a number of women pitch in to set food out while the men assemble chairs and tables. The other missionaries who sat with William are there, but he himself is at the temple. The flowers from the church are brought in, and set upon the tables as decorative centre pieces.

The mood is mixed, confused, as if we have all been summoned to a funeral and are surprised with a wedding, or we've dressed ourselves up for a nuptial celebration, only to arrive at a wake.

Jennifer, who has gone to fetch us some water, returns and saves me from a swarm of sisters, who continually remind me what a 'gift' this day is. I fear when the day is done, and the gift opened, we will gasp in horror at the macabre offering wrapped up in pretty little bows and ribbons.

"So? How long do you think this charade will last?" Jennifer asks me in hushed tones, as she sips from a small glass. A nearby sister, nosy and obtrusive, turns into our private exchange without a hint of shame.

"Some have a great deal to discuss with the Lord," she cheerfully explains, "and others are in and out in no time at all. Help yourself to a slice of banana loaf while you're waiting."

"How kind of you," Jennifer smiles to her, venom in her words.

We step outside to wander the beautifully maintained church grounds, admiring the hoarfrost that hangs upon the trees and shrubs. I gaze towards the temple, shading my eyes from the mid-day glare, and imagine the scene in there that everyone believes to be happening, yet no one has witnessed. Save, of course, for the Prophet.

"What could they possibly think is happening right now?" I ask Jennifer. "That little Jacob is perched on a chair, his legs crossed and his hands gesturing with every word? Does he invoke abstract images in his discourse? Make reference to literature? Art? Scripture?"

"Astonishing, isn't it?" Jennifer says, and we shake our heads at how ludicrous it all is.

"How painful the truth must be," I add, "that so many prefer this lie."

Jennifer nods slowly, once or twice, utters a cryptic "Indeed", then curls her lips over her teeth.

Returning to the hall, we overhear a group of women discussing the Prophet's speech earlier as they try to discern who will succeed as church president.

"He can't be more than twenty-six years old," says one, "since he would have to be young enough to have undergone an Induction Ceremony of his own. They've only been performed since eighty-six, isn't that right?"

"Eighty-seven," says another, "so he'd be about twenty-five."

"Or younger," says a third.

Each put forward possible names as they scan the room for potential candidates. I scan the possibilities with them, and see that there are at least a dozen well-turned-out young men, shining in their suits, their freshly combed hair glistening with wax and pomade. The young women still outnumber them six to one, I estimate - underestimate, most likely - but there are far more men here than in Emmett.

Just then the doors open at the opposite end of the hall and the family enters. They are immediately thronged by the hundreds of supporters gathered in their honour. I turn to see them swallowed up in the crowd, little spots of white amidst all the colours of ladies fashions and the men's dark suits. I cannot immediately discern if they've returned with the child or not.

I stand on my tip-toes, trying to peer over the rows of heads, but can only make out the odd face here and there. I look to Jennifer, to see if she's afforded a better view, but she is also at a loss. I then descry William and Clara's parents along with Daniel and his. Everyone's expressions are joyful, happy, exhausted, revealing nothing.

Making our way to them is like penetrating a mob, and we

both listen for word about the child. Nothing. There is not a single clue one way or the other, as if the outcome mattered to no one but Jennifer and I.

The throngs on either side of me, before me, behind me, are focused on the now, the family, and this most momentous of days for them. They know the joy of having a child selected to join his Heavenly Father surpasses the sorrow of a temporary loss. They also know that the relief of having a child stay on in this world is more than sufficient antidote to the disappointment of not having him to rear in the next life.

And they know how to hide their rage, whereas I do not.

I begin to seethe, and am far from Jennifer's calming touch.

Finally I arrive at the front of the crowd and come face to face with William, flanked on either side by Wooley's apostles.

"Tara," he says, his voice loud above the murmur. "You're here! I can't tell you how happy I am to see you."

He smiles that beautiful smile, his eyes glowing like two daytime stars, impatient for night to fall.

Clara, his sister, has her arm linked into his, and appears to be holding onto him for dear life. She is acknowledging a long line of well-wishers, expressing neither great joy nor sorrow with her smiles and nods.

The Prophet and little Jacob are nowhere to be seen.

I cover my mouth and run from the hall.

35

"Come in, Miss Hale."

Oliver Harris answers the door himself this afternoon, the quiet house betraying the absence of children.

"I'm sorry if Amanda was impolite yesterday. I'm trying to teach both my children the difference between being firm and being rude, but it's a lesson that's slow to be learned. The younger one stopped answering the door altogether last week. Visitors would come every day, sometimes two or three times a day, but it's died down."

I step into the house, and survey the spacious rooms and grand staircase before me. The signs of affluence and taste are everywhere, but coated in a thin veil of dust, with various books and newspapers scattered about, piled high on side tables. It is exactly the home my father would keep at the college were he bereft of cleaning help.

I am out of breath and overheated due to my run from the meeting hall. My hands are chilly, however, so I stand close to the fire burning in the parlour.

"I was expecting your return," he says, addressing me with formality. "Perhaps you already know, but I feel obligated to tell you nevertheless, for your own protection, that I resigned my position in the church some days ago, and have been quite outspoken in my reasons why."

"Yes," I say, "I am aware of that."

"As you can no doubt appreciate, such a defection was not met kindly in town, especially given my status and the status of my family, not to mention that of my wife's family. She's a direct descendent of the founding prophet of the church. You can imagine the difficulty my choices have put us all in."

My jaw drops open in silent awe. We sit in silence for a moment while I do some quick math in my head. The great, great grandchild of the so-called Prophet of God threw a stick for my dog yesterday. The thought brings a smile to my face, and I happily share it with Oliver Harris when he asks.

"Yes," he says with an easy laugh, "I'm sure your dog will remember it forever."

The shared laughter subsides, and Mr. Harris leans forward in his chair, interlocks his long fingers, and asks what it is I've come to see him about.

"I attended an Induction Ceremony today," I quickly divulge, as calmly as I can, "and ran out of the hall when the family returned from the temple without the child. I ran straight here."

Mr. Harris nods compassionately as I speak, taking his time to respond, his voice soft and comforting when he speaks.

"The Induction Ceremony can be quite the shock to the system. It's designed to be that way. Such dramatic efforts are calculated to illicit a certain response from the faithful, and it works wonders. For those who are connected to the faith but outside the fold, however, it can be a devastating experience. How much do you know about what the ceremony?"

I tell him all I've learned, doing my best to keep my voice calm and measured.

"I see," he nods, again rather stoically. "Yes, I can see how terribly disturbing this all must be for you."

"Can you explain something to me, Mr. Harris?"

"I can certainly try."

"How such a belief system exists at all? It's 1912! The twentieth century. We have science and discovery and proofs and measures. How can anyone hold to a medieval mindset in this day and age?"

He smiles. "The sad truth, Miss Hale, is the church is living in its *era of enlightenment*. It used to be much worse, and I fear it is regressing."

He proceeds to tell me of how he was born and raised in the heartland of the church. His grandfather was one of the first men to join the new religion and was closely tied to the founding Prophet.

Oliver recounts how he himself served a mission to Scotland, was schooled in business matters upon his return, awarded a prominent position within the complex business division of the faith, and married into church royalty at the age of twenty-four.

"I've been living with the faith for all of my thirty-six years," he goes on to say, "and it's only now that I am beginning to see what a fraud it all is, how duped I've been my entire life. It makes for a heavy reckoning, I can assure you."

"You have two daughters," I say, "Amanda and..."

"Louise."

"Are they your only children?" I ask.

He knows the nature of the question, what I'm really asking, and slowly nods in affirmation.

"Yes, thank heavens," he says, "it's just the two girls, though it hasn't been due to lack of trying. It should come as no surprise, but church families expecting a child are riddled with mixed feelings, though they work hard to keep their feelings hidden. Great relief is quietly, secretly expressed when a girl is born, but there is also a measure of disappointment because boys are considered more worthy and valuable members of the church and society. The arrival of a boy is met with great celebration and excitement, yes, but the secret gasp of fear accompanies their first breath because of what awaits them two years hence.

That gasp of fear is a well-kept secret, mind you, but it lingers on for the full term."

"I was party to the secret all night at the Glenn house. Each and every member of the family hid their fear admirably, to the point where I began to question if it even existed for them. But how could it not?"

"They would be inhuman otherwise," Mr. Harris explains, voicing my very thoughts. "As it is, they are well-prepared to behave normally under highly abnormal conditions. Such is the result of a brilliant system of indoctrination and inculcation."

A shudder runs through my body as I listen to him, and I have to grip the armrests of the chair for fear of lifting completely out of it. He notices my reaction, and slowly nods in approval, as if expecting it to happen.

"Your body will react like that to the truth, Miss Hale. The faithful, were they sitting here with us, would say that such a physical reaction is the result of Satan trying to take hold of your soul. Rest assured, it is more of a letting go. Can I offer you a glass of water? Or anything?"

I shake my head, and ask him the question I've been asking since yesterday.

"How did you come to leave the church, Mr. Harris?"

"My wife and I both believed in the Principle of Induction, prepared for whatever the Lord brought our way. We were happy to have a third child, but unable to become pregnant for whatever reason. A two-year gap between children is nothing to worry about, but a three-, four-year stint for a young family? That gets the attention of the church fathers. There's no rule, no divine order about how many children one should or should not bring into the world, but there is a tremendous amount of monitoring that goes on with Sunday services and home visits. Somehow a rumour made its way back to the authorities that we were deliberately holding back due to fear of the Principle. This was not true, of course, but you know how tongues can wag."

When he says 'wag', I instantly think of Millie. I quickly see her in my mind's eye, confined to the back yard of Clara's home.

"You know how a person will believe anything he's told until he's given a reason to doubt it, Miss Hale?"

"Yes," I say.

"My reason to doubt came the day after my return from Emmett," he explains. "We were at Church, as we always are on Sunday, when one of Wooley's apostles pulled me aside.

"This apostle, Brother Cannon," he continues, "had served as a young man with my grandfather years ago, and was very close with our family, working side by side with the founding Prophet. My own father died when I was a boy, so this man was the closest thing to a father for me. I trusted him implicitly. He took me aside and said that I had nothing to worry about in continuing the wonderful work I was doing for the Lord. 'Have more children', he said, 'the Lord sees fit to give you boys and have them stay with you in this world'. He laid his hand on my shoulder and said 'I give you my word', then walked away."

He sits back in his chair as I watch the blood rise up to his cheeks. His countenance changes dramatically, and I behold his calm exterior betraying a soul in turmoil.

I make a comment about that being great news, and what a relief it must have been to have such fears allayed by someone with so much authority, but he shakes his head vigorously at my words.

"Don't you see, Miss Hale? I spent my life believing the Induction Ceremony to be an act of God. My family and I built our faith around such prophecies and revelations. To have one man 'assure' me that I would be spared something, to have a mortal man speak on behalf of God and make choices in advance that would protect me was nothing short of devastating. It *is* devastating."

"But how can he make such a promise?" I ask. "I thought all members believed it to be a private conversation between Heavenly Father and His child, witnessed only by the Prophet himself."

"That's exactly what we should be thinking," Oliver assures me, "what they want us to think. But when you're as close to the centre as I and my family have been, such secrets become more and more transparent."

"How do you know he wasn't just giving you a vague sense of hope?" I suggest. "His wont, I'm sure, as a leader and mentor."

"Exactly my wife's take on it, which is why it's so difficult for us to stay together. She and I are divided on this. She wants to stay and continue on as before, have more children, undergo the Induction Ceremony like everyone else, and remain true to the fold. But I know this man, and I know he was sincere when he said he could spare me. It is within his power. Therefore, not in God's hands at all, but in his and in the hands of men like him. Once I understood this, then the whole infrastructure of my beliefs began to blow apart. A cozy little bird's nest subject to a heavy wind. I was physically sick for seven days and lost ten pounds."

There is a knock at the door. When Mr. Harris answers it, I recognise the voice immediately.

"I'm sorry to bother you this evening, but I seem to have misplaced my traveling companion."

Jennifer enters, and I introduce the two of them.

"Please, have a seat, Mrs. Ness."

Oliver pours two glasses of water, as Jennifer joins me on the settee near the fire.

"I'm sorry to have run out like that," I quietly say.

"No need to apologise," she assures me. "It took me a few moments to see that you had gone, then a few more to figure out where you had run to. Are you getting the answers you were seeking?"

"And then some," I assure her, then turn back. "If not decreed by the Almighty, Mr. Harris, then what is the purpose behind an Induction Ceremony? What could be the motivation of perpetuating a lie?"

"First of all, Miss Hale, you must understand the history of the rituals. The Induction Ceremony is based on a reference in scripture-"

"Chapter 32, verse 14," I say. "I've read your Book front to back."

"Ah. Well then, you know what I'm referring to. What you don't know, indeed what most members today don't even know, is that the Induction Ceremony took place long before it was *revealed* to President Wooley in these latter days. As did the Acceptance Dinner. The two, according to the prevailing mythology of the time, were linked in the most ghastly way."

I feel my stomach tighten. My hands begin to sweat.

"A story worthy of Euripides, and not for the faint of heart. The children selected to live with Heavenly Father at the Induction Ceremony, so the story goes, were killed and slaughtered, their flesh served up to the faithful at Acceptance Dinners, all done so without subterfuge. Everyone participated knowingly and willingly."

Oliver rises and pours himself a glass of water.

"Terrifying fairy tale, isn't it? Meant to frighten the faithful into submission of a much more necessary and practical purpose."

"Which was?"

"Population control, essentially. The same purpose exists today; they just go about it in a different manner."

Jennifer and I both exhale at the same time.

"The classic problem of any polygamous society," Mr. Harris explains as he resumes his seat, "is striking the balance of men and women. If it were a truly polygamist society, the numbers would work themselves out, but this church believes in polygyny: one man with more than one wife. The question thus arises of what to do with all the excess males. In ancient times, one either sent the boys off to war, or, if there was no war to go to… "

He pauses. A log in the fireplace cracks loudly, and I jolt in reaction.

"In these latter days, it's not so easy. The church leaders must look ahead, plan accordingly, and eliminate the problem at the beginning. By doing a little simple math, calling a private session with the Lord for every child born into the faith, backing it all up with cryptic episodes from scripture, it's not hard to see how they can easily control the population of their flock."

"The only problem with all of this," I say, "is that members aren't living the principle. Are they?"

"Not currently, no."

"So if they're not practicing plural marriage, then why the Induction Ceremony?" I ask.

"They're not practicing it *now*," he says, "but it will be back, it's just a matter of time. Like Hamlet says, '*The readiness is all*'. They want to be ready for harvest when the sun finally shines again. If not in this world, then the next. Ask any of the faithful, even the women. Ask my wife. They all still believe in the principle of plural marriage, despite it being in a period of stasis right now. It will start again with the new Prophet, slowly, quietly, very carefully monitored and controlled. Wooley's health is in decline, and he knows it. The last thing this church needs is its founder to die without a clearly chosen successor. But since the Lord calls a prophet for life, nothing can be announced until after Wooley's death, but it's already been decided."

A chilly flood washes over me all of a sudden, and I see the eyes and smile that beguiled me under the tent in September.

"William," I say.

A smile sparks to life on Oliver's face, and he raises his eyebrows in astonished wonder. His reaction is not nearly as surprised as my own. I have no idea what made me say his name, for the thought hadn't crossed my mind before this moment, but it comes with absolute clarity. William will be the next Prophet of the church.

"I flattered myself once upon a time that it would be I who would succeed Wooley as Prophet," he confesses. "I surely would have made an ideal candidate except for one small detail: I did not undergo an Induction Ceremony. The new presidency, his advisors and apostles, the new regime, will all be of the new generation, survivors of the Induction Ceremony, taking the church into the 20th century and beyond. You see? It all hinges on the Induction Ceremony. That's the key to the future for the church."

"President Wooley said as much today," I add, "in his talk at the church."

"A revelation?" he asks.

"I believe so, yes."

Oliver nods skeptically.

"I take it, Mr. Harris, you no longer put much credence in such things," Jennifer comments.

"I do not, Mrs. Ness," he confirms. "I've stood witness to many of them, and I'm certain Brother Wooley believes in them as much as anyone else."

"But you don't," I say.

"Miss Hale, it's hard to maintain one's faith in such behaviour when the matters revealed by God in such a flash of revelation have been secretly discussed and planned in advance, sometimes for years."

My stomach goes taut once again, as if a great leather belt had been laced through the muscles and membranes, and with each new piece of information, the belt is notched another loop tighter.

"How long have they known it would be William?" I ask.

"You must understand one thing, Miss Hale," Oliver continues. "The Prophet, his apostles, and everyone else holding office in the church are not dishonest men who knowingly deceive and hoodwink their followers. They *believe* in what they do, and do not question the legitimacy of their actions. They believe that God ordains these practices and principles, and exploit it to the greatest effect. It is only people like us who see it as deception. We who are on the outside. We see it as deception, they see it as information management."

I repeat my question, grabbing Jennifer's hand as I brace for the answer.

"President Wooley and his apostles take great satisfaction in record keeping, Miss Hale. I know. I was a prime agent in the organization of information. There are volumes of records, charts, and projections that fill many shelves of many rooms in the church archives. Every member, every baptism, every marriage, every birth. Everything."

He turns to me and repeats the word.

"*Everything*, Miss Hale. They have everything on file. Including an otherwise dull report from Charles Emmett Snow in September, describing a trip to Calgary for supplies and a brief excursion to the fair taken by William wherein he obtained a sketch of himself from a traveling artist."

"What?" I ask as I feel a chill scuttle up my back.

"A rather innocuous missive, in and of itself, until it connects to a later one. Reports of William wanting to return to Calgary to sit for a portrait. His constant pining for the artist. His daily devotions at the train station, waiting in hope that the young woman will arrive from Calgary."

"Surely you're not serious," Jennifer says, as I'm unable to find my voice.

"Then a report communicating the arrival of said young woman into Emmett, with an injury. Sister Snow is encouraged to exaggerate the severity of the injury, so that the young woman remains longer."

The room begins to spin.

"But why?" Jennifer, again, is the one to ask.

"The longer she stays, the easier the conversion. Also, if the young woman could be made to feel that Sister Snow had interceded on behalf of Heavenly Father to save her life, the young woman would feel indebted. Vulnerable. *Attached.*"

Oliver rises from his chair, like a professor delivering an animated lecture. I'm reminded of my father.

"And so on. Wooley pressed me for more, and I would press Charles. Normally, one conversion wouldn't merit such a concentrated effort, but this was all in response to William's infatuation. And William was the heir apparent. His falling in love with a non-member was an unacceptable option."

"So convert the young woman, and ensure the unacceptable doesn't happen," Jennifer concludes, then turns to me. "The audacity of these people!"

"When the young woman is ready to leave, Sister Snow conveniently invites her to church. The Owens girl is dispatched as confidante. A portrait is commissioned, ensuring the artist will stay longer. Then the invitation to the Acceptance Dinner. Anything to ensure her departure for Vancouver is delayed, all with the goal of her giving in and agreeing to baptism. All too soon, it became a personal goal for William. To convert you, as his first wife."

"*First* wife?" I ask, feeling sick to my stomach.

"He will usher in the new order. Plural marriage. The Owens girl was assured second wife status if all went smoothly."

"That deceptive little bastard," Jennifer growls, her calm and controlled exterior finally giving way.

"For what it's worth," Oliver responds, "I don't believe William was aware of any of this. He was - and as far as I know, still is - simply this: a young man who has fallen in love. He has no idea of the thousand and one machinations going on around him."

I feel myself sinking in the chair, the force of his words pulling me down deeper and deeper into another wilderness. Whether it is a wilderness of truth or lies, I cannot say, but I am helpless against the torrent.

"The potential calling of William Joseph Snow will not come

as a big surprise to anyone," he explains. "The son of one of the original four. A handsome, charismatic, vital young man whose easy sense of humour and relaxed strength endear him to even the most unlikely of potential converts."

I quickly inhale the reference to myself in his words, and feel the blood drain from my face as if I were a sacrificial lamb whose throat has just been slit. Oliver watches my reaction in silence.

"A gifted, head-strong, wilful daughter of privilege and education, from the very antipodes of Emmett; not just geographically, but politically, religiously, ideologically. It would be quite the achievement for him."

My lips move but no sound comes out, as if I'm mired in the webbing of a dream.

"Nothing is left to chance, Miss Hale, especially when a new Prophet is being groomed."

"But he risked his mission, didn't he?" Jennifer argues, "His standing in the church to come and see her in Calgary."

Mr. Harris laughs slightly at this, but soon his laughter transfigures into a sad and lovely sigh, as if he is on the verge of tears.

"He risked nothing. I myself would have advised the Prophet on this, and urged him to grant William leave to go. Someone else simply did it in my stead."

"Why?"

"He loves her," Oliver explains. "And believe me, a young prophet is much more malleable when there's harmony at home. Nothing happens in this church that's not in the church's best interests, rest assured. Nothing is left to chance."

"Was he instructed to tell me of the Induction Ceremony?" I finally ask.

He shakes his head.

"I gather his informing you of the Induction Ceremony was the one slip in an otherwise perfectly calculated attack," he says. "In a way, it's what saved you."

"Saved her?" Jennifer exclaims. "I'm afraid you don't give

this young woman much credit, Mr. Harris. Which frankly I find not only misinformed, but entirely inappropriate."

"He would have left for his mission as scheduled, and no doubt Miss Hale would have gone on to Vancouver to meet the artist she set out to find. A few letters here, a surprise visit from Sister Snow there. The church has its ways, Mrs. Ness. It behooves us all to not underestimate *them*. Miss Hale would have had quite the fight ahead of her. Separated from her own family. On her own. Searching for something that's missing in her. These are the ideal conditions that the church preys upon."

"I'm sorry, Mr. Harris, but I find some of this incredulous to say the least," Jennifer says as she stands.

"Such as what?" He asks.

"William's age, for one," she replies. "He's only just turned nineteen. How could he lead a church so young?"

"The founding prophet was only fifteen when he was called by the Lord. Jesus knew his mission at the age of twelve. Age, experience, innocence... such attributes are relevant only to man, not to God."

Mr. Harris turns back to me.

"You were the final test for William that none of us could have possibly manufactured. A truly divine intervention, as if you had been sent by God. Wooley and his apostles believe you were. I did too at the time."

"So you came to Emmett to… what?" I spit out the words. "Spy on me?"

"In a matter of speaking, yes. To see how the miracle of conversion was coming along. I had to push things along a bit, knowing you had not yet been invited to his Acceptance Dinner. I'm sorry now for the Owens girl. But I'm afraid her feelings at the time were inconsequential."

We are all of us silent. Outside the large bay window, the setting sun paints the sky a deep red, as though on fire.

"What happens to little Jacob?" I ask. "After his miraculous conversation with his Heavenly Father?"

He pinches the top of his nose between the eyes, and I finally see the exhaustion on his face, the sudden weight loss, the stress of all he's endured. Asking him to recount things he's working so hard to forget is onerous, but I must know.

"Little Jacob is either gorging himself on sweets, bouncing on the knee of a wet nurse, or napping right now. There's no more of a conversation going on than there is a game of billiards being played. Wooley will decide how long to make the family wait. William's connection to it all is a factor with this one. I have no idea when it will end. Or how."

"But once it does..." Jennifer urges.

"Once it does," he continues, "the boy will be returned to his parents to live a happy life as another obedient child of God. We hope."

"Hope?" Jennifer repeats.

"It's late," Mr. Harris says. "You should be getting back to the Glenn house before they come looking for you. I'd rather not have a team of members at my door if you don't mind. I'm sure you can understand."

"We will not leave here, Mr. Harris, until you tell us whatever it is you are withholding," I cry. "I've come this far, and I deserve to know the truth."

"Which one?" he quickly fires back, his words filled with remorseful irony. "In a secret society, all truths are possible, so please be specific, Miss Hale, else we'll be here all night. Which truth do you want? The impossible but acceptable one, or would you prefer the horrific and plausible one? It's all about choice, so choose."

He stares at my shocked silence.

"The church leaders will tell you that the children are translated," he explains. "That they become translated beings."

"Translated?" Jennifer asks. "What on earth does that even mean?"

"Ascension into heaven," he explains. "They disappear into the firmament - skin, bones, hair, flesh - and await their parents on the other side. That's the impossible explanation, and the acceptable one."

"But it's not the truth."

"Once you convince people to accept the unacceptable," he slowly utters, "then you have their fidelity forever. But no, it is not the truth."

"So what is then?"

My question burns out of me, its flames covering Oliver Harris, but he does not catch fire.

"Mr. Harris," I urge, demanding a response. "The truth."

"The truth is I don't know. Some secrets run so deep even one as high up as myself cannot access them. I hope for something far less malevolent than what the ancients would have us believe. That they're packed off in the middle of the night, perhaps, sent to any one of a dozen orphanages in neighbouring states. But I can find no evidence of that."

Jennifer holds me as my knees give out and I start to fall.

"Nor can I find any evidence of bodies. There would be hundreds of them by now. Perhaps thousands. What has happened to them?"

"Surely you're not suggesting-" Jennifer begins to say, but Mr. Harris holds up his hand to stop her.

"I am not in any position to make suggestions, Mrs. Ness. Nor can I draw conclusions. Not on this. Had I lost a son myself, I assure you I would have the motivation to keep digging. But I can hardly make demands on behalf of those who are at peace with losing theirs. Don't you see? They believe their children are with their Heavenly Father. If how they got there is a lie, it does not change the fact that they are there and cannot return."

"So you do nothing? Even with the standing you have in the church?"

"Mrs. Ness. I have chosen to remove myself from a delusion far more powerful than I. Let me assure you it was a very diffi-cult action to take. I've lost my family, my faith, my God. But to shatter the delusion for everyone? That effort would be nothing short of heroic. I am no Hercules. It would take a lifetime of sleuthing to find out what truly happens to them, so carefully guarded is this worst of all possible secrets."

WE STEP out into the evening, Jennifer and I, and stand motionless in the night. I see the snowy tops of trees, the white limestone temple standing on the bluff illuminated by the moon, the flickering street light poles, and everything begins to spin.

The tightness in my stomach softens into queasiness, as the meal on All Soul's Eve comes back to me in a fiery flash. I am there once again, laughing, listening to Chopin on the Victrola, talking, hearing stories of a wandering boy, enjoying myself. I am served dinner all over again. I see the ornate platter, and smell the aromas of the stewed meat once more. I take it to my mouth again, taste and chew and swallow again, repeating the act, over and over and over.

Nausea hits hard with the realization of what I now wish I had never asked about. I lean against a thick poplar tree and vomit with ferocious violence.

When I am somewhat recovered, I begin to walk away.

"The hotel is this way."

Jennifer, who has been holding me while I sullied the pure white snow beneath, reaches to pull me away from where I'm heading. "Don't go back there, Tara. There's nothing for you there. Come, let's be done with this horror and be gone. There's a train first thing in the morning."

But I can't. I have to tell William. I have to tell them all.

"I need to get Millie," is all I say to explain why I'm pulling away from her grasp. Jennifer protests, offers to go in my stead, pleads, but I keep walking.

She soon gives up and follows.

36

MILLIE, ALONE IN THE BACK YARD WITH HER WATER BOWL AND FOOD scraps, barks with elated joy upon seeing us. Despite Jennifer's attempts to hush her down, the family gathers at the back door and spills out into the yard to greet us.

Jennifer stands off to the side. My second, yes, but understanding this last battle is mine alone.

I can only imagine what I look like, and am thankful to have night's cloak to hide in. They have all changed out of their temple whites, and stand on the back porch with wools draped over their shoulders. William alone is still dressed in white, his sleeves rolled up on his arms.

"Miss Hale," Sarah Snow exclaims as she comes to my side, "you look an awful fright. Are you feeling ill?"

I give no answer as I bend down to Millie, using her as a buffer between myself and the conversation I'm sure none of us want to have.

"Are you all right?" Clara asks. "Do you need to sit down?"

"We've been looking all over for you," William adds, "wondering where on earth you could have gotten to all afternoon. I've only just come back now from searching."

"Excuse me," I say, more breath than speech. I then notice the bottom of my dressed is soiled with dried mud and vomit, and I try to brush it off with my hand. "My dress..."

"Yes, let me help you inside. I've something you can borrow," Clara says as she tries to take my arm. "You must be frozen solid."

I flinch and pull my arm back so quickly that it catches Millie on the nose. She cries in pain, but is quickly mollified by my apologies and petting. Jennifer discreetly calls her over to where she stands in the yard.

"Perhaps," Charles Snow calmly says, "if you tell us where you've been all this time, we can help you bear whatever this turmoil is that you are struggling with. Let us bring you peace, Miss Hale."

"No," I cry, almost screaming, as if blades were at my throat. "No more peace."

"What's the matter, Tara?" William asks, and then turns to Jennifer for an explanation. She offers none.

"Yes," Clara says as she takes another step towards me, "tell us what is bothering you."

"Where's your son?" I sharply ask her, and watch as the question ices over her face and body, freezing her to the spot. Her husband comes to her side.

"He's with his Heavenly Father," she says in a voice that blends stoicism, pride, defiance, and compassion.

"Translated," I say, unable to restrain the bitterness in my voice.

She does not respond.

"Perhaps we should all go inside," Mrs. Snow says as she reaches out her hand to me.

I turn on this woman who made me think she saved my life, who manipulated me.

"And yours," I cry. "Where are your sons?"

"There is venom in your words, Miss Hale," Mr. Snow accuses, "and we can easily guess the name of the viper who has poisoned you. I will help you rid yourself of the toxins, but I cannot stand by and allow you to address my wife, my family in this manner."

"You lied to me," I shouted. "You, your family, your town."

"Tara," William steps towards me. "What are you saying?"

"Did *you*?" I demand, staring into those eyes. "You said it would be beautiful. You and your damn ceremonies and rites of passage. What else did you lie about, William Joseph Snow? What else did you know? What *do* you know?"

I stand in the centre of the yard, my voice rising up to the moonlit night.

He looks to his father, who only shakes his head at him. Then to his mother, who also turns her focus down. "What is she saying?"

"When I met you," I cry, "you were pure light. Light and dark, shadows and shadings, black lines scarred upon white paper. You were Snow in summer. I was so bedazzled by the radiance, that I forgot – like an amateur – to take into account the shadow being cast."

"Tara, I don't understand what you're talking about," he confesses.

"No," I say, resigned, "I don't believe you do."

I look around at the confused faces watching me, their blank expressions struggling to hold back their fear.

"You're all so grateful for the glorious light of God in your lives," I say, unsure myself of what I'm uttering, "that you forget to see the shadow cast. You refuse to acknowledge that it's even there."

I feel the sob rise up in me and escape before I can stop it.

"You say you're seeking the truth, but you're happier to live with a lie."

"Miss Hale," Mr. Snow says, warning me with his words, "I would strongly suggest that you not start throwing stones at others for living a lie."

"No!" Jennifer's voice cuts through with authority. She steps forward and levels her eyes at the patriarch himself.

"What is going on?" William asks. "What lies? What is she talking about? Mother? Father?"

"Tell him, Miss Hale," Mr. Snow challenges me. "Since you're such an advocate for the truth. Tell him every truth you know. Beginning with your father."

"Enough!" Jennifer demands. "We're leaving."

"My father?" I blink the words out of my mouth, as I'm suddenly assaulted with the smell of sea air. I see bodies all around me again, in the curling rink. Back home. Far from here.

"Yes, your father," Charles continues. "After your embarrassing confession to Sergeant Parks the other night, he came to see me. He sent a telegraph to Halifax, to confirm that you were who you said you were. You see Miss Hale, when you live a lie - however well you think you're able to hide it - others begin to doubt you."

"Come, Tara," Jennifer is pulling on me. "It's time to go."

"I take it, Mrs. Ness, that you know the truth as I do," I hear him say.

"This is not the time or the place," Jennifer hisses to Mr. Snow. "Can't you see the state she's in? Have you no shame?"

"What's she talking about? Father, answer me!" William finds the authority in his voice. The authority that will no doubt serve him well for the life ahead.

"Your father is dead," I hear Charles say to me with firm and steady voice. "Drowned. A last minute passenger on an unsinkable ship. He never made it home."

I hear it, but can't respond. Someone grabs me as I fall. Is it William? Charles? Jennifer? A complete overloading of my cart, as if a star has exploded inside of me. Brilliant and painful all at once. Cold and blindingly bright.

"My god," William says with shock in his voice.

Everyone is silent. Everyone, that is, except for me. I wail and cry, burying myself into Millie's fur, who is trying to lick my tears as fast as they fall.

"Shame on you," I hear Jennifer berating Charles. Her voice is raw, angry, and fearless. "As a father, I would think you of all people would understand. Especially one who willingly gave up his own children. And now your grandson."

"You're wrong, my child."

This new voice, gentle and soft, yet able to cut through Jennifer's anger and my sobs, comes from the back doorway. I look up and see Prophet Wooley. Little Jacob, still dressed in white, held in his arms.

"Sorry, Sister Glenn," he says. "I hope you don't mind but I let myself in."

He looks to Clara whose smile is filled with wonderment, and she nods her approval. Next thing I know, the boy has wrapped his arms around his mother's neck and is holding on as tight as he can.

"For behold that all little children are alive in Christ," Prophet Wooley quotes. "I can't think of anything that fills my heart with more joy and peace than such a sight as this."

He takes a step down to the grass.

"One of the longest Induction Ceremonies I've ever witnessed. Jacob and the Lord had plenty to say to one another. It was a remarkable and beautiful afternoon. Wondrous things lie ahead for this little one," he adds, laying a hand on William's arm, "and for *all* members of his family."

I want to speak out, to protest, to challenge his words and practices, but I see Jacob nestle his face into his mother's bosom, and she clings to him for all she's worth. Grateful tears flow down her face. I am filled as much with joy as I was previously filled with anger.

"This, my brothers and sisters, is what we're all about," the Prophet says. "Spreading peace in one another's hearts, without words, without ceremonies, without truth or lies or faith or doubt. Just a simple act of love, freely given by a true child of God."

He lays his large hands on the head of the child in a silent blessing, and takes his leave.

Jacob moves his fingers up to his mother's eyes, and covers them. He holds his palms there for a moment, sticky from her tears, and then quickly pulls them away, and laughs, despite her inability to sound the familiar words of the game.

37

THE WALLS OF DRUMMOND HALL ON VANCOUVER'S PENDER STREET are literally covered with art: oils, watercolours, ink and pencil sketches. It is overwhelming to wander amongst such a quantity of work from one artist, and such exotic work at that, with names like *Tanoo, Tsatsisnukomi,* and *Klawatsis.* The bold use of line and colour flies against everything I thought I knew and understood about painting. The blues are bluer than anything I had seen in art or nature, the yellows unequivocally yellow, the reds truculent and combative, and the greens deeper than any Irishman could dare to dream of.

I am an unsuspecting Alice who has fallen through a rabbit's hole into a palette, making my way from colour to colour, line to line, pole to pole. This has been worth waiting for, worth everything I've endured and lived and suffered and tasted. For the first time in months, I experience a state of knowing only this, wholly forgetting William Snow, his family, Emmett, the church, and God.

The artist is present. She's older than I imagined, or at least looks older than I pictured her to be. I watch her from a distance, too shy and overcome to make her acquaintance just yet. I watch her speak with admirers. I listen to those who are less than impressed with her work, and wonder how she is accepting their lack of acceptance.

Emily Carr offers a long lecture on the totem poles she has painted and the various sources of her creations. I sit and try to give her my undivided attention, but it continually escapes to the forest around me. What chance have words next to pictures?

One part of the lecture beckons my attention back. It is a story about her trip to Yan by way of a small dugout Indian boat with an Indian woman and her two children.

"The mother sat at the stern with a baby in her lap," Miss Carr recounts, "while the other girl - twelve years old - manipulated a sail made of flour sacks. It was a wild, rainy day and a fire was made in the small hut at night. The woman told me stories of her life. She had had nine children and lost them all. The Indian women love their children passionately," Miss Carr explains after a long pause, holding her gaze out over the rapt audience. "To have no children is to be truly desolate."

She is a tentative and nervous speaker, and her statements receive little in the way of nodding heads or other signs of agreement. A far cry from the oratorial prowess of a Charles Snow.

"A young woman from Skidegate comes to her friend. She is the mother of five or six children, and brings two with her - a boy and girl - and gives them to the desolate mother to somehow console her. How many white mothers - though they might grieve for another's sorrow - would even dream of such a sacrifice?"

My mind escapes again - perhaps 'stolen away' is more accurate - to images of Sarah Snow and the dozens - hundreds - of other women who *sacrificed* their children to their Heavenly Father. I wonder where those children are now?

I think of my own father, and realize that today is the one year anniversary of his death. The significance of the date is not entirely lost on me, nor is it entirely understood. I am oddly comforted by it, and trust that I am at the right place at the right time.

While others come and go through the exhibit all day, I stay. Eventually I work up the nerve to approach her but remain silent, afraid to speak but wanting to meet her and exchange greetings.

"You've been here all day," she says after eyeing me for a moment.

"Yes," I reply, flattered that she noticed me.

"You and I are the only ones able to stick it out this long," she says, "and I for one am exhausted."

"It's no trouble for me," I tell her. "I can't seem to get enough of your paintings. Time disappears."

"That's promising to hear. They don't shock you?"

"Yes," I say without thinking of a better answer, adding "but I'm no stranger to being shocked."

She laughs heartily at this, her chortles filling the large hall, causing the small audience there to turn and look at the source of it.

"One concerned citizen wrote to the paper complaining of my vanity in thinking I could eclipse the Almighty with my bizarre work," she confides. "He accused me of trying to improve on nature. I wrote a suitable response back, I can tell you, Miss..."

"Hale."

She glances down at the sketch pad in my hands and sighs. The breath is barely audible, but I hear it. I start speaking before she walks away.

"Your paintings remind me of what I saw in Paris," I announce. "I was there last year."

"As was I," she acknowledges, brightening somewhat and resuming her role as gracious hostess. "I spent a summer in St. Efflame. By eight every morning, I would be in the fields behind the long beach, painting until noon. Then Harry would climb the hill and give me a lesson, every afternoon. Twice a week he would offer some criticism..."

As she talks about her experience, I look on in silent wonder at the canvases around us. Her words fill me with both humility and slight humiliation as I awaken to ideas and techniques - an entire universe of painting - that I know nothing about. The only words I can say at the end of this exchange come in the form of an appeal.

"Teach me."

She grows silent for a moment or two, studying me with those half-moon eyes.

"Are these your sketches?" she asks.

I nod and hold the book out to her.

"Let's go outside. The light is much more favourable and I need some air."

Millie leaps up when she sees me, her tail sweeping the street dust into a cloud. Some pedestrians passing by grumble their complaints, but Miss Carr immediately sinks to the ground and embraces Millie like a long lost friend.

"And who's this?" she asks, her voice filled with warmth and humour as Millie eagerly licks her cheeks.

"My best friend," I say. "Millie."

"Ah! Hello Millie. We share a name, you and I."

She sits on the curb with Millie rolling into her the way she likes to do, and reaches for my sketch pad.

"Let's have a look."

She studies the drawings - a mixture of exaggerated faces and some recent landscape attempts from Stanley Park - all the while scratching Millie's tummy.

"This one is interesting," she says. "I like it very much."

She holds a sketch I did shortly after the events in Cherry Creek.

I HOLD on to Millie a little while longer that night, silently squeezing her into me, hoping some of her pure innocence will transfer over and flush out the truth I've been told and that which I have chosen not to accept.

When I finally open my eyes, I see that everyone has returned back into the house. Jennifer helps me up, opens the gate, and leads me back to our hotel. We take the morning train to Calgary, and I stay with her until Christmas.

She had tried to tell me that she knew about my father's death. I knew it, but wasn't ready to hear it. She understood, as she does most things that I can only imagine.

After Christmas, I board a train back to Halifax, to be with my aunt. She too is alone in her grief. We are alone together. Millie remains with Jennifer.

There is a modest inheritance awaiting me in Halifax. After three months, I return back west. It feels like coming home.

THE SKETCH that Miss Carr finds interesting I drew aimlessly, mindlessly, circling my pencil over and over again on the page, until a picture started to form. A mouth, wide open like a cave. I didn't know whose mouth it was. Mine? William's? Everybody's? Nobody's? Though there is enough representation of the rest of a person – eyes, limbs, hair – the majority of the paper is the empty space between the teeth.

"It's the place where words come out," I say, struggling to explain the inexplicable. "Where food goes in. A place almost always in darkness except when it is open wide enough to let in some light. As it is now. Big enough to hold all the lies the world has to offer. And all the truth."

"*Truths*," Miss Carr says. "I believe that it's a word that should, by default, always be plural. Like trousers or scissors. It just doesn't work in the singular."

"I couldn't agree more," I say, and crouch down beside her and Millie on the street.

"You do caricatures very well," she says with authority. "The trick with them is communicating the truths you exaggerate. Most only show the exaggeration, not the truths. Yours are very good. Where have you studied?"

"Just classes here and there. I learned to caricature in Paris."

"There's some evidence of freedom in your work with those," she comments, "and I get a sense of you from them. The landscapes and other sketches are competent but academic in the worst possible way. Don't be discouraged, dear, it's not your fault. We all start the same way, especially in this slow and stubborn nation of ours." She buries her face in Millie's coat and lets my dog lick her lips without reserve. "Are you married?"

"No," I say. "I came close, but found out that he had been spoken for long before I arrived."

"Ah," she nods, "a painful discovery to make."

"He's gone now," I add, "out of the country serving a mission for his church."

Miss Carr loses herself in thought, trying to grab the frayed ends of a memory.

"In my house growing up, my sisters would constantly have various missionaries over, to the point that I would literally trip on them as I walked into the dining room for tea. I soon grew to dislike missionaries. Still do, I'm afraid. They believe that they've laid claim to your soul, and sooner or later they come to stake it."

She stands and brushes some of the dog hair off her skirts with the palm of her hand. Most of it remains and she appears entirely unbothered by it.

"She's a great ole' girl, your Millie. Full to bursting with love and affection."

"Yes," I say. "She's stood by me through the good times and the rough."

"Rough times," Miss Carr intones as she nods, settling those eyes on me once more. "I know all about those."

She stares ahead, across the street, and moves her lower jaw to and fro as if chewing on a thought.

"When the exhibit closes on the weekend," she confides, "I'm moving back to Victoria. I've a boarding house I'll be opening up there in need of tenants. If you're mobile, and would consider relocating, you can rent one of the apartments and use it as a live-in studio. Finding landlords who will tolerate both paint and pets is a challenge. I'm a lover of both."

"Victoria?"

"On Vancouver Island," she explains. "My home, where I grew up. A lovely place, but I'll warn you: it's very conservative, far more so than Vancouver even. I'd be happy to offer you some lessons there."

"You would?"

"And," she continues, "I may be able to help with finding you some simple employment. No promises, mind, but a news editor I used to work for has been hounding me to supply political cartoons for his paper again. I cannot go back to that work, but it might be just the thing for you, given your penchant for caricature. The pay, I can promise you, will be negligible. He's as cheap as they come."

My body fills with triple excitement at the thoughts of moving, studying with her, and selling my sketches to a newspaper.

"Yes, of course," I stammer out, "I'd love to. Thank-you. Thank-you. Thank-you."

"Very good," she concludes. "You'll find Hill House at the end of Simcoe Street, next to Beacon Hill Park. Again, no promises about the job, but I'd be happy to give you lessons and help with your development as an artist. Now, if you'll excuse me, I must get back."

She nods an unspoken goodbye to me, and indulges in a final embrace with Millie.

"I'll see you soon, ole' girl. Yes I will. Yes I will."

EPILOGUE

CROSSING OVER THE GEORGIA STRAIT, I WATCH THE SUN DESCEND IN the western sky, the playful dance of dying light reflected off the water. Night falls hard on land, but at sea, it lays down slowly, embracing the day like a lover until she is entirely enveloped inside his arms.

Millie sleeps in the seat beside me, her head upon my lap. Someone will come by soon enough and tell me that she can't be here. But for now she sleeps still and peaceful, my sketch book open upon her head.

I think of what Miss Carr said about missionaries. William will come looking for me when he gets home, to stake his claim. That much is true. I confess there is a small part of me that wants him to. Another truth. But most of me hopes he doesn't. Another.

There are more truths than I can carry on my own.

I relieve the weight of this overloading by thinking back to less confusing times, to Paris, and the I discovery made on that September afternoon.

. . .

WE'VE BEEN *in France for a couple of months, arriving by ferry from Rosslare, Ireland. I am no longer my father's little girl, nor have I begun any sort of life as an adult. We walk down the Champs-Élysées in sweltering heat to the glass covered Grand Palais where the Salon d'Automne is being held.*

There are hundreds of paintings, and even more patrons. We wander off in different directions, my father and I, and after a few hours I find him again, alone in a small room towards the back. He is standing in front of two vibrant landscapes. He puts his arm around me as if I've been beside him all along.

"Look, Tara. The artist is from Canada."

I GLANCE out the window of the ferry. The evening sky is beautiful. I twist my body to fully take in the subtle reds and yellows of the sunset, disturbing Millie in the process. She looks at me with her almond eyes, barely wags her tail, melts off my lap and drifts back to sleep on the seat opposite.

THE ARTIST IS FROM CANADA.

British Columbia. About as far from Halifax as Paris. Two pieces by a Canadian, surrounded by Europeans. Two pieces by a woman, surrounded by men. Inspiration arrives like a descending angel and takes possession immediately. I stand motionless for what seems hours, imagining myself as the other female Canadian artist with a pair of paintings at the Salon.

"Stay with me," my father says, "in Paris. Study painting here. Sketches. Art. I don't have to be back at the university until April. There's such life here, Tara. I want you to have it. To have it all."

We book passage home on the RMS Titanic for its maiden voyage on March the 20th. It is delayed. A voyage is then re-arranged for me on her sister ship, the RMS Olympic, for April 3rd. Due to the massive rush for tickets, we manage to obtain the last possible passage. First class.

"You deserve it," my father assures me. "I'll stay on another week, and take the second class cabin with the Titanic. I'll be home before you know it."

I'm excited to travel alone, unchaperoned, for the five day journey. At the port in Southampton, I give my father a kiss. He pats my back, and hands me a pair of gifts. A thin volume of poetry from a writer I've not heard of before, and a bottle of Bordeaux.

"You'll finish one long before the other", he says, "but they're both for the long journey ahead."

He makes me promise to wait for him to get home before I go trekking across the country to meet this artist. I promise that I will.

I can wait. I'm good at waiting.

BEFORE THE DAY outside gives over to total darkness, I complete a sketch.

A father with a child upon his lap. The child is speaking. He listens, rapt with wonder at the marvellous spell of words being cast over him.

I open my Emily Dickinson once more, and copy another bit of the poet's light onto the dark lines and shading.

Soon, I will drift away to sleep with Millie, sharing whatever dreams I can with her.

This is how I love.

> *Of whom so dear*
> *The name to hear*
> *Illumines with a Glow*
> *As intimate – as fugitive*
> *As Sunset on the snow –*

ACKNOWLEDGMENTS

First and foremost, my gratitude goes out to my editor Janelle. You steered this ship clear of many deadly icebergs, and for that I thank you.

My deepest thanks as well to the many readers, friends, and colleagues who have been with Tara and me along the way. You're all over the place in terms of where you live, but incredibly focused in how you love:

To Richard in the UK; to Lisa in New Zealand; to De in Australia; to Esther in Israel; to Caroline, Steena, Deanna, Graham, Jarrod, Nola, and heaps more in Canada.

To John, who is forever in my thoughts and memories. I miss you more than I can handle sometimes.

To the two Emilys, who continue to overload my cart with their beautiful words and colours.

To Addie - my Millie - who sat at my feet in the early days of writing this book.

To Rosie and Eloise, who are faraway nearby.

To Piper, who's probably at the beach.

And to Jess, who's always right beside me.

- bjt

One more thing…

Thank you for buying and reading this book. I hope you enjoyed it.

Please *take a moment and post a review.*

Thanks!

ABOUT THE AUTHOR

B.J. Thorson is a life-long storyteller and has written extensively for the stage, the giant screen, and a variety of publications. A native of Western Canada, Thorson now lives and writes in Sydney, Australia.

Please visit www.bjthorson.com to learn more.

Printed in Great Britain
by Amazon